"We ha

"Do we?" Aidan asked.

Natalie and Aidan had different perceptions of what was important. For her, raising the little boy in an environment where love and nurturing would help him blossom was everything. For Aidan, his status as uncle outweighed all the other benefits.

She jumped off the swing and sent him a smile. "Sometimes taking a moment to breathe when your world falls apart around you is a win. That's what Danny needs right now. A chance to breathe and find his support system."

"I'm his uncle. I'm his support system."

There was no denying he was Danny's family, but so was she. Danny had reached the top of the rock climbing wall for the first time. Celebrating that was important. A win for Danny was having someone in his corner.

For now, she was that person...

Dear Reader,

Friendship is such an integral part of life. During my first year of law school, three women accepted me into their study group. We bonded over study sessions, where we'd work and then share stories of our lives. We supported each other through disappointments and celebrations.

In *The Sheriff's Second Chance*, Georgie Bennett emerged as an independent heroine who accepted the friendship so many offered. This trilogy has highlighted friendship as Georgie, Lucie and Natalie have shared more than cookies. They've commiserated over their ups and downs.

This time, Natalie Harrison experiences good and not-so-good times. Natalie's world is upended when her best friend dies, and she becomes Danny's guardian. When Danny's soldier uncle, Aidan, arrives, he sees how Natalie's friendships have guided her through this time and questions whether he needs similar relationships in his life. Strong yet stark, Aidan struggles with how to relate to people, most of all Natalie.

This book is a celebration of friendships in its many forms. I'd love to hear stories of the friendships that have impacted your lives. Please feel free to email me at tanyaagler@gmail.com or catch up with me on social media.

Tanya Agler

HEARTWARMING

The Soldier's Unexpected Family

———

Tanya Agler

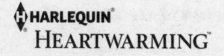

HARLEQUIN®
HEARTWARMING™

Please Recycle — This Product Is Recyclable

ISBN-13: 978-1-335-17980-7

Recycling programs
for this product may
not exist in your area.

The Soldier's Unexpected Family

Copyright © 2021 by Tanya Agler

This edition published by arrangement with Harlequin Books S.A.

For questions and comments about the quality of this book,
please contact us at CustomerService@Harlequin.com.

Harlequin Enterprises ULC
22 Adelaide St. West, 40th Floor
Toronto, Ontario M5H 4E3, Canada
www.Harlequin.com

Printed in U.S.A.

Tanya Agler remembers the first set of Harlequin books her grandmother gifted her, and she's been in love with romance novels ever since. An award-winning author, Tanya makes her home in Georgia with her wonderful husband, their four children and a lovable basset, who really rules the roost. When she's not writing, Tanya loves classic movies and a good cup of tea. Visit her at tanyaagler.com or email her at tanyaagler@gmail.com.

Books by Tanya Agler

Harlequin Heartwarming

A Ranger for the Twins
The Sheriff's Second Chance

Visit the Author Profile page
at Harlequin.com for more titles.

This book is dedicated to my daughter, Ellie. Every day, she makes my world brighter in unexpected ways, from dancing on the fireplace hearth to discussing history with passion and flair. I love you always, and I'm so proud to be your mom.

This book is also dedicated to my father and both of my grandfathers. The three of them served in the military and will remain in my heart forever. And to all four of my children and my husband, Jamie, thank you for your encouragement and supporting me through the writing and editing of this book.

CHAPTER ONE

"THIS IS GOING to be so much fun." Natalie Harrison flipped over the plans for the parade float and then twisted the papers one more time. Now the images were right side up, although she'd much prefer to toss the schematics in the park's trash can and start with a new and exciting design. Something with pizazz and flair and...

"Aunt Natalie, are you lying?" Danny tugged on her floral sundress, the pleading in his voice stopping her in her tracks.

She laid the plans on a nearby picnic table. The summer breezes from the North Carolina mountains cooled the morning air and her bare arms. She glanced at her six-year-old ward and sent him a smile. "Of course I'm not."

"My mom told me it isn't nice to lie."

Natalie brushed away a strand of her red hair, along with the wave of grief at the mere mention of Danny's mom. Shelby Murphy had been her best friend since their college days.

Three months hadn't dulled the ache left

from Shelby's sudden death from an unde-
tected brain aneurysm. As long as Natalie
lived, she'd never forget opening her front door
and finding Danny there, out of breath, tears
cascading down his cheeks, saying his mom
wasn't waking up.

With the Fourth of July fast approaching in
two weeks, Natalie would do everything in her
power to make it a great day for Danny.

Though bittersweet, what a day it was going
to be for everyone, considering Hollydale was
no longer the sleepy hamlet of her youth. Now
it usually ranked in the top three "must visit"
destinations this side of the Great Smoky
Mountains. The downtown district's renova-
tion brought tourists flocking to the shops and
businesses from now until the last leaf fell in
October. The influx of dollars had led to more
elaborate summer celebrations, with the parade attracting huge crowds that stayed for the
famous, or infamous, pie baking contest and
fireworks display.

Natalie ruffled Danny's thick brown hair,
the silver of her thin stacked bangle bracelets
chiming in the soft breeze. "Your mom was
right, but I'm telling the truth. We're going to
build the biggest and best float in Hollydale's
Boulevard of Stars Parade, and spending time
with you is always fun."

When Hollydale Elementary School Principal Marisa Garcia, her boss, had called and asked Natalie to supervise the construction of the float, she'd given every impression this project was further along than it actually was. Then again, with the original plans only calling for a stapled navy sheet to the wooden frame with Marisa dressing up as a woman suffragette, Natalie understood why more teachers hadn't been called on to help with the project.

If Natalie followed the current schematics, there'd be no theme, no sparkle, nothing to stand out in the crowd. If she'd learned anything from her seven years of teaching, it was encouraging her students to reach for the stars. Marisa knew this and surely expected Natalie to take the float to the next level when an out-of-town emergency required the principal's attention elsewhere.

Bright sunshine reflected upon the metallic red truck that would pull the float, which only had a few boards nailed together for a frame. After Marisa had emailed her the schematics, Natalie had taken a cursory glance at some websites, which had given her solid ideas of an eye-grabbing float with gold garland and a framed platform that would announce the theme of "Reaching for the Stars." This project would require more elbow grease than she'd imagined. Her bright pink cowboy boots sunk into the ground, but she refused to let her spirit sink as well.

She'd bluffed her way out of other situations in the past. Why would she let a little detail like not knowing what she was doing stop her now? Confidence and bluster would go a long way, as would the pack of volunteers she planned to bribe and cajole with free barbecue and beer the weekend before the big event. Between the teachers who were still in town and her friends, this float would come together and the school would break away from its reputation as having the most boring display in the parade.

While that sole weekend was cutting it close, she didn't have any choice because her parents' summer bash was this coming Sunday. An annual event, this year's had the added significance of doubling as their fortieth wedding anniversary.

Besides, having Danny ride alongside her on the finished float in a mere two weeks, throwing cinnamon candies to his classmates and the crowd, would be worth the effort. There would be enough room for several other teachers and students, although anyone who wanted to walk alongside was also more than welcome to do so. With some ingenuity and time, she'd have Danny laughing again.

Immediately following his mother's death, Danny had had nightmares to the point that he crawled into bed with Natalie all the time. Counseling had helped, but his progress was slow. Natalie shared legal custody of Danny with his uncle, who served in the military and was assigned overseas. The law might only consider her his co-guardian, a glorified baby-sitter of sorts, but their bond was stronger than that. She'd be there for him always, and his home was now in Hollydale. She wouldn't let the little boy down.

Speaking of guardians and parents, if she wasn't mistaken, that was her mother's gray compact pulling up to the curb. She'd extended the call for volunteers far and wide, but hadn't expected her own mom to lend a hand. Natalie wouldn't shoo her mother away, though. She needed as much muscle as possible for this project. Dreaming about the finished project was her forte. Others would ensure it would soar to the stars.

Sure enough, her mother stepped out of the car and waved, her white capris paired with a red-and-white tank top and matching sandals sporty and fitting for mid-June. Diane pointed to the pavilion where another picnic table sat, and they joined her there. She hugged Danny. "Good morning, sleepyheads! How are my two favorite people enjoying the first Monday of summer vacation?"

Danny hopped off the picnic bench and ran over to her mother.

Natalie's heart went out to Danny as he tried to hold everything together, grasping for something certain in an uncertain world. Natalie, more determined than ever to lighten his load and bring constancy back into his shattered life, sat on his left side while her mother settled on the right.

"Are we really your favorites?" Danny asked softly.

Her mother's arm navigated its way around his shoulders, and her hand reached out and patted Natalie on the back. "You're very special to me, Danny. You're family. And family's more than blood or a piece of paper. It's love and concern for each other that form the bond that holds us together."

"I guess you're right." Danny's gaze landed on the concrete, no smile lightening the features of his chubby cheeks.

Natalie missed the sound of Danny's laughter as much as she missed his mother.

Natalie reached for his hand, and they stood

up together. "We have to show you our project. Come on."

Excitement bubbled in her as she thought of the finished float and Danny's smile of approval. The dew on the grass shone as the trio approached the chassis. A blank slate awaited them. With an extra spring to her step, Natalie dug deep into her experience as a kindergarten teacher. If she displayed enthusiasm, Danny would catch on and respond in kind. Kids were sponges that way.

They circled what they had to work with, and Natalie ran through the unlimited possibilities, nailing down the final product as she envisioned its potential. She'd already forgotten Marisa's plans. "It might not look like much right now, but when we're done, it's going to be as colorful and lively as the fireworks."

"It looks like a wooden platform on top of a chassis." Diane ran her hand through her short auburn curls with interspersed silver strands.

Natalie and her identical twin, Becks, had inherited their mother's hair color. Becks kept hers short in a crop that flattered her while Natalie opted for longer locks.

"You gave me the impression this float was almost finished. This is a mere skeleton. Did you bite off more than you can chew again?"

"This is a good thing. Now I can put my imprint on it." Natalie released Danny's hand and walked up to the frame.

With a growing grin, she knocked on one of the wooden boards of the support frame. The entire frame dislodged from its studs and thudded to the ground. She jumped back and steadied her balance a second. Otherwise she would have fallen on her rear. Two-by-fours dotted the ground.

Danny moved in for a closer inspection, and Diane pulled him away. "Watch out for those nails!"

Natalie picked up the smallest beam. "Starting from scratch will let us build bigger and better anyway. I'm recruiting a crew of workers with the promise of free food. We'll get it done."

"I can help, Aunt Natalie. I'm a good helper." Danny shook free of Diane's hold and hugged Natalie.

Warm fuzzies filled her heart for the boy she'd known since the day he was born. She'd take on the world for him.

"Whose truck is this? It looks new." Diane peered into the windows.

"It's Marisa's grandfather's truck. He broke his hip a month ago and can't drive. She didn't want to assemble the float at his house since he'd insist on lending a hand. The great news is Marisa persuaded Mayor Wes to keep everything here at the park shed. She texted me his permission along with her proposed plans." Natalie squeezed Danny's hand and directed him toward the picnic tables.

Once he sprinted for the sheltered area, she began picking up the boards and placing them nail side down on the remaining planks of the trailer platform.

"Ah, plans. Now we're getting somewhere. Did you bring them with you?" Mom folded her arms and pursed her lips.

Natalie stopped from rolling her eyes at the vote of no confidence in her mother's voice. No doubt her mother would have smiled at Becks or her brother, Mike, in this situation, but instead, she'd question every decision Natalie made from the tissue paper colors to the type of candy tossed to the spectators. "They're on the picnic table, but I'm starting fresh with some new ideas. I'm thinking wire mesh stars and lots of flowers."

"Real flowers get pricey fast. And shouldn't you have a theme first?" Her mother's disapproving expression didn't waver as she helped with the remaining boards. "Did Marisa leave you a budget or materials to work with?"

Natalie waved away those concerns. "I wasn't planning on using real flowers. Even Mrs. Glisson wouldn't be that generous, and I should know, having worked in her floral shop through high school. We can make tissue paper flowers instead, using chicken wire to hold them in place. Trust me." She hoisted the last plank onto the platform and wiped her hands free of the dew and grass. "By the way, thanks for what you said to Danny."

"Any word yet from his uncle?" Diane picked up her purse from its resting place next to the truck's front tire.

"In his last email, he mentioned coming for Christmas if his assignment is complete. From what I remember from Shelby, he's a security specialist with a knack for languages and dialects." She leaned closer to her mom, not wanting Danny to hear what she was about to say. "Between you and me, if he does come home, he should agree to continue our present arrangement, Danny living with me full-time. I think it's for the best. Danny needs a solid support structure. Laughter and love will pull him through this. You and Dad always taught me to find the joy in the little things."

"Some days were easier than others."

A two-by-four fell onto the grass. Natalie picked it up and dropped it onto the platform with a thud. "I'm glad you knew where to find us this morning." She looked at the bent nails and winced. "Maybe Danny shouldn't be around this."

Diane situated her purse strap on her shoulder. "I agree. I'll take him to the splash fountains, where I'm meeting Georgie and Rachel in a little while."

Natalie admitted her mother was right. Danny would have more fun with Georgie, Natalie's new sister-in-law, who had married her brother Mike earlier this year, than helping her. Since Georgie worked most Saturdays as a mechanic, she usually had Mondays off. Hanging out with the three Harrisons would also provide an opportunity for Danny to grow closer to Mike's daughter, Rachel.

Natalie called to Danny and he moseyed over to them.

"Hey, Danny. Georgie's taking Rachel to the new splash fountain area. Why don't you tag along? I'm sure Rachel will enjoy spending time with you," her mom said.

"I'll stay with Aunt Natalie." Danny hovered behind her leg. "I'm strong, and she might need me."

In the past few months, Danny hadn't wanted to leave her side unless it was necessary. Even from a good distance, the new splash fountains beckoned with shouts of joy coming from kids of all ages. Spouts in the shape of jungle animals jutted water from the spigots in the concrete. After she was done for the day, she might cool off there. Features like this more than made up for an increased tourist presence.

Natalie reached for his free hand and squeezed it. "You'll have a much better time over there. I'll get some of the boring stuff done here, and tomorrow you can help me. The nails will be all gone by then. I'll be okay. I promise."

Danny let go, although reluctance hovered in his serious brown eyes. "I'm not going to wear my bathing suit."

Her mom reached for Danny's hand. "That sounds fine. Not wearing a bathing suit never stopped Natalie or Mike from enjoying the sprinklers, before Becks came in and told on them, of course. It's okay to break the rules every once in a while."

Over Danny's head, Natalie winked at her mom, happy for this small glimpse of rebellion from everyday norms.

"Only for a couple of minutes." He threw his arms around Natalie's waist, keeping the contact close. "I love you, Aunt Natalie."

Shelby had bestowed the title of honorary aunt on her before Danny's birth, and Natalie had no problem with keeping that the same, even though she was now his official guardian.

Diane led Danny over to the newest section of the park, which had been redone in the past couple of years. When Natalie and her siblings were growing up, there was a round playground spinner, a couple of swings and a metal slide that had burned her legs more than once, even in the cooler climes of the mountains. Thanks to the influx of tourist dollars, Hollydale now boasted the largest park for kids this side of Raleigh, with a new splash fountain area, two different playgrounds for all ages, a rock-climbing area, and basketball and tennis courts. Over the summer, she planned to spend many a leisurely morning here with Danny.

Once the parade float was finished, that was.

A new project to sink her teeth into. Something unplanned and spontaneous to get behind. Rubbing her hands together, she headed toward the picnic table for the printout of Marisa's plans. The sooner she evaluated her supplies, the sooner she'd have a sense of what else was possible and stop for the day. She hated to miss a minute of fun with Danny. Summer vacation was too short for her liking, although once August rolled around, she'd love the thrill and challenge of teaching twenty new students. She wouldn't trade her job for all the fried green tomatoes in North Carolina.

She grabbed the pages and saw a black car

parking alongside her mother's. The driver's door opened and a tall man in a blue dress shirt with rolled-up sleeves that highlighted muscular arms emerged from the car. Unlike the typical park runners in athletic shorts, tank tops and sneakers, this newcomer wore jeans paired with dark brown loafers. Sunlight glinted off his dark chestnut hair, its short length reminiscent of... He closed the car door.

There was also something familiar about the determination in his every step, but she still couldn't place him.

The oversize manila envelope in his hand caught her eye. For a second, she worried Danny's uncle was serving her with some sort of legal action in case he wanted to take his nephew with him once he returned stateside. Considering the uncle hadn't been involved the past three months, she wouldn't entertain that kind of negative thinking.

The man glanced at the envelope and headed back to his car. He must be lost. She transferred her attention to the plans. Movement caught her eye, and she looked up to find him heading straight toward her, no envelope in hand. His gaze gave the distinct impression he was looking for her. If she didn't know better, she'd say he recognized her. However, Hollydale was a small town, and she'd have remembered anyone with his commanding presence.

"Can I help you?" she asked.

"Natalie Harrison?"

They'd spoken at the same time, and she released some of her nervousness through laughter. She extended her hand, and his grip exerted the right amount of pressure, not too firm, but not too soft.

"Guilty as charged."

"I'd have known you anywhere from her description of you." He moved his lips into a straight line. She wasn't quite sure whether that was his version of a smile or not.

She racked her brain about who would have described her to a total stranger. Then she snapped her fingers. "I'll be the son of a sea biscuit. Marisa came through already, didn't she?" *Thank you, Marisa, for sending someone with muscles.* "I need all the help I can get with this float. You wouldn't believe the state I'm in with everything literally falling apart at my feet today."

"She's not the reason I'm here. My new assignment starts soon and—"

"Oh. If Marisa didn't send you, the mayor must have. You're the new city manager, then."

Mayor Wes had been all aflutter when Bob Woodley announced his immediate retirement.

Hollydale gossip speculated age had nothing to do with his decision. Instead, everyone believed he didn't want to judge the upcoming Fourth of July pie contest again, legendary in these parts thanks to the feud.

"You'll have your hands full since this is a tiebreaker year for the pie contest, but you look like you'll rise to the challenge. Besides, it's a change that will do everyone some good."

"I'm counting on that, but I'm not the city manager. Change is often necessary, and I'm glad to know I have your full support." He blinked, almost as if he hadn't expected to say that. "I didn't anticipate this type of welcome."

Hollydale surprised people that way.

"I'll support anyone who's here to help." She twisted the small disc of St. Michael on her gold necklace. "When the nails came off this wooden frame today, I came this close to landing on my rear end in front of Danny. Now that you're here, I won't have that problem anymore."

The man's demeanor didn't change, his back still straight as an ironing board. "I didn't realize you considered this situation a problem. Good to know."

"The truck chassis is over here, and you can see the state of the platform." Natalie wiggled her fingers, and he followed alongside her.

"Your arrival changes everything. Between you and me, however, I was on the verge of having to call in every favor folks have ever owed me, and for what? I dug a hole that's simply too deep. The nails are literally coming out at the seams. I didn't sign up for anything like this, but what's done is done."

"That's rather harsh." His low voice was deep and sleek.

"Not at all. I signed up under a whole different set of expectations." She halted a couple of feet from the truck and attached trailer. "Oh well, before I know it, this chapter will be done and I'll hand everything off. Life will then be all rainbows again. You have to look for the silver lining, you know."

The man walked around the truck and chassis, and Natalie kept her gaze focused on him. The man's piercing gray gaze seemed to be measuring up the situation, the wheels in his head turning, she imagined. He picked up a plank from the platform and examined it from all angles. "Just like that? No second thoughts, no regrets?"

About a parade float? She could use garland or premade decorations. However, creating puffy tissue paper flowers with Danny would give them something to do together. No way would she stay up nights second-guessing her decision to dream big. "When this is finished, I'll be able to live with myself just fine." *Better than fine if Danny's laughter is back.* "I'll have my summer ahead of me, free and unencumbered of the commitment. Late mornings, friends, good times ahead."

"You have some serious issues." He turned to her. Concern in his features mirrored something she'd recently seen, but she couldn't put her finger on what.

She'd seen those gray eyes somewhere before, but where?

He pointed to the nails sticking out of the end of the board. "Do you want my opinion about what went wrong?"

"Even silver linings need the right glue. You don't use finishing nails to hold support beams together." She picked up a board and tapped the nail. "When I drove the truck out of the shed for better lighting and more work space this morning, I must have jarred the frame enough for the boards to fall apart."

"Looks that way. Glad no one was hurt." As he spoke, he rolled down his shirtsleeves, unusual in this warm weather. Something running along his left forearm caught her eye, but he folded his arms before she could see whether the mark was part of a tattoo or something else.

"Don't I know it? When something harmful comes along, you have to move forward. I'm just the facilitator, so to speak, but I'll be counting on you in the future. I'm sure your energy and experience will yield dividends in the upcoming years." She tried to smile, but the man stared at her, his brow furrowing deeper with each passing second. Once again, a rush of familiarity flooded her, but she couldn't pinpoint why it seemed like she should know him.

"I had every impression you'd put up more of a fight."

"Why would I argue with you? You'll make life so much easier around here. By the way, I didn't catch your name. Mister...?"

Out of the blue, Danny rushed toward her, Diane on his heels. Whatever was wrong with Danny must be serious. "Excuse me a minute." Her cowboy boots smacked the pavement as she hurried toward the pair. "Mom! What's happening? Danny, are you okay? Did you fall down?"

Danny rushed past her, and she twirled around. The stranger stood a couple of feet away, awe and wonder lightening his hard face. Crouching down, he opened his arms wide for the sopping-wet missile heading his way. Danny flew into his chest, and the man absorbed the impact without falling down. Instead, he cradled Danny's head and held him tight.

Out of breath and wringing the wet towel, Diane reached Natalie and touched her arm. "He started running before I could find out anything."

No wonder the man's gray eyes looked so familiar. Natalie saw the same shape and seriousness in Danny's brown ones every morning across her breakfast table when Danny slurped down his favorite cereal and drank his orange juice. Danny's uncle, Major Aidan Murphy, had arrived in Hollydale six months ahead of schedule.

CHAPTER TWO

FROM THE SECOND Aidan walked into Natalie's small cottage later that afternoon, he'd been struck with a sense of home. A plump sofa with five bright pillows suited the colorful interior. Vivid abstract paintings lining the walls caught his eye. They matched her vibrant style, and his modern tastes as well.

He reached for the slightly blurry photo of his half sister and nephew on Natalie's mantel. Despite the poor quality, he made out the joy radiating from Shelby's eyes, her cheek touching Danny's.

It had about killed Aidan when his latest assignment had prevented him from attending Shelby's funeral and claiming guardianship of his nephew. Every day since he'd received the fateful call, he'd awakened an hour earlier to finish his work ahead of schedule, shaving months off his intended target date to reunite with his only remaining relative. This week the last clearances to return stateside came through.

Adjusting to base housing and Aidan's simple style might take some time, but Danny was young and resilient. Aidan had also lost his mother at the same age, and his father's steady hand had mattered a great deal more than his surroundings.

Though he wanted nothing more than to bundle Danny on the plane and move on to the next chapter of their lives, Aidan hadn't been stateside in a while. In the year since he'd spent the last Fourth of July with Danny and Shelby, who'd flown out to Fort Lewis near Seattle to be with him, the boy's hair had darkened to the same chestnut shade that greeted Aidan in the mirror, and he'd grown at least two inches. While a clean break from Hollydale would be best, he wanted to give his nephew enough time to adjust to his presence in his life.

That was why he wasn't wearing his official uniform. He'd checked in and changed at the Eight Gables bed-and-breakfast before he found Natalie's neighbor, who knew where she'd gone, and used the rental car's GPS to find Hollydale Park.

Listening to his sister's best friend talk about Danny as a problem easily solved meant he hadn't arrived soon enough. The redhead was pretty in a wholesome, friendly way, a free spirit, from the looks of her flowy floral sundress paired with bright pink cowboy boots. Any other time, he'd have found himself drawn into her blithe charm.

However, fifteen years in the army had taught him to always look below the facade. While Shelby had always raved about Natalie's caring nature, his sister had misjudged her friend's real character. Natalie obviously craved a return to her previous life when a child hadn't weighed her down. Aidan was only too happy to comply. Caring for Danny wasn't a hindrance around someone's neck. A reliable person and consistent schedule would instill in his nephew a sense of pride, a strength that would get him through anything else life threw his way.

"I snapped that photo of Shelby and Danny the day before she died. It was pure Shelby, ready for adventure and going for broke." Natalie's voice came from the breakfast nook area, and he replaced the picture and headed that way.

He reached Natalie a second too late to assist her with the full tray she lowered to the scarred oak table. A whiff of cinnamon and sugar reminded him how long it had been since he'd tasted apple pie.

"This is nice, thank you. But you didn't have to go to any trouble on my behalf. I won't be here for long."

One week ought to be just the right amount of time.

"Then you're just passing through?" She cut a big slice of pie and handed it to him on a bright yellow plate. "I was hoping you'd stay for the Fourth of July festivities. Hollydale goes all out to make it an unforgettable memory. I'd like that for Danny."

Taken aback at the way Natalie treated him like a long lost friend, Aidan reconsidered his approach to Danny's transition. At the military base in Germany, poring over every detail relating to reuniting with his nephew and cutting through the red tape, he'd decided to arrive unannounced. He hadn't wanted to alert Natalie. Her reaction was the one factor he couldn't plan for. But so far, things were a lot easier than he'd been anticipating.

She reached for the carafe already on the table. "Coffee? You might need it to keep up with Danny."

He blinked at how she seemed to read his mind about being tired. Jet lag must be muddling his brain more than he thought.

"I personally like coffee with my pie, but some people find hot beverages in summer overwhelming." Natalie poured him a cup and handed it to him.

He accepted the mug with sunflowers and

lowered it to the table, taking care to shield his left hand from view. "I love my nephew, Miss Harrison."

"Call me Natalie." She poured her own coffee and then sat, indicating for him to do the same. "I hope you can arrange for leave and stay longer at Christmas."

Stay longer? Once he and Danny boarded the plane, he had no intention of returning to Hollydale. Natalie was part of Danny's past. He was Danny's future.

He readjusted his weight in the hard oak chair and picked up the mug while keeping his left hand under the table. "I haven't given much thought to Christmas until now."

The first without Shelby. His half sister always sent him the same package with her homemade sugar cookies, an ugly Christmas sweater and some souvenir trinket she'd picked up on one of her adventures with Danny. Pain ripped through him at the thought that he'd never open another box from her.

This would also be Danny's first year without his mom. He'd plan something special for his nephew. They could go to the Space Needle or maybe the zoo.

"Too bad you won't be here for the Fourth of July. Everyone loves the parade in the morning and the pie contest in the afternoon. I like to think our fireworks celebration is the best in the state. And speaking of a little firework." She glanced upstairs. "I wonder what's keeping Danny. He's normally in and out of the shower in seconds flat. He's so quick that I have to check that he used soap and shampoo. Being a kindergarten teacher has taught me some of the tricks of the trade."

Her working with children seemed like a natural extension of her personality. He hadn't been around kids since Shelby traded her stuffed animals for a cell phone and her first boyfriend.

"Does he always take a shower in the middle of the day?"

Sipping her coffee, she leaned back, thumped her chest and coughed as though the liquid went down the wrong pipe. She lowered her mug and composed herself. "Most of the time it's all I can do to convince him to bathe, period. Running around in the splash fountains, though? That calls for an early shower this afternoon before our appointment. We love playing out in the rain, running through sprinklers, anything where water isn't contained in a tub or coming out of a showerhead. Showers are second only to broccoli on his yucky list."

From Natalie's observation, it sounded as if she knew Danny well. If that was the case, his nephew had been looked after well and Aidan was grateful. He shook his head, refusing to go down the road of warm fuzzies. If he did, guilt might swoop over him about leaving before the Fourth of July, and there was nothing wrong with him claiming custody of Danny. In fact, everything was right, considering Natalie wanted to live an unencumbered life, free of problems related to a six-year-old.

Hard to believe anyone so kind could be so cold and heartless about a young boy.

"However," Natalie continued, "he likes to look his best for his afternoons with Toby. Hence the shower."

He pushed away his coffee, the heat getting to him. "Toby? Given the circumstances, Toby's mother will understand if you call and cancel the get-together." The sound of the shower stopped, and Aidan rose. "I'll break the news to him."

"Excuse me?" Natalie came over and touched his arm, breaking off the contact after less than a second.

He recoiled at the tingle from a mere touch.

"I can't call Toby's mother since she's a seventy-pound golden retriever. Trust me, this visit with Toby is important to Danny and his well-being. I'm not canceling."

A visit with a dog was more important than

preparing for a life-changing move? Her stubborn attitude was the final part of the equation. The clean break he'd decided on for himself and Danny was for the best. Natalie's home might be cozy and welcoming, but there was something about Natalie that challenged what he wanted for Danny. The sooner his nephew was away from this place, the sooner they'd lean on each other to get over Shelby's death.

"Then I'm coming with you," he told her.

She looked at him, her deep blue eyes sizing him up. He'd withstood the stares of drill sergeants, four-star generals and enemy combatants. However, none of them saw through him like she was doing right now.

She raised her chin before giving a slight nod. "Good."

An afternoon of fun with a dog disrupted his schedule more than he cared to admit. They were on a tight timeline. Rolling with the punches wasn't his favorite way of getting the job done, but he'd do whatever it took to make his nephew happy.

Even if it meant playing with a puppy.

NATALIE CRUISED THROUGH downtown Hollydale with Danny and Aidan as her passengers. Volunteers scrambled to decorate the large gazebo with red, white and blue flag bunting. Others hung welcome banners from one side of Main Street to the other, attaching them to the tops of the new-and-improved bronze light poles. A nearby sign announced road closings while another flashed the early starting time for the parade. Glancing at her rearview mirror, she caught sight of a solemn Danny, quite different from the chatterbox she'd known four months ago. She'd give anything to have that boy back in her life.

Now his uncle was also part of her life. If she remembered the details Shelby mentioned, Aidan enlisted in the army straight out of college. Hollydale might seem a little dull to him. Meanwhile, there was nowhere else she'd wanted to live, teaching in Raleigh until a position finally opened at the local elementary school last year.

Driving slower than her usual Indianapolis 500 pace, she wanted to show off her beloved little town to Aidan. For some reason, she wanted him to view it through her eyes and like it as much as she did.

"If you look out your window, you'll see our courthouse that dates back to the year Hollydale was put on the map. Our town centered around the timber industry at first, but now we have our fair share of tourists. And that's the Main Street Pharmacy. Mr. Hoffman's been the pharmacist forever, and his tech, Tami, knows everyone by name."

Hollydale might be small, but the residents cared about each other. Missing out on the fun and love of her family made her decision to return that much easier. Okay, she'd been homesick in Raleigh and wasn't afraid to admit it. And Shelby, after visiting Natalie a couple of times with Danny, decided to make Hollydale her home and open a lunch café. The business property she'd purchased with a large chunk of her mother's life insurance policy proceeds still sat vacant on Pine Street.

"The town square is rather larger than I'd have expected."

"My brother married his wife in that gazebo five months ago." Natalie pointed out the driver's-side window, keeping a cautious eye on the newest traffic light, which brought the grand total up to four. "If you have time before you go, you have to try one of Miss Louise's ice-cream cones. When did you say you were leaving?"

"I didn't." Aidan's arms remained folded, with a guarded expression to match. "If all goes according to schedule, a week from today would be for the best."

"You're not staying with me?" The hurt in Danny's voice gutted her.

"I'm based in Seattle at Fort Lewis."

Her heart screamed out that his quick departure wasn't for the best. Danny needed more time with his uncle, a positive influence from the past, someone who knew Shelby when she was little. Her lips remained silent on the subject. With Aidan having a limited layover, it wouldn't do for her to put her foot in it like she had this morning. If only she'd recognized Aidan, she'd have gone out of her way to start his vacation on a happier note.

Although they had both connected through Shelby, they'd always missed meeting each other over the years. First in college, then in Raleigh, before Natalie moved back to Hollydale for good. Whenever she invited Shelby to her parents' home for the holidays, her friend had stayed behind, awaiting Aidan's visits, or she'd flown to meet him.

"We'll squeeze as much fun as possible into a week. A lifetime, so to speak," Natalie said.

She concentrated on the traffic light at the corner of Main Street and First Avenue, trying to ignore the effect Danny's uncle was having on her. Whether it was positive or negative, though, she couldn't say, as she turned left.

"Uncle Aidan." Natalie wanted to kiss Danny for breaking the tension building in her SUV.

"You'll like Toby. He's gentle and sweet and, if you sit still, he'll lick your hand."

Aidan's quick intake of breath wasn't lost on her as she made another left, this time onto Oak Street. This shouldn't come as a surprise to him since she'd kept him informed of everything through emails, not that he'd bothered to respond. If he knew how far Danny had come since he'd been seeing Toby, he'd be more accepting of Danny receiving counseling after Shelby's death.

Besides, Danny was right. Toby had stolen her heart the first time she'd laid eyes on him.

Natalie pulled into the parking lot. The long, nondescript commercial brick building was rather unassuming. For the longest time, this had been the local video store, until streaming became popular and the new owner turned it into a medical complex.

Aidan cleared his throat. "One of Danny's friends lives in an office park?"

Natalie turned toward Aidan, his scowl deepening the crinkle lines around his eyes. "I think you're under some sort of misunderstanding. This isn't a playdate."

"So far all you've told me about this activity is Danny will be playing with a golden retriever puppy."

Right. "Did you get my emails?"

"What emails?"

She winced.

They were already running behind, and Aidan deserved the whole story. She reached to her necklace and slid the clasp to the back of her neck again, touching Francisco's medallion for added confidence. "Let's get Danny and Toby together, and then I'll explain."

Danny clutched Natalie's hand as they neared the entrance of the Timber River Counseling Center. Aidan held the door open, and she ignored the questions in Aidan's gray gaze. He hadn't lived through the nightmares Danny had endured in the weeks after Shelby's funeral. While Natalie had hoped time and love would provide a level of comfort, it had become obvious Danny needed professional help.

Once inside, Natalie signed Danny in while he bounced on the big red exercise ball in the cheerful children's waiting area. The spot brought a smile to her face. The rainbow mural livened the other beige walls, and Danny always found something new in the bin of toys. She started for the middle chair but stopped when someone tapped her shoulder.

"This is a counseling center." Aidan folded his arms, a gesture Natalie had seen too often over the past couple of hours. "Toby's an emotional support dog?"

"A therapy dog," Natalie clarified and lowered her voice. "They tried play therapy first, but Danny relates to Toby best. We'll finish this conversation after they call him back."

The door opened, and a nurse with a gorgeous golden retriever in a vest called Danny's name. Danny jumped up and hurried to Toby's side. "My uncle came to visit me. Be nice to him. He's a major."

Natalie went over and spoke to the nurse for a few seconds before returning to Aidan's side. "Follow me. The nurse is going to take him for his monthly attention test before he settles in with Toby and the PA, who's subbing for his regular therapist today. We have a couple of minutes until Danny will be back."

She led Aidan to one of the therapy rooms and closed the door behind them. Parts of this room reminded her of her classroom, with its bright yellow walls and toy kitchen set. However, her room didn't contain a low-resting orange sofa across from an aqua chair where the therapist usually sat. She sank into the sofa opposite the major, who'd already made an impression on Danny. She only hoped he wouldn't be devastated when Aidan left in a hurry.

Protecting Danny and keeping him on the road to recovery were her top priorities.

"Why don't you start at the beginning?" Aidan scrubbed his clean-shaven face with his right hand. Then he lowered both sleeves to his wrists, but not before she again caught a glimpse of a faded but ragged scar running about four inches to the back of his hand.

"What happened?" Natalie pointed to his arm.

"*That* happened years ago and isn't important. Danny is. How long has he been coming here?"

That was as much of an answer as he was probably willing to give her at this point.

Her life centered around making sure kids could be kids. Too often the pressures of the world weighed them down too early. In Danny's case, he'd lost his mother so young, and Shelby hadn't listed a father on his birth certificate. Loss wasn't easy at any age, a lesson she'd learned the hard way, but Natalie would do her best to give him some semblance of a normal life from here on out. Love and laughter went a long way in childhood.

And in adulthood as well.

Natalie leaned back and fingered her necklace. His stare verged on becoming a glare, but she didn't wilt easily.

"Danny and Shelby were very close. His world caved in when she died. He hasn't laughed since then, and the nightmares started right away."

"You should have consulted me before starting the counseling."

"I tried. You didn't respond."

"That must have been for the few weeks I didn't have access to email. Either that, or yours went to my spam folder."

If he thought that steely look of determination would cause her to cave, he'd never been around twenty kindergarten students ten minutes before lunch when they were hungry and snapping at each other. She always kept her control around them, and she'd maintain her sense of calm now. "I'm a teacher, and I know when a child needs immediate help. He deserves a chance to be a kid, and I'm doing all I can to help him."

His jaw clenched, and she worried she'd crossed a line. In spite of everything, a judge could decide if Aidan, as Danny's sole living relative, should have custody over Shelby's wishes. Her focus had to be on Danny rather than his attractive uncle, who could make everything more difficult if he chose to do so.

"Then it's a good thing I'm here."

Finally, he said something she supported. He must be coming to his senses at last. "Then you'll arrange to stay longer? I'm no expert, but there must be some sort of bereavement leave, or something like that."

"It's too late for me to contact my superior officer at Fort Lewis today. You've opened my eyes to some details I hadn't considered before." He frowned and started to rise. "I'd best call about the arrangements tomorrow."

Natalie's heart soared at how reasonable Aidan was about extending his leave with only a slight suggestion on her part. The real benefactor in the decision was Danny, who'd bloom under his uncle's attention. "That's great."

"Who's the best person to talk to on staff about getting Danny's records transferred?" His words brought that level of wariness back into her spine.

"Why would you need to do that? Danny has his appointments scheduled for the whole summer. That makes it easier to sleep in or plan our adventures." Some of which would now have to include Aidan. A twinge of excitement at the three of them doing something together lodged deep in her, and she tried to push the feeling away. Aidan would return to his military base near Seattle too soon while she and Danny remained here.

Aidan rose, and she followed suit, thankful for the extra inches from her cowboy boots, allowing her to draw even with his taller-than-average height. "I'm not extending my leave."

Her stomach sank at how disappointed Danny would be at Aidan leaving so soon. She'd have to console him, and this might set his progress back.

"I'll arrange for Danny to continue his therapy at Fort Lewis. I'm taking him with me on Monday."

CHAPTER THREE

"THANK YOU FOR seeing us on such short notice, Ms. Romano." Natalie shook the attorney's hand and Aidan did the same.

"Call me Penelope. I'm glad I could fit you in this morning before my other early appointments." The petite brunette signaled for them to occupy the seats on the other side of her desk, and he and Natalie did so.

Part of him bristled at having to come to the law office when there were pressing matters at hand, like packing Danny's belongings and signing releases for his medical information. He was Danny's only living relative, and blood trumped everything as far as he was concerned, especially given Natalie's earlier words about how Danny was a problem she'd be glad to be rid of.

Aidan handed over the legal documents pertaining to Danny's custody for Penelope's examination.

"This shouldn't take up much time. Daniel Murphy is my nephew. Unfortunately, there were pressing matters that needed my attention before I could fly over and procure custody. That's been taken care of, and everything's in order. I'll be returning to Seattle next week with Danny."

Natalie shook her head, her red hair flying. "After Shelby's death in late March, I signed custodial papers with Mr. Mahoney. Shelby named me as Danny's guardian." Her voice trembled, and she inhaled a deep breath and smoothed the silky fabric of her sundress. "You should have a copy of the custodial order. We came straight here after dropping Danny off at my mother's, so I don't have mine with me."

"Thomas made some notes here in the file. I need a moment to review them." Penelope extended a tight smile before focusing her attention to the paperwork.

Natalie crooked her finger, and Aidan leaned toward her, catching a whiff of her light floral perfume. "Thomas is Mr. Mahoney, who was like an institution in Hollydale since he'd practiced law here before my father was even born. He suffered a heart attack a couple of months ago, sold the firm to Penelope and moved to Arizona."

For some reason, Natalie was intent on telling him every detail about every resident of this town. He knew his taciturn demeanor usually dissuaded people from wanting to chitchat. Instead, he usually only heard the strictest of confidences. So this was a new experience. While he could wrangle details out of others, he tried to keep his own conversations short and businesslike.

Penelope cleared her throat, and he snapped to attention. Sitting ramrod straight, he tried to glimpse some of the paperwork in the file, but Penelope was having none of that.

"I'm not sure where the confusion has come from, but it seems both of you are under some misconceptions." Penelope doffed her wire frames and placed them alongside the file.

"Apparently some of my emails and other communication didn't reach me while I was on a mission, but she's indicated she's only too happy to relinquish custody of Danny and get on with the rest of her summer." He'd had quite enough. He hadn't flown over four thousand miles for this. Natalie had a way of getting underneath his skin like no one had in some time, but he needed to settle this now and take Danny with him.

"I did no such thing." There was fire hidden in those happy, calm depths of her eyes.

"You said you were looking forward to having the whole summer ahead of you, free and unencumbered. You agreed that my coming here helped you."

"A summer with Danny after the parade is finished. I thought you were the new city manager, remember?"

"You called Danny a problem, and you said you had dug a deep hole."

"You're twisting my words. I can see where some of what I said might have sounded bad when taken out of context. I meant I'd dug a deep hole in agreeing to work on the float. I never meant anything bad about Danny. I held him the day he was born, and he's a part of my heart." She turned toward him, her voice raised. "I'm Danny's legal guardian. I signed papers to that effect. That has to count for something. Shelby wanted him to grow up with a family, with love."

Penelope patted the desk with her hand, and he broke eye contact with Natalie. "I don't have a gavel, but it's important to remember we're here for a reason. The legal standard for a court to decide custodial cases is what is in the best interests of the child."

"I'm Danny's uncle, his flesh and blood."

"I'm his legal guardian. I've helped him with school and tucked him in every night since Shelby passed."

Penelope replaced her glasses and glared

at each of them until he and Natalie quieted. "From what I understand, Shelby Murphy listed no father on Danny's birth certificate." She looked Natalie's way and received a nod for her efforts. "And she moved to Hollydale earlier this year, since she had a support network."

"Danny's father was never in the picture. Since Aidan's in the military, Shelby didn't want to move to Seattle in case Aidan was transferred yet again. She had enough moving as a child, and she wanted Danny to stay in one place. When she visited me, she loved Hollydale and decided this was where she wanted Danny to grow up. She was going to open a lunch café, Snickerdoodles. It was her pet name for Danny, since those are his favorite cookies."

"When she completed the paperwork to purchase the property on Pine Street, Thomas asked her to complete a will."

Aidan leaned forward at Penelope's words.

"She names Aidan Murphy, that's you, as Danny's financial guardian."

He breathed in the sedate smell of old books combined with a scent of the fern on the corner of the desk and relaxed. "Thank you. Are there any papers I need to sign to extinguish the previous guardianship forms?"

"Hold on. I'm not finished. There's more."

Aidan's stomach roiled at Penelope's precise diction. He could have used someone of her caliber when dealing with rogue new recruits.

"She also named Natalie Harrison as Danny's co-guardian in the event you were still in the military. Is that the case?"

He nodded. "At least until next summer and my reenlistment date."

"Your sister expressed her sincere desire that Danny remain in Hollydale if anything should happen to her prior to his eighteenth birthday or his high school graduation. Before you ask, it's legal in the state of North Carolina to have unrelated co-guardians of a minor child, unusual but legal."

"Danny's supposed to go with me to Seattle on Monday. I have to report to Fort Lewis. It's in Danny's best interests to remain with family." Aidan didn't recognize his voice. He'd worked all around the world on many difficult missions, and this was the first time his voice sounded weak, as though he'd lost all control of the situation, which he had.

Penelope shut the file and folded her hands. "I suggest the two of you come to an understanding about what's in Danny's best interests and where his permanent residence will be. It'll mean more in the long run if you two are in agreement without involving legal counsel or the court system. May I suggest a follow-up meeting next Tuesday at the same time with your decisions?"

Nothing was going as planned on this trip. Instead of returning to Fort Lewis with Danny early Monday, Aidan would have to call his commanding officer and request family leave time.

Penelope glanced at Natalie, and Aidan turned her way as well. Natalie nodded, while Aiden let out a silent sigh.

Somehow, he had to convince Natalie before next Tuesday at 8:00 a.m. that he was the best guardian for Danny.

CHAPTER FOUR

AIDAN WAS STRUCK by how blue the sky was as he walked down Main Street on his way to the Eight Gables bed-and-breakfast. To his left, Natalie matched him stride for stride, her bright pink cowboy boots thumping along the sidewalk. His sister had left custody of her son to a woman who wore cowboy boots in summer.

It wasn't that Hollydale seemed like a bad place to raise a boy. His maternal grandmother had lived in a small town like this, and he'd enjoyed a couple of weeks each summer with her exploring her farm before his mother's death. Then he'd lived with his father, who was in the military and transferred on a yearly basis, and hadn't visited her again.

He'd moved on, and so would Danny.

At this point, there was no other option. He needed to contact his superior officer for that extra time away to convince Natalie and Ms. Romano he was the best choice to be Danny's guardian. There wasn't a moment to spare.

In doing so, he'd be going against Shelby's wishes. Should Danny stay with the person who'd cared for him over the last three months?

Everyone in the military knew you didn't leave a soldier behind. Aidan wouldn't leave Danny behind either.

That brought some relief.

"I hope you don't mind my walking with you. I stopped at Eight Gables, intending for us to go together to Penelope's office, but you'd already gone, so I left my car there and headed over to the law office. It's such a gorgeous day, not too hot and no trace of rain."

He turned toward Natalie, who sent a smile in his direction.

"Besides, there's something special about seeing the Fourth of July decorations go up, don't you think?" Natalie tapped his arm, and a shiver of awareness at her touch stopped him in his tracks.

Her carefree charm struck him at his core, and he understood why his nephew might be captivated by someone whose blue eyes sparkled with enthusiasm. However, her innate trust and easy acceptance of total strangers threw him, and he wasn't sure whether she was naive, in light of some of the horrors he'd witnessed, or wonderful.

While he'd like to err on the side of wonderful, something gave him pause, and he kept walking.

"I haven't thought about it. I haven't been stateside for the holiday in a while."

"I'd like you to see Hollydale like I do, since this is your first trip to the place where Shelby wants Danny to grow up. If you take the time to look around you, you'll understand why. Then it will be easier to go along with what she wanted." Natalie's voice was as warm as the sunbeams radiating the town, giving no sign of nervousness that he'd be taking Danny away permanently. "There's the town square with the gazebo and people enjoying the fresh air. Or if buildings are more your thing, check out the architectural details on our City Hall. When was the last time you strolled along, soaking in the beauty of what's around you? Look at the mountains, breathe in the sweet air, feel the sunshine on your skin."

Somehow, she made being alive feel like a big thrill. Military life had jaded him—the sight of children clutching a blanket and knowing that was their only remaining possession or the sight of a mother burying her child drove home reality in a way he'd never be able to forget.

And yet, Natalie wanted him to revel in decorations? He wasn't sure he was ready to do that. Diverting attention away from him was a wise tactical move. Focusing it on Danny would be even better. "You were right about talking without Danny around."

"My mom was happy to watch him. You should consider Shelby's wishes and let him stay here."

"I can't leave my nephew in the hands of a total stranger."

She recoiled and moved her hand away. "I'm not a stranger to Danny. You're more of a stranger since you haven't seen him much over the years."

"I'm his uncle, and he's my family."

"Family is more than skin-deep. Take my parents. They loved Shelby and took her under their wing. They've done the same with Danny."

He had to concede her point about families. After college, the army had become his family. "And Fort Lewis will care for Danny in the same way. Besides, I won't be in the military forever."

"If memory serves me right, you have another year. That's a long time."

"Yes, and it's five if I want to take full retirement. Actually, I've been in talks with a private security corporation in Washington, DC, about a position that would utilize my linguistic skills in conjunction with their military contracts. My reenlistment date is a year from now, and they're willing to wait for me." While the job offer was impressive, he'd decided against taking it and instead had planned to finish his remaining years in the military until his retirement. Now, however, with Shelby asking for Danny to live in one place, he'd contact the company and see if the offer was still open.

And Ms. Romano couldn't fault the idea of a Virginia suburb for Danny, which would offer everything from the finest schools to easy access to museums and stadiums for catching a ball game together.

Someone called out Natalie's name. She waved and yelled out a greeting before returning her attention back to him. "That's still twelve months away."

"It might hurt him more in the long run to form a deep attachment to Hollydale and then leave."

"His therapist says this is a crucial time for him. He needs a support system."

Support systems could let a person down. He knew that too well. His father had remarried after his mother's death. Shelby's mom, Cathy, had possessed the same ability as Natalie to make friends at first sight, the rare exception being his young self, who'd chafed at someone taking his mother's place. As soon as Shelby came along, it was easier for Cathy to devote herself to her baby than a sullen kid. It was sometimes hard to believe they were all gone, as his father and Cathy had died in a car accident the summer before Shelby started college.

"Fort Lewis will provide that, too." He glanced at her, the wrong thing to do with the slight breeze ruffling her pretty sundress.

"Hollydale is already providing that. Name me one aspect of the town you've noticed since leaving Penelope's office."

"The sign explained how hollyhocks are the reason behind Hollydale's name, the historic post office, four cars in the parking lot next to the coffeehouse, an SUV in the drive-through at the utilities office, and four parents and toddlers entering the library indicating some sort of story time hour."

"I'm impressed. Sometime I'll tell you about Deb, who owns the coffeehouse, and Kate, the new librarian." She widened her smile, one crooked incisor only adding to her charm. "It's hard to believe I've only just met you. I've heard so much about you from Shelby over the years that it seems as though we're old friends."

Yet their paths had never crossed. Something always came up. A military assignment on his part, a family emergency on hers. The kicker was that the one thing that had finally brought them together also caused each of their worlds to turn upside down.

"Natalie! Wait a second!" A woman's voice heralded from the front porch of a yellow Victorian, and he and Natalie came to a stop.

The woman ran toward them. Natalie met the blonde halfway, embracing her before grasping her hand and pulling her to the sidewalk where he stood. "I want to introduce you to someone."

Natalie resumed her place by his side, and it was almost as if she already belonged there. "Lucie Spindler, meet Major Aidan Murphy, Danny's uncle."

Lucie extended her hand, her firm grip lasting but a second. "My twins, Mattie and Ethan, want to know if Danny can come over next week for a playdate. You're more than welcome to tag along, Major Murphy."

"I should warn you about her miniature pigs, Fred and Ethel. They stole the limelight at her wedding." Natalie squeezed his arm, and he couldn't help but wonder why he was drawn to her. She didn't fit in with his schedule or his plans for Danny. "Ethel tends to flirt with attractive men."

Natalie finds me attractive?

Lucie stepped back and waved. "I have to run. Call me and we'll schedule that playdate. Glad you've finally arrived in Hollydale, Major Murphy."

"Call me Aidan, and Danny might…" He stopped when he found himself addressing Lucie's back. Not for the first time in Hollydale, he claimed a deep breath and recovered his bearings, the bed-and-breakfast his destination for now.

Natalie fell back into step alongside him. "She's right, you know."

"About what?" *Only a block to go.*

"It's about time that you arrived in Hollydale." She gave him a curt nod and walked on.

She was no longer next to him, but he refused to feel sorry she was no longer there. Best not to go down a path he had no intention of traveling. Once he left the military and began private security work, he'd find someone on his timeline, someone more practical, whose hair wasn't the color of rubies. "We're almost at the Eight Gables," she called out. "There's an area in Reception where we can talk uninterrupted about Danny."

Within five minutes of first arriving at his temporary lodgings, he'd scoped out all the entrances and exits and uncovered every nook.

Though he wasn't wearing his uniform at the time, it didn't make him any less aware of his environment. Even now, he could identify the five adults, two Labrador retrievers and one stroller with an infant in a police lineup.

They arrived at the bed-and-breakfast, the cream exterior showing signs of recent painting. According to the information on its website, the farmhouse traced its origins back to early last century, when it was a hotel for temporary timber workers, and the eight gables gave it its name. The side porch featured two rocking chairs, both of which were occupied by an older couple with an equally ancient mutt at their feet. Even in the daylight, the porch lanterns glowed a golden beam, beckoning tourists and locals alike for afternoon tea, which the owners included in their lodging fee. He hadn't come to Hollydale, however, for tea.

Natalie bounded up the steps with him as if this were a new adventure rather than likely a serious discussion with consequences for all of them. "I hope we're in time for tea. Ginny's lemon squares are legendary."

He drew in a deep breath. "Life isn't all bunting and lemon squares, Miss Harrison."

"There's never anything wrong with making each day special, Aidan." She stressed his first name as he opened the front door for her, shooting him a look that said they were well past formal last names. "Life is too short to do anything else."

He gave a clipped nod as she passed. Anything so she wouldn't guess the turmoil within him. Going against Shelby's last wishes. Finding a nephew who was undergoing counseling with a therapy dog. Fighting an attraction to a woman who took a different approach to life. "Wait here. I'll be right back."

Approaching the registration desk, he wondered if he was doing this backward. Informing Lieutenant Colonel Thrasher should have come first, but with Natalie watching from a few feet away, firming up his itinerary gained priority. Extending his reservation would settle his nerves.

Aidan rang the bell and waited. He tapped his loafer impatiently against the cherry hardwood. Once he extended his stay past Monday, he'd start acclimating Danny to a new routine. It seemed like he was forgetting something, but for the life of him, he couldn't remember what.

A light touch at his wrist proved Natalie could walk with stealth when she needed to. "There's something you should know."

He heard footsteps rushing along the corridor, and Ginny hurried over to the desk. "Major Murphy. So good to see you. Is everything satisfactory with your room?" The owner, who was most likely in her sixties, beamed as she wiped her hands on the lacy apron covering her linen pantsuit.

"I need to extend my visit. One more week ought to do it." Pressure increased on his wrist, but he kept himself from looking at Natalie, knowing there might be a frown or other disapproving look on her sweet face. If she thought he was going to draw this out, however...

"I'm very sorry, but we're totally booked. I have your reservation confirmed until Monday, but you'll have to make other arrangements after that." The owner tilted her head and lowered her eyebrows along with a sympathetic smile. "Your original call came on the heels of a last-minute cancellation. Because of the circumstances with your sister and nephew—" her lips turned into a sad semblance of a frown "—I bumped you ahead of the people on the waiting list."

Natalie almost cut off the circulation in his right wrist, and she jerked her free thumb toward the porch. "I think I might have the solution."

He'd seen her small cottage. While her sofa invited a person to settle in with a good football game and maybe a bottle of beer, it would make for poor sleeping. Still, he followed her outside, organizing a polite rejection speech for whatever she suggested.

"Before you say no, hear me out." Her voice contained the smile he already associated with her.

"What made you think I was about to say no?"

She laughed and pushed back her wavy hair. "Your shoulders, your eyes, the way you're leaning against the siding with your jaw clenched."

Moving away from the building, he tried to relax, but his shoulders refused to cooperate. Good thing, given how she already read him better than most new recruits. "While sleeping in the same room as Danny or on your sofa would facilitate getting to know him more quickly, I'll find other lodgings."

"People make reservations around here weeks or months in advance. Summer's a popular season, much to my brother's chagrin but my sister-in-law's delight." She must have seen the look of confusion he couldn't hold back. "My brother is the sheriff, and Georgie is a mechanic. More people bring more trouble, and more tourists need Georgie's services. Still, I have another place in mind."

"What's your suggestion?"

"Shelby's house."

NATALIE PULLED INTO her driveway, only too aware of the man driving the rental car behind her. Somehow, she had to convince him she was the best thing for Danny.

Which she was. He just didn't know it yet.

Too often she caught people off guard. They assumed she was flighty simply because she liked to see the good in folks and the world around her. Francisco was one of the rare ones. From the moment they met, they laughed and bolstered each other's strengths. She reached up and touched the pendant on her necklace for encouragement. At least time allowed her to smile at his memory now.

She was confident that someday she'd be able to say the same about losing her best friend.

From the parked car, she tried to see Shelby's house through Aidan's eyes. Since it was next door to hers, she mowed both lawns at the same time. Even though the yard was in tip-top shape, the house looked forlorn, she admitted, lost somehow without a family of its own. She exited her SUV at the same time he emerged from his rental. He strode toward her.

"I thought you were going to drive me to Shelby's house." He reeled off an address, and Natalie shook her head.

"That's her business address downtown."

Natalie pointed at the blue craftsman, and they walked over to it together. "This was her residence. She used the small insurance policy your mom left behind to make a dent in the purchase price of the business and the rest for the down payment and a year's worth of mortgage payments. Originally, she considered living above the café, but she wanted Danny to have a yard. I think she really wanted her own room and didn't like the idea of sleeping on the couch."

Rummaging through her purse, Natalie shoved aside a couple of granola bars, Danny's favorite Matchbox car and some pencil grippers until she found the spare set of keys Shelby had foisted upon her. She unlocked the door and stood back, but Aidan remained rooted on the porch.

"What happened to the café?"

Natalie removed the key from the door and handed it to him. "The space is empty at the moment." She paused, remembering how excited Shelby had been when she'd come up with the name for it. "In fact, it never got going. You have the financial authority, according to Mr. Mahoney. I have no control over that." She held up her hand and cut him off before he defended himself. "I know. You were off the grid or it went to spam. Your sister set everything up to give herself one year to make the business work."

Shelby had loved to plan while Natalie often flew by the seat of her pants, something they had oddly bonded over. Shelby had been shocked when she found herself with two blue lines on a pregnancy test, but she never looked back, working hard to provide a loving home for her son.

"The place looks well-maintained. Thank you."

"I asked Danny if living so close by was okay with him and he insisted it was. He said it kept him close to his mom." And she'd been trying to coax Danny back to life ever since, a hard enough proposition. "The utilities are off, but it's still daylight, so you should be able to see."

"I'll contact a Realtor before I leave town."

"Or you can keep it and stay here whenever you visit your nephew."

He opened his mouth to protest, but she cut him off.

"Hear me out. This town is great for Danny."

"I beg to differ. Fort Lewis has many strong attributes."

"Talk to your commanding officer, then stay here to see why this would work so well for Danny. Hollydale may be small, but this close to the Great Smoky Mountains, there are so many opportunities for you to get to know Danny better. Hiking, the Fourth of July festivities, you name it." Natalie escorted Aidan inside.

Even with the passage of three months, it still seemed hard to believe Shelby wouldn't emerge from the kitchen or the back of the house. Since Shelby's passing, Natalie had brought Danny over whenever he wanted a toy he'd left behind or to pick up a special T-shirt or other item he wanted. Shelby's home no longer smelled like cinnamon and little boy. Mustiness now tinged the air, and a fine layer of dust coated the coffee table.

Aidan made a beeline for the mantel, and her stomach twisted at witnessing his getting acquainted with his sister's memory.

He traced his finger over the bright pink photo frame. "She displayed this here? My father snapped this picture. It was the first time I held her when she was only a few hours old." Then he moved to the next photo and picked up the wooden frame decorated with green camo. "This was the day I graduated from boot camp. She and my dad and Cathy traveled all the way from Cincinnati."

Natalie crept closer, the thick carpet muffling the sound of her cowboy boots. "She was proud of her big brother. I didn't know you called your mother Cathy. Shelby always called her Mom, of course."

"Cathy was my stepmother." His shoulders stiffened as he placed the frame back in its spot. "Shelby and I are half siblings."

In all the time she'd known Shelby, not once had her friend ever said anything about that. Shelby always referred to him as her brother. Always. Even though she hadn't known him long, his cracked voice let on how much seeing all this affected him. From the way his shoulders were hunched over now, it became clear he wanted some time alone. She backed away.

"I'll be next door if you need me." She winced. From everything Shelby told her, Aidan only let a few people into his inner circle, choosing not to depend on many folks. His loss.

However, for Danny's sake, she was glad he had found a way to let Danny into his life. The catch was convincing Aidan to maintain everything the way it was.

"I'd like to spend some time with Danny later today." Aidan kept his back to her, his tone low.

"Of course. What should the three of us do together? Go to the splash fountains? Have lunch at the Holly Days Diner? Want to kayak on Timber River?"

He turned around, stoniness reflected in his gray gaze. "Just Danny and myself."

Aidan didn't add anything further. He didn't have to. The tilt to his chin, the stiff manner of his shoulders, everything indicated he believed Danny would board the plane with him eventually.

She couldn't let that happen. Shelby wanted her son to grow up in Hollydale, and Natalie intended to follow through with her friend's decision.

Still, Danny did need time with his uncle. "He doesn't know you, and you don't know him yet. You need me as a go-between. Everything doesn't have to happen at once. Danny's just now sleeping through the night again."

"He knows me from visits and phone calls."

"None of which have been a factor in his life since his mother died. How about meeting us at the park around noon? Give me your phone for a second, please." She programmed her number into his cell. "Text me later so I have your number, too. If you take him to lunch, I'll work on the float and be close by if you need me. A compromise of sorts."

"Eleven works for me."

"Eleven thirty it is." Natalie sent a smile his way and closed the door behind her.

Maybe she was worrying over nothing.

Maybe Aidan would come around to the idea that Danny needed them and they needed Danny, *in Hollydale*. She intended to keep everything the way it was.

Except, she'd add more laughter. Both Murphy men needed more of that in their lives.

CHAPTER FIVE

NATALIE SWUNG THE huge duffel bag full of supplies onto the picnic table. This was the type of day she loved. Some late morning runners sprinted along the paths, and the mountain air held a kiss of summer without the melting heat. Pink and purple petunias lined the path, bright colors heralding her favorite season. Danny hovered nearby, a scowl taking the place of the sad expression she'd seen too often over the past three months.

"Stay here," she cautioned, before running back to her SUV and unloading the chicken wire from her trunk.

The wire didn't weigh that much, but its unwieldy bulk made it difficult to carry. A car door slammed and footfalls on the pavement made her pause. Aidan reached for the rolled-up wire and handled it with ease, carrying it the rest of the distance to Danny.

"Good morning. As someone who's used to getting up extra early, it feels like the day's already half gone, but we'll make the best of this late start." Aidan moved toward Danny and hesitated, probably noticing the boy's expression. Aidan seemed unsure whether to embrace Danny, shake his hand or do nothing. He stepped back. "All ready for a fun lunch?"

Danny shuffled his feet and mumbled a reply, unintelligible to Natalie's ears. Her heart went out to Aidan. He was trying, and yet, Danny had been through so much. If he moved away with Aidan, she wouldn't be there for him. And she'd be letting Shelby down.

"What's wrong? Yesterday you were happy to see your uncle." Natalie knelt beside Danny, her bare knees touching the still wet grass.

Danny shuffled his feet once more, a far cry from the cheerful child who'd once given away hugs like they were going out of style. "If I'm with Uncle Aidan, I can't be with you."

Her heart zinged. He had to stay in Hollydale. She squeezed his hand. "We have lots of time." *I hope.*

If she couldn't convince Aidan that Hollydale provided Danny with much-needed stability, could she stand in his way, Shelby's instructions to the contrary?

"I'll be right here while you have fun with your uncle, who will come get me if you need me."

"I want to stay with you."

Danny clung tight, and she glanced over her shoulder at Aidan. She mouthed, *Help*.

Aidan came over and patted Danny on the shoulder. "I like your attitude. Work first, play later. We'll have more time for outings now that I'm staying in Hollydale for a month. Lieutenant Colonel Thrasher approved my request."

A small spark ignited in Natalie at his intention to remain here for a longer period. A month to get to know the enigmatic major. A month for him to get to know Danny and see the benefits of consistency with a side of fun thrown in for good measure. Then again, she tamped down that spark. He was staying for Danny's sake, not hers. In fact, this delay might cost her dearly. What if she and Aidan formed a bond? The beginning of something between them wasn't lost on her.

Then where would she and Danny be when he returned to active duty?

Danny stood back, and she gave him a smile for reassurance. "We can work with that, right?"

Aidan removed his windbreaker and placed it on the wooden table. "So, where's the plan? What are you using the chicken wire for?"

Plan? She had it all in her head at this point.

"This morning I'm improvising and modifying the original plan and taking it up a level.

Once the structure is built, the overlay will involve more glitter and color. Next will come the frame and wallboard. It's going to be a reach for the stars extravaganza." She walked over to the duffel bag and unzipped it. Reaching inside, she pulled out wads of tissue paper and scissors. "Today I'm working on the part that will go around the sides and hide the frame. It's an idea for making the display more colorful and eye-catching. I hope it works."

Aidan raised an eyebrow. "Tissue paper? What if it rains?"

"Then the parade will be rescheduled." Natalie brushed an imaginary piece of lint off her colorful tunic. "Holidays are such happy celebrations. And represent everything you're fighting for."

She had to keep believing that. This float was more than just a float. It was a way forward. She missed Danny's laughter so much. Others might find her silly for putting this much weight into prepping a simple parade float, and yet, sharing and laughing and just being together in a special moment counted for so much.

"Paper schematics? An inventory list? Supplies on hand?" Aidan glanced at her duffel bag. "Some of the engineers I've worked with have taught me a thing or two about simplification. We can examine whatever you have and find ways to streamline your project."

His expression implied she was supposed to have a detailed plan and a backup and maybe even a plan C. She shrugged. "It'll come together." Searching the nearby ground, she found three smooth pebbles and picked them up, laying them atop the piles of red, white, and blue tissue paper. "I planned to cut these into long strips while you frolicked at the splash fountain."

She and Danny turned toward Aidan. His outfit of pressed cargo shorts paired with a long-sleeve shirt with a collar was hardly conducive to getting wet.

"You're not wearing swim trunks."

He returned her shrug. "Your text said he'd get wet. You didn't mention anything about me."

"Next time, I'll be more specific." Before the words were out of her mouth, she knew that was a switch. It was Aidan's tendency toward details, not hers. Her tendency was to dream big, the bigger the better.

Aidan arched his eyebrow but added little else while sitting across from Danny. She showed them the length and width of what she had in mind, and the three of them got to work.

Aidan's nimble fingers made quick work of his pile.

"So, Danny, how was kindergarten?"

"Okay, I guess."

Aidan looked at Natalie. "Is he ready for first grade?"

While Hollydale Elementary was smaller than average, it did boast four kindergarten classes. She hadn't had the pleasure of having Danny in her class. Still, she knew everything about him, including how he doodled anywhere, anytime, but put off reading for hours.

"Yes, he's smart and expresses himself best with a sketch pad and pencil." She filled Aidan in on Danny's educational progress. By the end of his pile, Danny had started opening up to Aidan.

Danny placed his scissors on his pile of completed strips. "Before you leave, Uncle Aidan, I'm gonna draw a really nice picture for you. This time you'll remember me and won't stay away so long."

Aidan rolled up his sleeves before rushing to lower them again, his scar peeking out for a second. "I've never forgotten you. You're a piece of my heart." He looked at Natalie. "Didn't you tell him…"

"I think Danny's earned a break." Natalie jumped up and stretched her legs. She didn't want Danny to know she and Aidan had different viewpoints on where he should live. Not just yet. "How about we walk to the playground? See if the swings are free?"

"What about all these strips? They might fly away or someone might take them." No sooner did the words come out of Aidan's mouth than a gust of wind blew some of the tissue paper off the table, scattering the strips about the grass.

Once they'd gathered and secured the tissue paper in the duffel bag, the three of them set off toward the playground. Danny skipped ahead, and she glanced at the handsome man walking alongside her. If it weren't for his standoffish glare, it would almost be like they were a couple on this beautiful summer day, the birds chirping, the slight breeze ruffling the light fabric of her tunic. Any hopes for a partner of her own had disappeared with the solemn news of Francisco's death from his parents.

She pushed the memory away and focused on Danny. She was so proud of the brave little boy.

"Hollydale is prospering and coming into its own. Timber River is better than any amusement park, and the hiking trails around here are second to none." Inside, Natalie groaned as she sounded more like a tour guide than a teacher.

"Good to know." Aidan jammed his hands in his cargo shorts pockets and marched along the path, his gaze never leaving Danny. "Why did you interrupt me back there? I have the distinct impression he doesn't know I plan to fight you for custody."

The man was direct. She'd give him that much.

"Aunt Natalie!" Danny climbed to the top of the slide. "Watch me."

She clapped when Danny slid to the bottom. Then she pointed to the empty swings, the silence in contrast to the cheerful cries from the splash area. "Want to join me on the swings?"

Danny shook his head and shouted, "You guys swing," before he ran over to the rock-climbing area.

She reached for Aidan's hand and pulled him along. "Come on. When was the last time you went swinging?"

Her cheeks warmed at her awkward phrasing, but that didn't stop her from escorting him over to the swings anyway.

"Are you always this persuasive?"

"Only on days ending in *y*." She smiled as she climbed onto her swing, making sure he joined her on the one next to hers. After pumping her legs a few times, she glanced over and glimpsed a small glimmer of a smile before he masked his face again. "You can have fun in Hollydale. It's not only allowed, it's encouraged."

"You keep mentioning the town." Aidan's gaze wandered over to the rock-climbing area, and Natalie didn't have to look in that direction to know he was watching Danny.

"If you give the town half a chance, you'll find it's a great place to raise a family." She wasn't only talking about Hollydale. It wasn't often she had to prove herself to someone, yet gaining Aidan's trust was worth it. "Shelby wanted Danny to grow up here."

"Young children are resilient. He won't even remember Hollydale by the time he's grown up."

His words sent a chill through her, and he seemed oblivious to what he'd said. If Danny had no memories of Hollydale, he'd have no memories of Shelby either.

Aidan kept pumping his legs, and she didn't know how to get through to his heart.

"Danny's therapist says this is a delicate time." She switched her attention from the uncle to his nephew, whose heart she did seem to impact. "Anything unexpected can rattle him, more than we even realize. Until the custody and living arrangements are finalized, telling him about our differences will only worry him."

"Differences? That's a light way to phrase it. Only one of us can get what we both want." The defensiveness in Aidan's voice rose, not that she blamed him.

How he was holding it together so well was beyond her. These adjustments would devastate anyone with less inner strength than the man beside her. His quiet gentleness had made a positive impression and, if it had been any other situation, she could have found herself rooting for him to take his nephew with him.

She shifted her weight, continuing to move her legs back and forth. The breeze in her hair invigorated her, the sweet smell of summer filling something deep within her, something that had been dormant since her fiancé Francisco's death. The man beside her had an edge to his quiet intensity. Letting down her guard might allow him the chance to become who he needed to be and she needed to have in her life.

A mother arrived with her two children and looked grateful for a few minutes alone on the bench while they played. Natalie kept her voice low. "Danny has great potential. Taking him from me and my home, which has become his

in the past three months, could be devastating."
For him and for me.

Guilt rippled through her at thinking of herself when she should only put Danny's needs first. The truth was, Danny needed Natalie and Hollydale, and they needed him. There was nothing wrong with that. At least she hoped there wasn't.

"Having him told his uncle doesn't care enough to take him with him could also be devastating." The undercurrent running through his words meant Natalie wasn't quite sure whether he meant that for Danny or himself.

This day was slipping away, just like her hold on Danny's future. "When was the last time you had fun for fun's sake?"

"We're talking about Danny." Aidan clenched the metal links of the chain so hard his knuckles turned white.

"Are we?" Natalie tried infusing their conversation with the same bright intensity of the sun peeking through puffy white clouds. Although there was no sign of bad weather on the horizon, she'd nip any sign of bad blood between them if she could. "I was under the impression we'd found something in common."

"Something other than Danny or Shelby?" Irony laced his voice.

"Neither of us wants to let go first."

"You mean lose. You don't strike me as the competitive type." Aidan slowed his pace as his feet dragged along the dirt.

"Appearances can be deceiving. From the way I see it, though, you think winning is the best alternative to losing, whereas I've learned there are other ways not to lose. It's the how you play the game that changes your perception of what a win is."

Growing up with a twin who was a star soccer player should have dulled her competitive edge. To a certain extent that was true. However, she'd also learned there were other strategies to winning besides scoring more than the other person or landing on Park Place and Boardwalk. "Danny's not a game or a sport. We have to work together."

"Do we?" Aidan asked.

The trouble was, she didn't know Aidan well enough to know how to appeal to his sense of compassion. Besides, Danny deserved better than a compromise. He needed someone in his corner who'd teach him what was important in life.

She and Aidan had different perceptions of what was important. For her, raising Danny in an environment where love and nurturing would help him blossom was everything. For

Aidan, his status as uncle outweighed all the other benefits.

She jumped off the swing and sent him a smile. "Sometimes taking a moment to breathe when your world falls apart around you is a win. That's what Danny needs right now. A chance to breathe and find his support system."

"I'm his uncle. I'm his support system."

There was no denying he was Danny's family, but so was she. Danny reached the top of the rock-climbing wall for the first time. Celebrating that was important. A win for Danny was having someone in his corner.

For now, she was that person.

Aidan wiped away a bead of sweat with the fabric of his long-sleeve shirt. How did he get stuck sawing new wood for the frame of the trailer chassis? Somehow, Natalie had crooked her little finger, and he did her bidding. From the utility shed, they'd taken two sawhorses and made a makeshift construction zone where he now worked.

He was a major in the army, a trained military ops specialist. Under normal circumstances, he delivered orders in one of six languages. Military training had impressed on him the importance of teamwork, and he thrived on a set timeline and instructions to achieve every goal. A place for everything, and everything in its place.

Natalie was turning his settled world upside down. More than ever, he longed for the shelter of the plane that would take Danny and him back to the world he knew. Even he could see the irony in wanting to return to a military base for safety and security.

The latest overseas assignment had occupied his every moment for three months, allowing him to keep his grief at bay. Seeing Shelby's favorite blanket on her couch and not hearing her voice had shaken him to the core. Why had he survived fifteen years of military service, including two tours in Afghanistan, while his sweet sister died of natural causes before her thirtieth birthday? The reality of Shelby's death had sunk in at her house.

So, too, had his resolve to have Danny near him. Aidan had been there when Shelby lost her first tooth and when she cried over their father's last army transfer. Danny had her smile and made the same eye-squint whenever he concentrated on something. Aidan couldn't miss out on the rest of his firsts, too.

Exerting extra force on the board snapped it in two a bit sooner than he'd have liked for a smoother edge. No matter. He'd sand down the rough edges.

He opened the toolbox Natalie had provided and checked the supplies. While the hammer and screwdrivers had wear and tear on them, the quality was good. He rifled through the sandpaper, passing over the extra-fine pieces and choosing a square of medium coarseness.

Sitting with his back to the side of the shed and his legs bent, he made himself as comfortable as possible. This seemed as good a way as any to pass the time until Natalie and Danny returned with lunch. He'd gladly agreed to this tradeoff. He would do dinner with Danny tonight instead, and in return she'd wrangle volunteers and write down revised plans for the float.

The rhythmic motion of passing the paper over the rough surface calmed him like little else so far on this trip. He wasn't sure whether the reunion with Danny or meeting Natalie riled him more. There was something in the air whenever he sparred with the pretty redhead, and he needed to focus his entire attention on his nephew. He didn't do anything halfway, and he wasn't about to break that streak now.

"Excuse me. Major Murphy?" A bald man in khakis paired with a light blue shirt and navy blazer approached.

"Yes, sir, I am."

The no-nonsense gait, along with his jacket,

created an air of authority, triggering Aidan's curiosity.

The man closed the rest of the distance and extended his hand. "Welcome to Hollydale."

Aidan set the wood and sandpaper beside him and rose from the ground. He waited until after the handshake to dust the dirt off his legs. "Thanks, and you are?"

"Wesley Grayson. Everyone calls me Mayor Wes."

Aidan's gaze wandered over the construction area. "Before I leave, I intend to clean up my mess and put away the materials. If the sawhorses—"

"This does involve the parade, but not in the way you're thinking." The mayor laughed and ran his hand over his jaw. "Glad to see you're helping with the elementary school float. Marisa Garcia called me last night with the update that Natalie was taking over and going with the theme of 'Reaching for the Stars.' I like that. You're staying in our good town for the parade, then?"

By the Fourth of July, he and Natalie should be able to come to some sort of agreement regarding Danny's future. It would be his first stateside Independence Day in a couple of years. "Yes, sir."

The mayor's smile widened. "Do you like pie?"

Is that some sort of rhetorical question? "Can't say as I've turned down many slices of pie in my day."

Mayor Wes came closer and patted Aidan on the back. "I have an offer you'll hopefully find hard to resist, son. All the pie you can eat by some of the finest cooks around."

"What's the catch?"

"No catch. It's an honor. I'd like you to be the official pie judge for this year's contest."

"Surely someone else, someone who lives in Hollydale, would be a better choice." Aidan wiped the sawdust off his fingers.

The mayor shook his head and smirked. "Believe me, you're the best choice. You're an important visitor. A fine military man. What do you say?"

It had been a long time since anyone had valued Aidan's opinion for something other than as an expert interpreter. When the mayor put the offer in those terms, it sounded like it was Aidan's patriotic duty to accept. His stomach already thanked him for the privilege. "You've got yourself a judge."

Something like relief spread across the man's face. "Thanks. See you around."

Mayor Wes practically sprinted away.

CHAPTER SIX

AIDAN SNAPPED THE measuring tape back into its metal carrying case. *Measure twice, cut once* was one of the first lessons his father had taught him. Now he'd be teaching Danny about tools and passing on those same lessons.

He walked over to the long boards and grabbed the top one on the pile. Consulting the rough diagram of oversize constellations he'd drawn from Natalie's sketches after the mayor's visit, he was satisfied with his choice. Same as his stomach would be satisfied, no doubt, in a couple of weeks after getting his fill of pie.

Natalie might be right. There might be something about Hollydale that defied expectations. There were other people in town more connected to the community who would make a suitable judge. And yet the mayor seemed to have singled him out. Maybe there was something to small-town life, something similar to military life but without the carousel effect of people coming and going. He knew that feeling too well, considering he was the fourth generation of Murphy men to join the army. His father hadn't accepted an honorable discharge until Shelby was Danny's age and they'd settled in Cathy's hometown of Cincinnati.

Whistling, he laid the board on the sawhorses and fetched his saw. As soon as he retrieved it, Natalie and Danny returned. Her red hair glinted in the rays of the sun. There was a freshness about her that sparked something in him, the part of him jaded from the impact of all he'd seen over the past fifteen years. Her gaze narrowed in on the neat pile of cut wood near the chassis.

"Look at what you've accomplished since we've been gone. If you weren't holding that saw, I'd give you a huge hug."

It was easy to see why any parent would consider themselves lucky if their child landed in her kindergarten class; her tone was encouraging without carrying any condescension.

He laid down the saw. "I'd have been done by now if it weren't for the interesting offer that came my way while you picked up lunch."

Her smile widened, and she leaned forward as if she couldn't wait to hear what he had to say. "Good news?" She gestured for him to join her at the pavilion, where Danny had already started eating his sub. He should mind the familiarity, even be wary of it, but he was coming to understand her openness was just a part of her.

Allowing himself this one distraction, he slipped his hand in hers. In the normal course of his work, he'd be winding down the training of recruits, simulating different scenarios, using his foreign-language skills, the main reason he'd already been recruited for his postmilitary career. He felt like he was playing hooky with the blue skies, chatter and laughter nearby and the sweet mountain air filling his lungs.

And yet? He didn't want to feel guilty. Natalie's vitality added something he couldn't put his finger on, but he had to stop noticing her. The optimism she radiated from head to toe brightened his afternoon, and he pulled back from the unexpected attraction. This was his sister's best friend.

He glanced at Danny, who was cramming two chips in his mouth at once. Instead of telling him to eat more slowly, he let it go. Though he felt like he was getting soft at his old age of thirty-six.

Getting along with Natalie and smoothing the transition would benefit Danny in the long run. So for the next few weeks, he'd make those his top priorities.

"Aidan? What's your good news?" She tapped his arm.

"Mayor Wes stopped by, and I'm going to judge the pie contest on the Fourth of July. Danny can be my helper." Good thing his leave did come through.

Her lips curled up, and she brought her hand to her mouth before she bent over laughing.

He held out his palms. "What's so funny?"

One more laugh escaped before she smoothed the ruffled edge of her tunic. "Please tell me you rejected his offer."

There was underlying concern in her voice, the type that usually meant someone cared. Still, why the concern over judging a pie contest? "Any reason I should have?"

"You have no idea what you've committed yourself to, do you?" She whistled and reached for her lunch. A loaded submarine sandwich with all the extras, the same way he'd ordered his. "For the past twenty-six years, Hollydale has gone all out celebrating Independence Day. It's one reason this is my favorite holiday. The town comes together and throws a big party. Everyone contributes something."

From what he'd seen so far, he could understand that. People and parties suited her, while he'd like nothing more than to take a couple of days and hike the mountains alone, maybe do a little kayaking.

"Nothing seems amiss to me. Can no one in Hollydale bake a decent pie?" Maybe that was the problem. Pretty town, bad bakers. Now he could end up with indigestion, or worse.

"Belinda Chastain is known as the Pie Queen in these parts. She bakes the most delicious cherry lattice pie." She smacked her lips. "Flaky crust, fresh sweet cherries. It's heaven on a plate."

He wondered if he should get back to work. "Good to know."

Natalie patted his arm, and he settled on the bench once more. She handed him his lunch bag. "And then there's Hyacinth Hennessy. Her lemon meringue pie is scrumptious. The meringue is so light, and the lemon curd is simply to die for."

"As judge, I'll get to try both, along with all the other entries. Nothing wrong with that." Her hand remained on his upper arm, and he wanted to lean in. He kept back, however, as it wouldn't do to get used to anything in Hollydale other than Danny. He pulled out his sub and began to unwrap it.

"What other entries? No one else ever dares submit a pie. Hyacinth has thirteen blue ribbons, same as Belinda. It's gotten to the point where it's almost unbearable to live around here for a year until there's a tie again. What's worse is the judge who does break the tie moves into the doghouse with the family of the losing baker. Norm Braswell had to drive to and from Asheville for a year to buy his fish bait when he declared Hyacinth the winner since Belinda's husband owns the local gas station, which is also the site of our best local bait shop. Mary Anne Whitten was banned from the garden club for a year when she declared Belinda the winner."

She settled back, and he crammed a bit of sub into his mouth and chewed. "So, I'm it, the fall guy." Something about that rubbed him the wrong way.

Here Natalie had been trying to sell him on Hollydale, and now? His opinion of the town turned on a dime. However, he'd made a commitment, and he'd see it through.

He wrapped up the remainder of his sandwich for later and jumped off the bench, more determined than ever to finish sawing the wood for the frame.

"Aidan, wait!" Natalie caught up to him quickly.

"I want to complete this part of the project first."

She tapped her cowboy boot. "Listen to me first. Now that I've thought about it, you're the perfect choice. You're calm and you inspire confidence in those around you."

"If you believe all of that, why fight me about Danny? I'm his uncle, and I should be the one who inspires confidence in him in the future."

She glared at him before looking over her shoulder and then returning her gaze his way. Danny gave no signs of having heard them. Instead, a chocolate chip cookie held his complete attention. "You promised you'd give Hollydale a chance. Shelby felt there was something about this town that could give Danny stability and a home. There's more to the town than what's on the surface."

The underlying context didn't escape him. She wanted him to give her a chance.

The sky darkened, gray clouds rolling in out of nowhere, an afternoon shower in the immediate future. He quickened his pace.

She turned around. "Danny, stay there. We're going to clean up so we don't get caught in the storm. They come up quickly here in the Great Smoky Mountains."

Arriving at the area with the sawhorses and piles of wood, they reached for the same board, their fingers brushing each other's. His awareness of her heightened.

He pulled back and picked up the tools from the ground. "I'll keep an open mind."

She smiled, and a distant rumble of thunder cut off any further explanation as they worked together to protect the supplies from any damage.

NATALIE SLIPPED HER hand out of Danny's as they entered her mother's kitchen the day after a whopper of an afternoon storm. Unlike her bright yellow kitchen, Diane had painted hers bright red to match her ceramic rooster collection sitting atop the cabinets.

Every Valentine's Day, her dad presented her mom with a new addition to the rooster collection, and her mother laughed and placed it alongside the others. Each time, Natalie saw the love reflected in her father's eyes for his wife. Becks and Mike had always groaned and left the room when the parents started hugging, but Natalie remained, soaking in the love in this space, hoping someday someone would look at her the way her parents looked at one another.

For a while, she'd found that someone when she and Francisco were engaged. Then he died too soon, and her dreams fell by the wayside.

Bubbling water on the stove sparked Natalie's curiosity. The starchy smell of potatoes greeted her, and she glanced at her mother, who rested her paring knife alongside a big ceramic bowl.

Diane rose and greeted Danny with a warm embrace. "I'm so happy you came over to help me this afternoon. Nothing like a handsome fellow to make the cooking more fun." Diane winked at Natalie.

"Thanks, Mom, for watching him so I can work on the float. You're an angel."

"Where's Aidan?"

"He's meeting with the Realtor about Shelby's house and her downtown property. He texted me the electricity's back on, but the water and gas have to wait until Monday."

"Glad I can help, then. Danny can peel the eggs, so it worked out for the best." She winked again, this time in Danny's direction.

Natalie headed off, intending on a quick getaway, but her mother wasn't having any of that.

She shoved a chopping knife her way. "Your father wanted a test run of potato salad before our big family picnic this weekend. Out of the three of you, for some reason, yours always comes out the most like my mom's."

"Probably because Becks follows the recipe too closely and measures everything, and Mike makes a goofy joke and always forgets to add something." Five minutes couldn't hurt much, and Diane was doing her a huge favor.

Natalie settled onto the wooden chair across from her mother. Danny sat next to her at the oak table, which had seen more than one food fight between her and Mike before Becks ran for Mom. Natalie discarded the first Vidalia onion and the second before settling on the third.

"Why that one, Aunt Natalie?" Danny propped his arms on the table.

Natalie waited for her mother to say something, but there was only silence from the other side.

Natalie reached for the two discards and showed them to him. "This one has a black spot, and this one is too soft in the middle. For me, it's touchy feely. That's how I get the sense of which one's right."

Danny touched each of the rejected ones. "Why not use the good half of these?"

Diane reached over and ruffled his hair. "You've got old-fashioned common sense. Natalie's going to have her hands full in a couple of years with you."

Natalie's stomach twisted at the thought of Danny growing up anywhere other than Hollydale. Shelby had wanted Danny surrounded by people who'd give him roots and pass on something as simple as the Harrison Family Potato Salad recipe. She sliced the onion with an expert hand. At least now, if any tears fell, she'd have a good excuse.

"Danny's here!" Her father announced his presence, and Natalie popped out of her seat.

"So am I." For right now, although the park was starting to call her name.

Dad met her halfway and gave her a side hug. "Hey there, Nattie-girl." Only he was allowed to call her that. "Hey, Danny, want to go work on catching that baseball some more?"

"I'm supposed to peel the eggs." Danny reached into the small bowl, pulled out one of the hard-boiled eggs and turned it around as if he didn't know what to do next.

Natalie reached over and showed him how to peel one and then caught her father tapping his foot, as if waiting for her permission. How times had changed. "Go ahead outside and have fun."

With a second glance her way, Danny waited until she gave a slight nod. Then he jumped out of his chair and hugged her. "Thanks, Aunt Natalie. You're the best."

If Aidan had his way, Danny would be on a plane to Fort Lewis outside Seattle, perhaps even as soon as the fifth of July. Natalie chopped her onion with that much more force.

"I have the feeling those aren't onion tears." Her mom's hand neared her own before backing away. "Does this have anything to do with Shelby's brother returning?"

Her mother always had a sixth sense about her children.

Natalie laid the knife on the cutting board. "He wants full custody of Danny."

"I see."

Do you? If her mother could bring all of this into one neat bundle so she and Aidan could do the right thing for Danny, Natalie would love to hear it. All night she'd struggled with balancing Shelby's final wishes with Aidan's ties to his nephew. It might have been easier if she didn't think she and Aidan had some sort of connection, something unrelated to the young boy at the center of all this.

Ignoring that connection made the most sense. Admitting there was something between them made her more vulnerable than she already was.

Besides, Danny fit in perfectly with her family. Even now, her father set aside time to teach him how to throw a ball. Would Aidan do the same?

"You can make this potato salad in your sleep. I'll be back to pick up Danny in a few hours."

Mom laid her hand over Natalie's and, for

the first time, she met her mother's gaze. "We'll support you no matter what. You know that, right?"

Somehow, Natalie didn't have the heart to hear the rest of that speech, the unspoken "but" giving her pause. She'd heard that same tone whenever she'd suggested having cake before dinner, bringing the ducks in from the rain or staying up all night in order to see the sunrise. "I have to go build the best float in the Hollydale parade. Something fun and bright."

"Are you biting off more than you can chew?"

And there's the rest of that speech. Her mother would never have asked the same of either Mike or Becks. Natalie jumped out of her chair and grabbed her purse from the hook on the wall. "Shelby thought I was up to the task. I can bring something special back into Danny's life."

She stopped short, unable to leave but unable to face her mother, the person she thought would be the most understanding. Without turning around, she knew her mother was behind her.

"Sweetheart." Her mother touched her shoulder.

Natalie didn't flinch.

"I wasn't talking about Danny. I was talking

about the float. Maybe you should call Marisa and tell her something's come up."

Facing her mother, Natalie became that much more determined in her quest to make the holiday special, not just for Danny, but also for Aidan, who needed to see the people around her coming together to build something good and lasting. And that he could see she wasn't wrapped up in herself.

"Everything's going to turn out for the best." Her own words didn't sound all that convincing, so she reaffirmed them in a stronger way. "This isn't just about me. It'll come together, maybe not as I expected, but life is filled with twists. Just wait and see."

CHAPTER SEVEN

NATALIE HELD THE door of The Busy Bean for Danny, and he slipped in under her arm. Only ten minutes late this morning, and this delay wasn't even her fault. At least, it mostly wasn't her fault. Her sister had called especially early considering Becks lived in California, so Natalie couldn't cut her off. No matter how much Becks insisted she only wanted to chat about her baby daughter, there was something wrong with Becksher. Natalie was sure of that.

Just like there was something wrong with Danny, although she couldn't put her finger on what was amiss, same as Becks. The Busy Bean was one of his favorite places, right up there with Miss Louise's Ice Cream Parlor, yet he hadn't mustered any enthusiasm for this morning's trip.

Catching sight of his scowl concerned her. Many times he called Deb's hot cocoa "the bestest in the world," and Natalie'd indulged him with weekly visits. Food and drink were no replacement for a mother's love and attention, but the comfort of the cheerful coffee-house, with its delicious aromas of chocolate and sugar, seemed to buoy his spirits. The residents who smothered Danny with love made it almost like a second home and well worth the trip.

She looked the other way when Mitzi Mayfield, the owner of A New You hair salon, sneaked Danny his favorite flavor of lollipop from her not-so-secret stash after a haircut. And Miss Louise always added sprinkles to Danny's cone when Natalie hadn't even paid for them, shooing her away when she tried to do so. From the Summer Country Music Series to the Spring Fling, there was and always would be something for Natalie and Danny to do.

Had Hollydale been the best place for Shelby, though?

Guilt fluttered through her about how she'd convinced Shelby to open her lunch café here rather than in Raleigh, like she'd originally planned. If Shelby had experienced those headaches in an urban setting, would it have been easier to seek medical attention sooner? Could that have prevented her untimely death at such a young age? Natalie would never have an answer to those questions.

For now, however, she'd have to explain to

Aidan why they were late. She scanned the coffeehouse until her gaze settled on Shelby's attractive brother. Aidan glanced at his watch, as if he didn't expect them to show. When he spotted Danny, he smiled broadly, showing off a dimple in his left cheek she hadn't noticed until now. She pushed the thought away. Falling for this man, or any other military man, wasn't a good idea.

Besides, Aidan's smile was for Danny, not her.

Aidan strode toward them, and Danny pulled back. The little boy's reaction made no sense.

"Danny?" Aidan reached for his nephew, but Danny grasped her leg with the grip of a boa constrictor.

Hurt was reflected in Aidan's steady gaze. Natalie ached for Aidan over the rejection. "Danny, why won't you tell us what's wrong? Your uncle just wants to talk to you."

"He can go home now." Danny looked frustrated, which was unlike his normal good nature. She wondered if he meant the opposite, too. "He didn't come when Mom went away and he's just gonna leave again anyway."

She leaned down to look Danny in the eye. "He's traveled a long way to see you now. He had a job to do, or else he would have come sooner."

"Danny." Aidan finally spoke and moved toward his nephew, the anguish clear in his voice. "Your mom was my sister, and I miss her every day. I made a commitment and couldn't break it. Do you know what a commitment is?"

"Yeah."

"What is it?"

Natalie urged Danny forward, and he scuffed the floor with his sneaker. "I dunno."

"It's a promise to follow through on something." Aidan moved his hand as if he was about to reach out, but then he pulled it back and folded his arms together. He tilted his lips in a half smile, and she stood close enough for that dimple on his left cheek to imprint itself onto her heart. "I made a commitment to the army that I'd keep people safe. I take that promise to heart every day."

"But I don't want you to go back." Danny contradicted what he'd just said, but Natalie understood. He craved a sense of security.

This time, Aidan rubbed Danny's arm before meeting Natalie's gaze. The air crackled as he seemed ready to address the custody arrangements. "I contacted my commanding officer so I could have more time here with you.

We can get to know each other and make decisions after that."

Natalie jumped in. "Thirty days, you'll be here, right? So much can happen in a month." Like proving to Aidan the intrinsic value of the town. *A cinch, really.* "And the Fourth of July is only eleven days away."

"Speaking of the Fourth." Aidan pointed to the table where he'd been sitting when they arrived. "I drew up new plans for the float. Thought we could take a look at them."

"I'll let you in on a little secret." There was something trustworthy about Aidan that made her believe he'd never reveal anyone's secrets without cause. At the same time, there was something mysterious about him, so she wanted to urge a few of his own out of him. "I function much better after I enjoy one of Deb's scrumptious pastries, along with my morning coffee. Then again, that's not really a secret. Oh, I know, we love ice cream in winter and hot cocoa in the summer, right, Danny?" Danny grinned. "What about you, Aidan? What's something most people don't know about you?"

He blinked as if she'd caught him off guard. "That today is my treat. I'll order while you two man the table." He reached for his back pocket and pulled out his wallet.

She shook her head. "You don't get off that easily. One small secret, that's the price of admission."

Danny gave a quick nod as if he, too, wanted Aidan to answer.

"See, it's unanimous. One simple fact about you that isn't common knowledge."

They made their way to the counter while Aidan looked snared in a bear trap with no way out. He tugged at his shirtsleeve until it covered the small dot of white near his palm. "Give me a minute." Then he glanced at Danny and released a deep breath. "Well, I like hot cocoa and ice cream, too."

Natalie knelt beside Danny and scrunched her nose. "Ernk. Strike one." Danny nodded, and they glanced at Aidan once more. "Try again," she said.

"What's wrong with that? Not everyone likes those things." Aidan folded his arms.

"I said it first. You have to come up with a simple fact about yourself that's original." She stood and brushed her wavy hair behind her ear.

"So many rules!" He sighed but looked game for another round. "And I usually thrive on order and discipline. This morning, I wrote out my agenda for the day, which included going over ideas for your float."

"Ernk. Strike two." She liked making that sound a little too much. She'd have to incorporate that one into her kindergarten repertoire. "I knew that about you within five minutes of meeting you. One more try."

"What about my mommy? This can be about my mommy and you." Danny stepped forward and pulled on Aidan's shirtsleeve. He gave a shy smile but stifled a laugh.

She placed her hands on his shoulders and ruffled his hair, taking note of the length. Time for another trip to Mitzi's salon soon. "That sounds like an excellent suggestion. I approve."

"While you two order, I'll think of a story." He ushered them toward the short line.

"Danny!" a little girl called out from a table on the other side of the coffeehouse. Her former student Gigi ran over, her cornrow braids bobbing around her. She gave Danny a big hug.

Natalie should have known she'd run into Gigi here as her grandmother, Deb, owned the place, and her mom, also a teacher, helped out by making summertime deliveries.

"Hi, Gigi," Danny said.

"I haven't seen you since school let out. My mom promised she's taking the afternoon off just for me. Hi, Miss Harrison! I missed you, too."

Gigi leaned forward and hugged Natalie.

This was part of what made teaching worth all the early mornings. That, and the joy when something clicked in a child's mind, whether it was reading for the first time or counting out play coins to buy something in Natalie's kindergarten classroom shop.

"Gigi, this is Danny's uncle, Major Murphy. He's visiting Hollydale."

She glanced at Aidan, who turned up the corners of his lips for a tight smile, that dimple nowhere in sight. "Hello."

"Come on, Danny." Gigi tugged at Danny, who followed. "You can draw a picture for Grandma Deb's new community board."

Aidan stepped toward the pair, but Natalie reached for him and pulled him back. "We'll be able to see them, and I know what Danny wants. He'll be fine."

He hesitated as if thinking of an objection.

"It'll give you more time to think of a great story about Shelby."

Aidan nodded.

Gigi led Danny to her table, and Natalie and Aidan soon reached the front of the line. She introduced him to the owner and barista, Deb. "I definitely see where Gigi got her sense of style. I love that scarf, Deb, so light and airy for summer." Natalie smiled and read the blackboard with the morning offerings.

Deb took her order, accepted Aidan's card and turned to Natalie. "By the way, Gigi loves drawing and was beside herself last night when that pencil thingy you gave her broke. Where can I buy one?"

"No need to buy one. I have extra." Natalie opened her massive tote bag of a purse and rifled through until she grasped two rainbow-colored pencil grippers. "Love your new community bulletin board idea. Would you mind if I post a sign in the fall asking for donations for my kindergarten classroom store? Little extras like stickers, picture books, small toys, anything arts and crafts."

"I don't see a problem with that. Remind me then." Deb waved and started preparing their order.

Natalie followed Aidan to his table. She'd have been able to pick out which one was his in her sleep, the neat pile of paperwork next to his phone opened to his calendar app. If she'd learned one thing from Francisco, it was how you could take the soldier out of the military but never take the military out of the soldier. Touching the medallion on her necklace for a second, she then lowered her tote onto the back of the chair before sitting.

"You surprised me just now." Aidan reached for his coffee and sipped it, indicating he'd been here awhile as Deb's drinks were usually piping hot.

"How?" Not that she was letting him off the hook for revealing one personal fact or story.

"You love your job, and you plan for contingencies." He placed his cup beside his phone.

"I won't argue with the first part, but the second?" She swallowed a laugh. "Hardly. I throw everything into my purse, knowing I'll need what's in there someday. Sometimes I surprise myself with what I find in there. Life's more fun with surprises, don't you think?"

"Depends on the surprise." His jaw clenched, and a shadow fell over his face. Aidan regained his composure and played with the plastic lid on his disposable cup. "I don't want Danny blindsided. We need to tell him about my intentions."

"Dr. Laurel Hargraves, his regular therapist, has emphasized the balance between a steady routine and old-fashioned love." Natalie leaned back and fiddled with the ends of her hair. "If you take him away from all this, it could be harmful."

"Could be, not will be." Aidan straightened everything on the table until it was neatly in order.

"You like plans. I get that. So let's stick to ours for the time being and not rush anything.

A couple of weeks getting to know you, and then a couple of weeks for us to hammer out an arrangement."

He tapped his pencil against the table as though he was finally letting her words sink in and giving them careful deliberation. "Fair enough, Plan B it is."

"I hope this plan includes more relaxation and downtime in your life. You need those, too, you know." Natalie looked around, wondering why her order was taking so long. She saw Danny coloring and turned back to Aidan.

"I'm quite content with my life as it is."

"Are you? Then why change it? Why fight me for custody?" She met his gaze, and something akin to electricity sparked the air.

She must be imagining the tension. There was no way she'd ever let another military man into her heart, even if Aidan had any thoughts about her other than as Danny's guardian.

Thank goodness Deb chose that moment to arrive at the table with a tray. The obvious look of relief on Aidan's face probably matched her own. She placed Danny's order at the empty chair and delivered Natalie's coffee.

Natalie shook her head when Deb also set a strawberry scone in front of her and one in front of Aidan. "These must be for the couple in front of us. I didn't order these."

Deb merely smiled. "A happy surprise for each of you. Yours is on the house as thanks for the pencil grippers." She turned to Aidan and patted his back, the thump audible where Natalie sat. "And word is getting out around here about you. I'm a navy vet myself, and I appreciate your service. There was one time I wasn't able to get home for a family funeral, so I understand your sacrifice. The scone's nothing compared to what you do for each of us."

After Deb left, silence descended for a minute before Aidan picked up the top sheet of paper and handed it to Natalie. "Here's one sketch I made based on your chicken wire idea."

There was something about his resolute look that made her heart thump. His humility was humbling.

"Why did you enter the military?"

"What? We were discussing chicken wire."

"No, you brought up chicken wire as soon as Deb walked away. She paid you a compliment, and you changed the subject. I'm just trying to find out more about you."

The subtle clench of his jaw proved she was right. He didn't like talking about himself. She picked off the corner of her scone and popped it into her mouth, the delicious strawberry flavor the perfect taste of summer.

He replaced the paper and straightened the stack once more. She resisted the urge to reach over and throw the pile up in the air. "My father was in the military. Same as his father and so on."

"There must be more to your decision than it's the 'family business.'"

He sipped his coffee and then craned his neck, checking on Danny, and then scoped out the entrance. "In college, I discovered I have an ear for languages. Since I'd been in ROTC as long as I could remember, the choice was obvious."

She broke off another piece of her scone and savored the flavors. "Were Cathy and your father in the accident before or after you enlisted?"

"Long after. I wouldn't have enlisted if Shelby had still been a minor."

That said so much about his character. She polished off her scone. "How will a little boy fit into your life on base? Who will take care of him if you're called away to another overseas assignment?"

From the way he recoiled, she knew her point hit home. The tension between them was back, but this time the flutters in her stomach weren't hunger and they weren't nerves. Instead, she liked the man sitting across from her, and that scared her.

There was something in his face that bolstered her opinion, signaling the feeling was mutual, but she couldn't allow that. Danny rushed back to the table, his eyes lighting up at the hot chocolate and sausage biscuit in front of the empty chair.

"I like hot cocoa in summer, too, just like Aunt Natalie." Danny smiled at her, and her heart squeezed at the prospect of not seeing that sweet grin every day. Already this year there had been too many days when he didn't smile. "Have you thought of a story about my mommy yet?"

Natalie glanced at Aidan. He met her gaze head-on, that spark close to becoming a full sizzling current. When she'd allowed one military man into her heart, his death had devastated her. This soldier held the fate of someone dear to her heart in his hands, and extinguishing the flame before anyone suffered irreparable scarring was best for all involved. As hard as it was for her to shutter her feelings, almost impossible as she'd never had to do so before, she averted her eyes and picked up the top sheet from the stack.

She reached for her tote hanging off the chair and rummaged through it until she found what she was looking for, a red pencil. She sketched her adjustments while Danny repeated his question about Aidan's secret. Her ears perked up.

"There's something about your mom that's important for you to know. Your mother was like me, and she liked to plan everything…"

"That was strike two, remember? Ernk." Danny made the sound, though no laugh followed.

She tightened her grip on the pencil. As hard as it was for her not to blurt out the custodial arrangements, so Danny could hear it from her lips rather than Aidan's, she kept silent. Their deal had to go both ways.

"You have a good memory. I…" Once again, hesitation halted the major's forward progress. He scrubbed his clean-shaven jaw with his hand and downed the rest of his coffee as though caffeine was liquid courage. "Shelby threw her whole heart into organizing events. One time she asked your grandma, Cathy, for twenty dollars but wouldn't say why. Your grandfather didn't want Cathy to give Shelby the money, but Cathy believed in your mom. She told your grandfather that Shelby must have a good reason for the money and we had to trust her. A week later, Shelby surprised all of us with a family picnic. She'd prepared all the food from scratch."

That sounded like Shelby to the core. Creating a plan while keeping everyone in the dark about her ultimate goal. It wasn't until Shelby had arrived in Hollydale, lease in hand, that she'd confided the truth about Snickerdoodles to Natalie, saying she didn't want to jinx anything.

The pencil point snapped, and Natalie flinched. Her friend's ulterior motive in naming her and Aidan as co-guardians wasn't apparent to her, and she was sure it wasn't apparent to Aidan either.

This time, however, there was much more at stake than twenty dollars. It was a little boy's heart.

AIDAN STEPPED OUTSIDE The Busy Bean. The sun shone full on his face, warming him after the cool, air-conditioned interior of the coffeehouse. Summer had always been his favorite season. The amount of daylight bolstered his reserves, allowing him to get more acclimated after long winters at the base wherever he was stationed. All around Hollydale, the vibrant colors of the season greeted him. Perennials in dark purple and bright yellow lined the walk from the building to the street. The patriotic red, white and blue of the street banner announcing the parade and other festivities for the Fourth touched something he hadn't connected with in quite a while. Considering he'd arrived on empty, that wasn't hard.

Hollydale could grow on him if he let it, the memories of his grandmother's farm returning full tilt. Early mornings, fresh eggs and milk, and her cheerful bustle as she cooked breakfast and finished her chores so they could drive into town in the afternoon. For a special treat, she'd taken him to a matinee complete with popcorn and soda. The brick storefronts of the surrounding businesses on Timber Road resembled those of his grandmother's hometown, except for the new renovations that propelled him back to the present. He kept searching their shadows, finding nothing out of place.

Danny skipped ahead on the sidewalk, leading the way to his friend's house, where he'd spend this Thursday afternoon while Aidan and Natalie worked on the float. Other volunteers from the school would be joining them to help with decorations for Natalie's theme, "Reaching for the Stars." A good message for young students. The words to tell his nephew how much he cared had been on the tip of his tongue. Then again, he'd best wait. He'd made Natalie a promise to let Danny become reacquainted with him again. Promises meant everything to him.

They turned onto Main Street. "Hold up a second, Danny." Natalie stopped in front of the River Art Gallery. "Come look at this painting. See how your eye is drawn to the primary colors, yet there's much more there."

Aidan contemplated the canvas, then turned his gaze on Natalie. The same could be said for her. There was more to her than what was on the surface. From her interaction with Gigi, it was obvious she cared for her students. He'd bet she was one of those teachers whose name her students would remember long after they finished school.

The sun glinted off her auburn hair, the gold highlights as vibrant as Natalie. Somehow, she conjured up happy endings, summer mornings and flights of fancy, seemingly untouched by the complexity of the real world. With her around, it almost seemed possible to balance the light and the dark, grief and joy. However, harsh lessons always infiltrated. He'd found routine the best answer to getting through the day without resorting to the messiness Natalie favored. His father had taught him that, while navigating the rough patch after his mother died. *Consistency is the hallmark of strength*, his father said, greeting him the same way every morning. Aidan thought he might start Danny's day the same way. It would keep his nephew safe and help him become a man Shelby would be proud of.

"You met Lucie already. She's one of my best friends." Natalie's voice broke him out of his reverie.

Is everyone Natalie's best friend?

"She's great with kids and animals."

"I thought the idea, though, was for Danny and me to spend time together." Aidan started walking and fixed his gaze on his nephew as Natalie presented more dangers than enemy territory.

"Her husband, Caleb, organized this outing a while ago. He's showing them his metal detector and letting them use it. When he was dating Lucie, Mattie found a coffee tin with toy soldiers and an antique watch. I don't want to disappoint Danny. He loves all of Lucie's pets. And the twins are great." Natalie stayed by his side, pointing out tidbits about each of the buildings and the people who worked in them.

"Glad we're doing this today, then. I can only be at the bed-and-breakfast for the length of my original stay. Monday I'm moving into Shelby's house temporarily."

Four days from now, the local Realtor would meet him so he could sign papers to list the house. Danny skipped ahead, and Aidan continued sweeping the area. The architectural cornices of the government buildings on Main Street caught his eye before the downtown district gave way to a residential section.

The rhythmic humming of lawn mowers provided a steady buzz, the aroma of fresh-cut grass filling the air. They passed a yard filled with wind chimes of every imaginable color and size. He stopped in sheer fascination. Blue metal elephants graced one tree branch while a sun and moon twirled on another. One with glass prisms caught the rays of the sun, splaying rainbows on the sidewalk.

He counted twenty-eight when Natalie finally tugged at his arm. "Come on. Hurry up!"

A window on the lower story of the white carriage house swung open. A woman with long curly gray hair tied back with a wide tie-dyed headband stuck out her upper body and waved her arms. "Yoo-hoo!"

Natalie muttered something under her breath, the first time he'd seen her out-of-sorts, and sighed. "She's one of my favorite people, but she likes to talk." She cupped her hands to the sides of her heart-shaped face. "Hold up, Danny."

The woman shut the window, the shrubs under it perfect green boxes of hollyhocks. In less than a minute, the bright blue front door opened, and she appeared, swaths of dress fabric whirling about her legs. "Aren't you Major Murphy?"

He almost snapped to attention. "Yes, ma'am."

"Stay right there. Don't move a muscle." The woman ran back inside, slamming the door behind her.

Aidan's muscles twitched. He blinked and glanced at Natalie. She placed her arms around Danny's shoulders, his brown hair, so like Shelby's, ruffling in the breeze. "Get comfortable. We'll be here a while."

Danny wriggled out of her grasp. "Which wind chime is your favorite, Uncle Aidan?"

He scanned the yard. The simple gray metal one appealed to him with its austerity. Then a bright sunflower one made of stained glass caught his eye. It had shiny copper chimes. Sunflowers had been his mother and grandmother's favorite flower. He pointed at it. "That one."

"I like that one, too." Danny clapped and jumped up and down.

The woman emerged, carrying a cake carrier. "Major M., it's a pleasure to meet you. Welcome to Hollydale. If there's anything I can do to be of service, please don't hesitate to ask. Having someone active in the army is going to light up our Fourth. Do you like red velvet cake? It was my husband's favorite. He said no one in North Carolina made red velvet cake like me."

His mind reeled at the speed with which she delivered all of that without stopping for a single breath. He accepted the carrier. "Um, thank you, but I didn't expect anything, Mrs.…"

"Hyacinth Hennessy. If you don't like red velvet cake, I have a hummingbird cake that makes the sirens sing."

Her chirpy voice reminded him of a bird, but since he wasn't sure what hummingbird cake was, he'd stick with this one. "Thank you for the welcome. Appreciate it."

"Don't mention it. Friends stick together. Any friend of Natalie's is a friend of mine. People are like nature in that respect. Plants grow best with tender loving care. Take my roses—"

Natalie rushed over and patted Hyacinth's arm. "Aidan will be here a month. He has a full schedule, what with helping me with the float this afternoon and then moving into Shelby's house on Monday."

"You're moving into Mommy's house? Does this mean you're staying forever?" Danny's eyes grew wide and he rushed over and threw his arms around Aidan's middle. It was all Aidan could do not to drop the cake.

Hyacinth reached for the carrier, and Aidan let go and hugged Danny back. For a second, he closed his eyes and reveled in having his nephew's arms around him. He might not have much experience with children, but he wanted to be a part of every aspect of Danny's life. "My leave is only for a month."

Danny's body tensed, and he let go as Aidan opened his eyes. "Oh."

That one word said so much more. Once Danny moved to his new home at Fort Lewis, they'd adjust to this new normal together. He caught Natalie's gaze, her clouded expression at odds with her sunny openness.

Hyacinth fluttered about like a hummingbird, handing him the cake carrier again. "Do you do much gardening, Major M.?"

What does gardening have to do with cake? "Can't say I have the time."

"It's very restful. My husband was a military man, air force, you know. At first, he was skeptical of the benefits of gardening until he studied it in depth. That was his character, always learning, always striving for knowledge." Hyacinth's hands kept moving, flapping like a bird's wings. "Soil composition, new composting methods, optimal placement for sunlight. He loved the challenges."

Aidan nodded and now understood why Natalie had urged him to hurry. He held up the cake carrier. "Thanks for the cake."

Hyacinth waggled her finger at him and planted herself in his path. "Yet for all his planning, there's so much more to gardening, you see. There's so much life teeming underground, but the time and effort to bring forth beautiful blossoms are worth it. When the flowers bloom and the yard is a riotous wonder of color, I love to come out here with a slice of pie and revel in nature's beauty. You have to take the time, though, and see the whole picture. A month is nothing to military men, but it's an eternity for a gardener. We're patient and see more than what's on the surface, you know. Enjoy the cake, Major M. You, too, Natalie. Say hello to your folks and Becks and Mike for me, won't you?"

She flounced along her front path until she disappeared inside, away from view. Aidan glanced at Natalie, unsure of what had transpired.

Natalie reached for Danny's hand. "If we're lucky, maybe your uncle Aidan will share his bounty with us." She glanced at him and winked. "I have a feeling, though, that's just a taste of what's to come."

"What do you mean?"

She only laughed. "You'll see."

AIDAN RAN HIS hand along the cool metal of the toolbox, content with a few hours of honest labor ahead of him on the float. He needed to lose himself in sweat and exertion. Hollydale had him turned every which way. A coffeehouse owner who gave away strawberry scones as a thank-you for doing his job. A gardener who gave away a red velvet cake for the same reason. Thank goodness Natalie's friend hadn't given him Ethel, although the miniature pig had made a positive impression on him.

This sense of community overwhelmed him, and he wasn't used to it. Despite his training and the camaraderie he found in the service, the warmth of Hollydale was something special, something different. People in this town surprised him with their kindness, and he didn't like surprises.

Aidan snapped open the lid to the toolbox and located the laser pointer and measuring tape. Palming both, he closed the box and headed toward the trailer chassis, the shouts from the splash park a dull enough roar not to disturb his attention. Movement in the picnic pavilion caught his eye. Some of Natalie's teacher friends were off in the distance creating wooden crates to decorate with hawks on one side for the elementary school mascot and stars on the other for the front of the float. In spite of himself, his gaze was drawn to Natalie, a picture of summer in her sundress and gladiator sandals.

Through it all, Danny responded to her like a moth to a porch light. How would Aidan be able to console Danny for losing Natalie's presence in his everyday life? Would he have to stay connected to her, to the town, for Danny's sake? He strode the rest of the way to the chassis, whipped open the measuring tape and glanced at the plans. At the front would be the mascot boxes and at the back, crates decorated in primary colors with numbers painted on them. In the middle would stand the overarching display of a rainbow of stars. First he had to ascertain the distance from the trailer platform to the ground in order to know the dimensions of the apron frame, which would then accommodate Natalie's chicken-wire-tissue creation that would decorate the sides, hiding the wheels and frame.

Nearby a car door slammed with an excessive amount of force. He jerked up, sizing up any threat to the immediate area.

An older woman in a red polo shirt and blue jean capris stormed toward him with a cake carrier. What was it with the residents of Hollydale? Did they always walk around with homemade cakes? He glanced around, wondering who her target was. She zeroed in on him and pointed toward the picnic tables.

"Major Murphy, I presume. Join me at the pavilion." She held up the cake carrier. Although her fluffy gray hair projected the image of everyone's favorite grandmother, her no-nonsense demeanor reminded him of his first drill sergeant. "I'm Belinda Chastain, better known as the Pie Queen in these parts."

He sighed and placed the tools and plans atop the trailer platform. With the constant interruptions, this float might be ready for the Christmas parade.

There was a hint of bemusement on Natalie's face. "So, you happened to be in the neighborhood with your famous three-layer lemon coconut cake?"

Belinda shot her a look of pure disdain, which would have made him drop and give her twenty pushups in boot camp. "Don't be impertinent or I'll order Major Murphy not to share."

"Aidan." He lowered his shirtsleeves and

folded his arms. "Another member of the Welcome Wagon, I presume?"

"You'll count your lucky stars someday and place moving to Hollydale atop your list of blessings." Belinda gave a curt nod for emphasis.

Why was everyone assuming he was moving here? "I'm just visiting."

"We'll see." Belinda handed him the cake carrier, and she bobbed her head, her hair not moving an inch. "My daughter moved back recently. Smartest thing she's done in years. You don't seem like a dumb chicken to me. You'll come to your senses."

"Thanks." It came out more like a question than an acknowledgment, and he cleared his throat. "Lemon coconut's my favorite."

A sly smile spread over her square face. "Good. Best news I've had all day." She turned toward Natalie. "You know where to return the carrier. See you on the Fourth, if not before."

Belinda marched away, and Aidan found himself at a loss for words. He glanced at the volunteers, who appeared to be fighting a losing battle not to laugh. They saw him and hastily went back to assembling their parts of the float.

Natalie's musical laugh brought him back

to earth. "Mattie and Ethan will be so disappointed Caleb turned down Mayor Wes first."

"I'm not following what Lucie's family has to do with this." His mouth watered at the sight of the cake now resting on the wooden table in front of Natalie. "Why bring them up?"

Natalie patted the bench and he settled next to her. Her sweet strawberry scent almost knocked him off the bench, and he narrowed in on the cake.

"Lucie told me Mayor Wes approached Caleb about accepting the position of pie judge first. Her new husband turned him down before Mayor Wes finished the question." Natalie swung her legs the other way and stared at the cake. "The twins will be upset Caleb said no, thereby depriving them of the chance to receive Belinda's and Hyacinth's bounty of baked goodies. They love Belinda's cakes."

The pieces of the puzzle clicked. "So they weren't welcoming me to Hollydale? These are bribes." *Where's the mayor's office?* Committing to something was one thing. Committing to something with strings attached changed everything. "This wasn't part of the deal."

He began to rise, and she reached out, her hand winding around his arm. Her presence touched something inside him best buried. "Hold on." She released him, and he missed her connection immediately. She unlatched the sides of the carrier and opened the lid, the smell of lemon and sugar enticing and sweet. "One thing you should know about Belinda and Hyacinth. They may want that blue ribbon, but they're honest to a fault. Neither one of them has a dishonest bone in her body. Devious, yes. Dishonest, no."

Aidan accepted his fate, knowing he was up to the challenge. He'd survived fifteen years in the military; he could handle the likes of Hyacinth and Belinda. "Okay, I won't back down. By the way, you and Danny can come over tonight for dessert. I have plenty."

"I'll make you a deal. You're still staying at the Eight Gables, aren't you?"

"Until Monday, but there's a reception area where we can share the cake."

"How about you come to dinner tonight at my house instead? There'll be more than plenty. The invitation especially stands if you bring the cakes for dessert."

It would beat eating takeout alone in his room. "What time?"

"Six works for me." Natalie glanced in one direction and then the other. Then she tapped his arm, a playful expression brightening her face. "When was the last time you did something for the sheer fun of it? Other than the swings the other day, of course."

Why did Natalie keep harping on him having fun? Fun wasn't going to get that float accomplished or prepare Danny as he grew up.

"Do I come off as stuffy or something?" He shifted in his seat. If he was going to take on the role of guardian uncle, an air of formidability was a necessity.

"A little." The admission was wormed out of her as though she hated to admit it. "But your demeanor has nothing to do with what I'm about to do. Belinda's cakes are legendary around here." She dipped her finger into the coconut icing on the side of the cake and then licked it off. Bliss radiated from her face as she closed her eyes, obviously savoring the deed. Then she opened her eyes and laughed. "Mmm, delicious. I couldn't resist. I dare you to try the frosting, although I don't think you'll take me up on it."

His finger darted out and swiped a swath of frosting before he smoothed their indentations over. One taste and he was hooked. "You're right. That is good. I won't tell Danny we did that if you don't."

"Deal."

She licked her lips and missed a speck of coconut that still lingered next to her mouth.

His gaze was drawn to her pink luscious lips. He swallowed the urge to kiss her. *Kiss her?* Where had that thought come from? One surprise after another greeted him, and the biggest surprise of all was sitting next to him, making him lose his equilibrium. Getting involved with Natalie would be trouble, and he had enough going on in his life. He made the mistake of meeting her gaze. Her eyes widened, and the air around them stilled. Natalie leaned forward as if she sensed the same feelings and was willing to act on them.

For Danny's sake, he staunched the attraction flowing through him. Romance was part of his future, once he was settled with a safe job and a house.

He jumped off the bench. "Don't want to ruin my dinner. I'll get back to measuring. Measure twice, cut once." He never babbled, yet words were flowing from his mouth like raging rapids. He stepped backward and almost stumbled where the concrete gave way to grass.

"Somehow, I think I've managed to ruffle the unruffable Major Murphy." She stole another glance at the cake before looking at him. "Don't forget. Bring both cakes. I'll work up an appetite with all this work, and Danny's always hungry."

Her blue eyes twinkled again, and he appreciated her attempt to put this back on firmer ground. He'd go along with that. "The way you say that, I'm not sure if you're inviting me or my cakes."

"A girl has to have some secrets." She winked and then sent an adoring glance toward the cake. "Decisions, decisions. Red velvet or lemon coconut? I'll be wavering all day."

He recognized the opportunity for a quick getaway and picked up the measuring tape. Snapping out the first foot, he was certain of one thing.

One taste of Natalie's lips, and he'd be hooked.

CHAPTER EIGHT

WITH ONLY A few minutes until closing time, Aidan exited the water utility office in Hollydale's City Hall. Frustrated, he shut the door with a little too much force and the glass window rattled. Coming in person hadn't yielded the results he wanted. He would have liked to have moved out of the bed-and-breakfast sooner to be closer to Danny, but Monday was still the earliest the water and gas would operate at Shelby's.

At least he hadn't canceled his remaining nights at Eight Gables. Besides, Ginny's afternoon scones were delicious, so good he'd have to resume his morning runs soon. He turned toward the exit that would lead him out to Main Street.

"Major Murphy!"

Mayor Wes stopped him in his tracks. He turned and saw the tall man striding toward him. "You found me."

Should he mention Hyacinth's and Belinda's *gifts* that bordered on bribes? "Mayor Wes, there's something you should know about the pie contest."

"All in good time. Let's make ourselves comfortable, shall we? Have a minute?" Aidan hadn't nodded before the mayor steered him in the opposite direction. "My office is this way."

Before Aidan knew any better, the mayor's assistant handed him a bottle of water and he was ensconced in a comfortable padded chair near the impressive chestnut desk.

"Thanks for the water." He uncapped the bottle and took a sip. "You treat your pie judges well. Speaking of judging, in full disclosure—"

"Our city manager is retiring, but he has to hold on a little longer for his complete pension to kick in. He needs his health benefits, too." The mayor steepled his fingers, genuine concern on his face, so Aidan decided to hear him out. "For the most part, that hasn't been a problem. However, there is one situation that's come up, other than the pie judging, that is."

"About Hyacinth and Belinda, there's something you should know—"

Once again, getting a word in proved impossible. "Any security detail in your training?"

Was the mayor serious? One look at the discerning eyes in the jovial face proved he was. "Yes, sir."

"Good." The mayor shuffled some papers and produced a business card. "Here's Bob Woodley's info. We have a project I bet is up your alley. It concerns the security details for the parade route. I'd like a consultant's view of the weaknesses before the tourists arrive. They start arriving about now and continue until the last leaf falls off our trees. We have a smaller group of visitors trickle back in the winter for the snow resort ten miles away."

Aidan accepted the card with some trepidation. "Wouldn't a job like this require bids? Background checks? Detailed strategies?"

The mayor snapped his fingers. "Knew you were the man for the job. This is only a minor temporary assignment but a vital one. You'll review the latest police report for strengths and weaknesses."

"I've worked in security, but I'm more geared toward linguistics."

"Good. An extra set of eyes on a security plan never hurts." The mayor reached for his reusable water bottle and took a long swig. "Woodley's at the station now, coordinating the parade route and logistics with the new sheriff, Mike Harrison. Woodley's expecting you, and he'll get you set up."

Aidan leaned back, perplexed at how he was getting more and more caught up in the town's web. Then again, having a side project might keep his mind busy and help him cope with all he had to do in the upcoming month: going through Shelby's belongings, listing her house and the downtown building, and planning activities with Danny.

"I'll need clearance from my commanding officer." Aidan leaned forward and tapped Woodley's business card on the desk.

"Of course." The mayor scribbled something down and handed him another business card. "Here's my private contact information. Your commanding officer can get in touch with me directly. Sheriff Mike Harrison will give you the paperwork you need for clearances and fingerprint you."

Considering the mayor always seemed to be flying by the seat of his pants, this was thought out and well-planned.

"About Belinda and Hyacinth." What would the mayor's answer to this conundrum be?

"They're great, aren't they?"

"I think they're bribing me." Aidan winced at how silly those words sounded.

"Nonsense." The mayor shook his head and waved his hand, dismissing Aidan's concern. "Besides, the pies aren't labeled. You won't know who baked what. Good news is we've received other entries this year, too." The mayor rose, moseyed around his desk and extended his hand. "What do you say? Are you on board?"

It would give his mind something to think about other than an attractive redhead. "Yes, sir."

The handshake was brief, and the mayor went and sat at his desk. "Woodley's expecting you."

With his marching orders, Aidan was out the door and in the hallway in no time flat. Mayor Wes had played him like a fiddle and taken Aidan's participation in this security venture for granted.

He wasn't sure if he should be annoyed or flattered.

AIDAN PATTED HIS STOMACH, full of Natalie's chicken fried steak and gravy. She wasn't just pretty, kind and creative, but a good cook, too. Any cake would have to wait until after a little exercise.

He scooted his chair away from the table and smiled at his nephew. "Feel like getting outside in the fresh air for a walk?" He looked at the dishes still on the table, minus the ones Natalie had already started taking into the kitchen. "After we help with cleanup first."

Aidan stacked bowls and placed them on his

plate. Crossing the threshold into the kitchen, he almost bumped into Natalie. Her silky sundress brushed his skin. Her eyes widened before she hustled back into the kitchen and found containers for the leftovers.

He glanced around her kitchen. Colorful curtains in shades of purple and blue and bold patterns weren't what most would expect in a breakfast nook, but the brightness suited her style. Her house burst with color in every shade of the rainbow, but it came together.

It looked like home.

She glanced over her shoulder as she turned on the faucet and poured dishwashing liquid into the water. "You're right about getting out of the house and doing something. Fresh air sounds delightful."

Danny joined them and scraped off his plate into the trash can. He wrinkled his nose. "Walking is boring." His eyes lit up. "What about soccer? With Uncle Aidan on my team, I might be able to win."

Natalie rinsed off her plate and reached for Aidan's, their fingers touching. Even with her wet soapy fingers, the spark between them was palpable.

He pulled his hand away. "I have to warn you. I was on my high school soccer team. Maybe the two of you should play against me."

Danny clutched at Aidan's T-shirt, and Aidan looked down. "Aunt Natalie is really good."

She shut off the water and turned toward them, reaching for a towel. Tonight she wore her hair up, and a few tendrils now graced the sides of her face. The effect was quite beautiful. "Thanks, Danny. However, I'm too self-conscious on a soccer field. How about baseball or basketball instead?"

Aidan's curiosity was piqued. "What's the deal about soccer? You owe me a detail about your life."

"I didn't know we were keeping score from the coffeehouse, but okay." She sighed and threw the towel onto her counter. "My twin sister, Becks, played soccer professionally for a couple of years. She lives in California with her husband, Jack, and my baby niece, Pippa. I'm nowhere near her level, but you can't grow up with Becks without learning a few moves. She always kept her attention focused on one sport. I liked to diversify, and I don't take soccer as seriously as she does."

That was fine with him. "That chicken fried steak was delicious, and the person who cooked that meal definitely gets to pick the game."

"Thanks." She washed the pot, and he picked up the towel from the counter and dried.

He liked the way they worked in tandem.

"What about basketball?" she asked.

"I'm not on any basketball teams. Sounds good to me, and I'm already wearing sneakers. What about you, Danny?"

Aidan placed the pot on the counter and watched Danny pump his fist. "Yes."

Natalie put the pot in a drawer below the stove. "There's a court at the elementary school a couple of blocks away. Five-minute walk, tops." She turned toward Danny. "You and me on the same team?"

Danny nodded with too much emphasis for Aidan's liking. Severing their connection might not be the positive remedy Aidan hoped it would be. Something akin to frustration bubbled up in him. This was supposed to be quick, easy and simple, none of which described Natalie.

He supposed the best way to get her out of his system was accepting his time here and then moving on. That was how he'd lived his life until now, and that had worked for him.

Except for the nights that felt empty.

"Where's your basketball?"

Natalie thumped her chin and then snapped her fingers. "It's in the garage. Danny knows where." She glanced at her sandals and her floral sundress. The blue flowers against the pink background brought out the deep blue flecks in her eyes. "I'll make a quick change and meet you there in ten minutes."

He tried to keep his mind off the delicate fabric swooshing around her as she headed out of the kitchen. "Come on, Danny." He held out his hand, happy of the reminder of who had to come first. Everything had to be about Danny for now.

His nephew led him into Natalie's garage, boxes and bins lined up against the wall. Aidan was impressed at the organization.

Danny went to a clear tote and brought forth a basketball. When he tried to dribble, however, the ball stayed on the ground, a dent in one side, proof it had deflated. Danny's face fell before it suddenly brightened again. "Mommy bought a ball last fall when I played with my friends. I scored six times, Uncle Aidan!" Danny searched him for signs of approval, and Aidan held up his hand for a high-five. Danny slapped his hand harder than anticipated. Danny's smile proved he'd done the right thing, and Aidan breathed a sigh of relief.

He had so much to learn, and fast. "We'll have to wait for Natalie to get into Shelby's house."

"I know the code for the garage. Come on." Danny motioned with his hand, and Aidan texted Natalie to let her know where they were going.

They walked next door. Aidan hesitated in front of Shelby's garage, unsure of why he stopped. He'd already been inside her house, so that wasn't the issue. The box to punch in the numbers was out of Danny's reach. Good thing the electricity was turned on. "What's the code?"

"My birthday. It's—"

"I know your birthday." He'd missed that day as he'd been stationed in Afghanistan at the time, unable to procure leave for his nephew's arrival. He punched zero-nine-zero-two into the keypad, and the whir of the motor filled the air. Shelby's teal compact sat there as if waiting for its owner.

It would be too impractical to drive it cross-country, but he could return his rental now. He'd ask Woodley if he knew anyone who would buy it from him after Aidan left town. The city manager might be able to give him a lead.

Danny ran into the space and found the basketball. He bounced it up and down. "You'll get hot in that shirt. Do you want one of my mommy's shirts?"

Aidan bit back a laugh. "I'm good."

"Is it because you don't want me to see that

line on your arm?" Danny kept bouncing the basketball, the resounding echo consistent and purposeful. "Does that have anything to do with why you didn't come home when Mommy died?"

Aidan stilled. Until now, he didn't know Danny had missed him. Sadness swept over him as yet another wave of grief that he hadn't properly said goodbye to his sister hit him like a tsunami. He rubbed his arm and sat on the car's back bumper, patting the spot next to him. This parenting thing wasn't as easy as it looked, and Danny was only six. The next few years stretched before them. There were so many ways to mess it all up.

Army strong. The motto flashed before him. He'd made it through so much already, he could manage this. Or at least try.

"Um." Sweat formed on his forehead, caused by mental anxiety rather than the weather, and he hadn't even stepped foot on the basketball court yet. He wiped away the beads of perspiration with his sleeve. The easy way out would be a distraction or a pithy excuse. Whenever he asked his father questions after his mother died, his father had always blurted out something off the cuff and changed the subject. That was, until he met Cathy. After they married and had Shelby, he'd opened up a little more.

"Can I see the line?" Danny scrambled closer to Aidan and stared at his sleeve.

The unexpectedness of his question caught Aidan off guard, but he recovered and rolled up his sleeve. The scar had faded to a pale white line, an old injury that hadn't been serious enough for a medical discharge. When the incident occurred nine years ago, the nightmares had been worse than the pain. Occasionally he woke up covered with sweat, but those nights were few and far between.

"So..." He steeled himself, waiting for some sign of revulsion on Danny's face but found none.

"Does it hurt?" Danny reached out as if to touch it but drew his hand back.

"You can touch it. It won't hurt." Aidan stretched out his arm. The scar, only four inches, was now simply a part of him, even if he preferred wearing long sleeves to cover it up. "It happened a long time ago. Before you were even born."

He'd been quite fortunate the knife wound hadn't severed any tendons. He'd downplayed it to Shelby, but this and the inherent risk in the military might have been part of the reason she didn't name him as Danny's sole guardian.

Truth was, his visits with her had grown less frequent over the past couple of years. Different missions had kept him off the radar for months. This new training assignment at Fort Lewis changed all of that. Unless something unexpected happened, he would remain stateside until he sought an honorable discharge next year.

Danny reached out and traced the jagged line with his finger. "Why'd this happen?"

Aidan noticed he'd asked why, and not how. "This occurred during a mission where I assisted with interpreting different dialects of a certain region during sensitive and classified negotiations between rival factions."

"Huh?" Danny pulled back. "What does that mean?"

"I was the translator for my boss. I listen to someone else and tell my boss in English what the person said. I speak six languages. What's different about me, though, is I'm adept with a variety of dialects and pick up slang easily." That was one reason the security firm in DC wanted him. He saw the confusion still written on Danny's face and tried to make it even easier for him to understand. "I was caught up in the moment and failed to ascertain the threat from the enemy combatant."

Translating for his commanding officer was easier than talking to a six-year-old, and Aidan stopped while he was behind. He glanced up and found Natalie standing at the frame of the garage door, a glimmer of a smile lurking in her blue eyes and a duffel bag at her feet. However, it was the way those athletic shorts showed off her tanned legs that deprived him of speech for a second.

"What your uncle is trying to say is he's good at talking to people. He got hurt when he was trying to help make life safer for everyone."

"Oh, okay." Danny nodded and jumped off the bumper. He turned to his uncle and hugged his arm. "Thanks, Uncle Aidan, for helping the world."

Natalie smiled at Aidan. "Ready to go?"

Danny passed the basketball to Natalie, who dribbled it on the driveway. "First team to ten gets to pick out tonight's cake flavor." A challenge lurked in her words, same as the challenge to connect with Danny.

And he wasn't one to pass up either challenge.

Soon the sun would set and the night would cool off a great deal because of the proximity to the mountains. Crickets chirped their mating calls, trying to find that special someone. Right now, though, magic sparkled in the twilight, the balmy air close to perfection.

With the basketball game complete, Natalie

enjoyed the night that much more. She wiped the sweat off her forehead with her towel and then sipped water while resting on the bleachers. She took another sip and drank in everything around her.

She loved those rounded mountaintops, her little cottage and, most of all, her friends.

Until Shelby's death, she'd spent every Tuesday night at the River Bar and Grill, shooting the breeze and darts while munching on nachos. Once Danny joined her family, her parents had noticed her grief and instituted Sunday night dinner, with Mike and Georgie bringing Rachel, as long as Sheriff Mike wasn't busy.

Natalie reveled in summer, the long stretch of time away from the classroom to recharge. Fall would come soon enough, along with a new batch of kindergartners to keep her on her toes. She wouldn't trade her job for anything.

Except keeping Danny close by.

That was one of the few things she'd give anything to make happen. She loved Shelby's son as if he were her own. Now, for all intents and purposes, he was. She'd promised Shelby she'd take care of Danny if anything happened to her. A promise made on gossamer wings as Shelby had been the picture of health, but a promise all the same. Promises were dreams come to life, and she would do whatever was within her power to fulfill a promise.

Something clicked, and bright lights illuminated the basketball court and nearby baseball field. The lights must be on a timer. Swigging another sip of water, Natalie held the ball under her arm and eyed Aidan with some suspicion. She and Danny had beat Aidan at basketball. "I think you let us win."

He shrugged, bent over and tied his sneaker. "Maybe I didn't want to be the person to make such an important choice about which cake to eat for dessert." He stole a glance at his nephew. Something akin to apprehension crossed his face. There was something mesmerizing about Aidan's solid frame. His confidence lent substance to his handsome features. She could get used to him and after-dinner basketball if she let herself.

The more she was around him, the harder it was to see him as Shelby's brother or Uncle Aidan or Major Murphy. Now he was just Aidan.

"After this much exercise, I say we deserve both."

"Two slices of cake. Awesome." Danny tightened his hands into fists and punched the air.

Natalie picked up the ball and started dribbling. "Just so you know, Aidan, I'd kick your butt in a game of one-on-one." She kept a playful edge in her voice. She needed to keep this on a superficial level, rather than letting it evolve into a deep conversation like the one she'd overheard earlier in Shelby's garage.

Aidan laughed and shook his head. "In your dreams."

Danny jumped between them and clapped, still coming up short of a genuine laugh. "I'll be on my best behavior on the bleachers. I promise."

"What exactly are you promising and why?" Aidan asked the boy.

"I'll be nice while you two play. I like to watch. I think Aunt Natalie's going to win."

She glanced at Aidan, who met her gaze. Then that confidence was back in his eyes, and a shiver of awareness shimmied through her. Then, her competitive edge, squashed from always coming in second to Becks, kicked in and she dribbled the ball, passing it behind her back and then in front of her. "I'm game."

"Isn't it Danny's bedtime?" Aidan tapped his watch. "A consistent schedule is a cornerstone of a child's foundation."

"It's summer vacation. Relaxing the rules a little allows the child to have freedom and know to trust that adults can show flexibility and a willingness to go with the flow." She went over and peeked at his watch. "Besides, his bedtime isn't for another hour and a half."

"And I had a shower last night. I don't need one tonight," Danny shouted before scrambling to the second row of the bleachers.

Aidan pursed his lips. "If Natalie and I play, you take a shower tonight. Proper hygiene is important, and you should be bathing every night."

"Aww, that's no fair. I like to be dirty." Danny rolled his eyes, and his bottom hovered an inch off the bleachers. "Okay, but I still get both types of cake since I won, right?"

"Right." Natalie dribbled past Aidan and shot, executing a perfect layup. The basketball bounced off the backboard, circled the rim twice and then dropped into the basket. "Two points. First person to twenty wins."

"That's not fair. I wasn't ready." Aidan jogged over and scooped up the ball.

"You were born ready. Besides, you have a good four inches on me. You ought to have this in the bag in no time." She held back a giggle. She was downplaying her skills on purpose, trying to have him underestimate her. She'd restrained herself during the previous game as it was obvious he was letting her and Danny win. All was fair in love and basketball. When you lived with Becks and Mike, you learned that fast.

He narrowed his gaze as if assessing her. Would he see the light and frivolous side she loved presenting to the world or would he dig deeper and find the complete portrait she only showed to a few? Didn't matter as she intended to win tonight.

He dribbled in a deliberate manner, and she swooped in and stole the ball, executing another layup. Danny clapped, and she gave a bow. "Four to zero. Your ball."

"Way to go, Aunt Natalie!" Danny clapped and cheered from the stands.

Aidan rebounded the ball, and she set aside the antics. She concentrated on the matter at hand. Most of the time she only played sports for fun, for the thrill of working in tandem with a team. Tonight, however, tension built as she felt his judgment weighing on her. For some reason, she wanted to exceed expectations, wanted him to see her as a serious competitor, one who wouldn't bow out on a whim.

He cut one way before breaking back and shooting, the ball sinking into the basket with a neat swoosh. She admired his move before retrieving the ball from its resting place.

"Way to go, Uncle Aidan!" Danny let out a

whoop from the stands. Joy lightened her heart at the bond forming between them.

Aidan exerted more pressure this time, and her shot bounced off the backboard with Aidan reaching over her head for an easy rebound. Within seconds, he scored again, tying the game. They traveled up and down the court, each missing a couple of easy shots while succeeding with more difficult ones. At ten-all, she called for a timeout. Both approached Danny and grabbed their water bottles.

Sweat dripped off Aidan's brow, and he dipped his head while taking a sip from his reusable water bottle. "You held something back when we played with Danny."

"There's a difference between playing for fun and playing for keeps." Their gazes met and, once again, tension simmered under the surface. While she was referencing the game, they both knew there was more on the line.

Aidan swallowed. Danny reached into her duffel bag and handed him a towel. Taking his time, he wiped off his brow. "For me, there's no difference. What you see is what you get all the time."

Truer words might never have been spoken. Even though he spoke six languages, she wasn't sure subtlety was in his vocabulary. She grabbed the ball from its resting place and jogged toward the court. "Don't worry. I'll wait for you this time, but no more Miss Nice Guy. No holding back."

He laughed and climbed off the bleachers. "Somehow, holding back doesn't seem to be part of your personality."

Funny how they'd each reflected on the other's attributes. She tucked away the implication and dribbled the ball. So far, he tended to favor the right side of the court as if he was waiting for her to make a mistake, rather than poaching in for the steal. Breaking to the left, he extended his arm and stole the ball. He sank another basket, going ahead for the first time in the game.

She admitted his skill was formidable, but she'd grown up with two athletic siblings and had a trick or two up her sleeve. When she reached midcourt, he guarded her. She moved one way, then circled and cut the other way, passing by him and sailing the ball in the air for a basket.

The same pattern followed for the next several baskets.

"That's eighteen-all. Next basket wins. My ball." Aidan dribbled, his fierce look mingled with respect as he seemed to concede she was more of an opponent than he'd expected.

She held her breath and moved under the basket as he shot the ball, which bounced off the rim and missed its mark. With a quick move, she recovered the ball, despite him having the height advantage. He moved back to defend, and she remembered a tip her father had whispered in her ear when she played her brother, who'd gone through a growth spurt and had a good six inches on her at one point.

From the half court, she aimed and followed through, hoping for a miracle as this was never her best shot. She kept her gaze on the ball as it swished through, eliciting a loud cry from Danny.

"Way to go, Aunt Natalie!" Danny climbed off the bleachers and ran her way. When he came close, he gave her a high-five. "I knew you could do it."

Aidan retrieved the ball and came over, his hand extended. "Good game, Harrison."

"Thanks, Murphy." Something like respect dwelled in his eyes, and she'd earned every bit of that out on the court. She smoothed back the long curl that had escaped from her ponytail, and she cringed at how her frizzy auburn hair must look to them. Didn't matter, though, she realized.

She glanced at Danny. His head drooped, and he leaned against her enough for her to know he was tuckered out. Cake for him would have to wait until tomorrow. "We'd better get this little one home."

Home. A funny feeling gripped her heart. Danny and Aidan were making her believe again that she could have a family of her own. One thing she liked about teaching was the constant turnover. She got close enough to make a difference without being so close as to risk losing someone.

With a glance at Aidan, who was depositing the water bottles and towels in her duffel bag, she wavered. He and Danny had a connection no one should sever. *Who said anything about severing?* Perhaps Shelby wanted Natalie as an intermediary to ensure their relationship flourished.

Somehow, she had to accomplish that while keeping her heart out of this equation, a tricky proposition, to say the least, as there was something about Aidan that spurred her to reach for more. Not to mention she tended to throw her heart into everything.

"Ready to go?" Aidan broke into her thoughts. The sheen of sweat dotting his forehead shouldn't have been as appealing as it was, making him that much more attractive.

"I'm tired, Aunt Natalie." Danny reached up, wanting her to carry him.

Aidan offered her the duffel bag. "How

about a trade?" He motioned for Danny. "Come on, sport. I'll carry you for a couple of minutes. That should give you enough energy to walk the rest of the way."

Natalie kept from laughing out loud. Aidan must not have had much experience with children. Once he started carrying Danny, he'd be on the hook the whole way.

"I can walk. I'm a strong little fellow. That's what Aunt Natalie says every night." Danny shrugged and walked ahead of them.

She reached for the duffel bag, but Aidan looped it around his shoulder, his jaw clenched, the progress made during the game gone in a split second. "I've got this."

They walked along in tense silence. Natalie fidgeted while keeping an eye on Danny. The bronze streetlights bathed the sidewalks in a soft glow, and stars popped up in the dusky sky. "Wait up a sec," she called out to Danny.

He waited for her and Aidan. She knelt alongside Danny and pointed at the North Star, the star that had led her back to Hollydale. "Did you make a wish? How about you, Aidan?"

Aidan cleared his throat. "Why? Do wishes come true in Hollydale?"

His intense stare would have given her pause a week ago. Now she knew that was just part of his personality. "Of course. If you make them happen, that is."

"How does it go again, Aunt Natalie. Star what?"

"Star light, star bright, the first star I see tonight. I wish I may, I wish I might, have the wish I wish tonight. Make a wish, Danny."

"I'm wishing hard." He screwed his eyes tight, concentration radiating off his too-serious face. He opened his eyes and smiled. "I wished real hard for..."

"Don't tell me. It won't come true." She rose and gripped Danny's hand. Then she turned to Aidan. "Did you make a wish, too?"

He arched his eyebrow and, before he had a chance to answer, some friends shouted a greeting.

Natalie waved back and yelled in their direction, "Don't forget. Hollydale Park. The weekend before the Fourth. My mom's fried chicken and Lucie Spindler's chocolate chip pound cake."

After they promised, she began to stroll, keeping hold of Danny but returning her attention to Aidan. "Well, did you?"

"If I tell, it won't come true."

Aidan Murphy made a joke?

"Then say no more." She nudged his side, the duffel bag swinging and bumping her shin.

"If I'm out of line here, you can tell me to buzz off, but how long ago was your injury? How bad was it?"

The thought of him suffering the same fate as Francisco brought a heavy weight to her limbs. Danny had her and her family always, but what if something happened to Aidan? Then Danny would lose his last living relative.

And what about Aidan himself?

His droll sense of humor, his honor, his willingness to commit where others said no? More reasons for her to step back from him. While she'd do anything for Danny, and she could easily wish upon the star for a chance with Aidan, relationships were built on compatibility, trust and more than moondust.

Although there wasn't anything wrong with a little moondust.

"You look worried, but you shouldn't be. It's nothing," said Aidan. "Just a flesh wound."

It figured he wouldn't tell her. "Buzz off, it is."

"It happened nine years ago. A lifetime, really. A young kid, probably not old enough to shave yet, attacked me with a knife while I should have been more attentive. I don't talk about it much."

"I think Shelby wanted to know everything that happened to you, the good and the bad. She talked about you, and how you and I never met before is sort of a mystery to me, but I came home to Hollydale for holidays, whereas you sent her a plane ticket to visit you at the base wherever you were stationed." She stopped, her words fading into the night. Had she met him sooner, would she still have felt this pull toward him?

They were already on Marigold Lane. In seconds, they reached her front door, and she opened it. Danny disappeared in a flash.

"You don't lock your door?"

"We were gone less than an hour. I do lock it at night."

Aidan settled the duffel bag on her porch and folded his arms against his chest.

She shifted her weight. "Okay, I'll start locking it whenever I go somewhere."

"Security is important to me. Yours and Danny's security is important to me."

He included me.

She reached out and touched his arm. What felt like electricity zapped her, and she jumped back. "My security is important to you?"

"Natalie." He moved closer, and her world tilted on its axis. The smell of him, sweat mixed with something like citrus, filled her senses, already rocked with the revelation that he was concerned for her welfare.

She didn't break the connection between them. For some reason, this soldier, who shouldn't be reigniting her love for moonbeams and stardust, something she thought was lost forever, stood on her front porch with the summer melodies of crickets and river frogs blending together for a sweet song.

There were a thousand and one reasons for her to step inside her house and shut and lock the door. And yet she moved closer just as he stepped toward her, as if some magnet was drawing them together instead of pulling them apart. The lyric sounds faded until only his breathing, steady and consistent, roared in her ears, that same breath caressing her cheek.

"One kiss might prove this is just summer magic," she said. One that was casting a spell over them rather than a real connection that would bind them together.

"Or it might complicate everything, especially if Danny came outside and saw us," Aidan said.

There was more stopping them than just Danny. Here was Aidan, a man who wore a watch and lived by a schedule, the last person she wanted any relationship with, and she was a kindergarten teacher who prided herself on leaping into whichever good idea came to mind. She needed people to like her, whereas, from everything she'd observed, he depended on himself, valuing his lone-wolf status.

She couldn't give in to a moment that would only lead to more heartache and pain, no matter how much she wanted to believe in moondust again.

She cast her gaze to the concrete. At the same time that she stepped back, he did the same, as if he'd figured out this kiss wasn't on his schedule. She blinked and dismissed that last part. There was more to Aidan than a day planner.

"It's just the front porch, it has this effect, you know. Summer and the smell of roses and an inviting porch," she babbled, reaching for anything to lighten the tension between them.

"I don't buy that." He stretched his arm until it made contact with the house, inches away from her. "I don't think you do either."

"I like things uncomplicated and light." And Aidan was the epitome of complicated. "I live for the moment, you know." She inched closer to the door, gripping the knob, the warm metal reminding her of home and what had to be most important for her now.

"So, which did you choose? Red velvet or lemon coconut or both?"

Her breath caught in her chest, still racing from the mistake she'd almost made a second ago. "It's too late for that much sugar." She closed her eyes, aware of how that might sound, before opening them at the same time she opened the door. "I think the simplest solution is for you to go back to Eight Gables now. Good night."

He stared at her and nodded. "Security first. Check all your windows and doors. Make sure they're locked before you go to bed."

He pulled his shirtsleeves down, hiding the scar. She watched until his figure had retreated down the street and faded away.

She slipped inside the house, too aware Belinda and Hyacinth had given him, and not her, the cakes. She didn't care much that she was poaching what belonged to him. She'd made the shot, and she deserved a slice of red velvet and a slice of lemon coconut. Everything else could wait until tomorrow.

CHAPTER NINE

AIDAN SCANNED THE area until he spotted the water fountain near the gazebo. He jogged toward it and refilled his reusable bottle. After a long swig, he stood back and wiped the sweat off his brow with his terry cloth wristband. Pink and purple ribbons streaked against the soft gray sky, a sure sign sunrise was on the horizon.

The rounded mountaintops didn't quite touch the clouds but still stood regal and proud. There was something about the stillness of this early time of day that touched him, the fruition of the previous day's work, the promise of new plans, new challenges.

The biggest challenge in his current path had to be Natalie. He'd avoided her yesterday. Instead, he had met with Woodley and Sheriff Harrison and updated them on some needed measures for the parade route and future steps to fix the problems he'd already identified. They'd scheduled a follow-up meeting for next Wednesday. The work had helped keep his mind off Natalie as he'd come close to doing something spontaneous when his cheek was mere centimeters from hers the other night. Good thing he'd backed away at the same moment she had. Getting involved with the spirited beauty wasn't in his plans.

Aidan stretched his leg muscles on the gazebo steps, almost ready to resume his run. He was about to reinsert his earbuds when he heard someone call his name. He turned and found Hyacinth jogging on the path or, more accurately, being pulled along by two boxers that ran ahead of her.

Hyacinth was a mass of color with a tie-dyed shirt and starburst leggings. "Good morning, Major M.! You don't mind my calling you that, do you? Which do you like better, peaches or plums?"

"Peaches, I guess." The women in this town flustered him like no other, and the jury was still out on whether that was a good thing.

"Good to know. Enjoy this glorious Saturday morning. I'd stay and chat, but Athena and Artemis prefer a nice, long run to start the weekend. Toodle-oo." She raised her arm in a jaunty wave without breaking her stride.

He blinked and tried a few more stretches before hitting the pavement again. This time, more early birds dotted the sidewalks, some running, others jogging. To his surprise, many shouted out greetings that involved calling him by his first name. In a town this size, he must be the story of the week after accepting the least popular job around, that of pie contest judge.

He logged another couple of miles before he veered into the Eight Gables' driveway. Only two more days until the gas and water were turned on at Shelby's house so he could move in for the duration of his stay.

Ginny bustled in the dining room, a large area that reminded him of his grandmother's in that it was fussy with knickknacks but not ostentatious. An antique mahogany table seated fourteen, with the matching cabinet displaying bone china with little pink flowers. A gleaming silver tea service was the centerpiece of the sideboard, where Ginny arranged baskets of muffins—apple cinnamon if his nose was correct.

He announced himself, and she turned around, her hands crossed against her chest. "Major Murphy! Did you have a nice run? Did you enjoy the sunrise? It's so beautiful with the backdrop of the Great Smoky Mountains."

He nodded and waved, intending to get an early start to the rest of his day. Then he stopped, unsure of what that comprised. Until the rest of the utilities were turned on, sorting through Shelby's belongings would have to wait. And he'd left Natalie's house before making plans to do something with Danny on this Saturday.

For the first time since, well, middle school, he didn't have his entire day mapped out. While Natalie would approve, his fingers itched at the very thought.

"Major Murphy?" Ginny came over and laid her hand on his arm. "Are you alright? You're almost pale."

The owner, who was around the age his mother would have been if she were still alive now, seemed genuinely concerned about him.

"Thank you. I'm fine." Although his smile was a little rusty, he'd used it around Natalie enough for it not to be broken. Come to think of it, he'd smiled more around Natalie in these few days than he had since his last stateside visit.

Ginny frowned as if he wasn't convincing, but she tucked the empty silver tray under her arm. "Once you shower and change, there's a continental breakfast available." She hustled toward the door leading to the kitchen and called out, "Feel free to bring that nice nephew of yours to tea this afternoon."

Aidan breathed out a sigh of relief as he

strode up the stairs, taking them two at a time. Something to do, and someone to do it with.

NATALIE TAPPED HER foot against the concrete slab of the picnic pavilion, a slight breeze ruffling through the piles of cut tissue paper next to her on the wooden bench. She adjusted the rocks so none of the paper would scatter and get ruined.

"Earth to Natalie, come in Natalie." Her sister-in-law's voice broke through her reverie as Georgie waved her hand in front of Natalie's face.

"How do you know something's a mistake or if it's right?" Natalie reached back for her water and sipped it before adjusting the chicken wire alongside her legs.

Georgie frowned and stopped sanding the two-by-four. "If this is about Danny…"

"Never." Why did everyone assume she was talking about Danny when she asked questions about the future? Her mother gave every impression Natalie was biting off more than she could chew, and now Georgie seemed to jump to the same conclusion. "I love Danny, and I'll always treat him as my own." Because he was hers. Shelby entrusted him to her, and she'd take care of him and love him always.

"That's a relief." Georgie glanced at her watch and then wrinkled her nose. "Are you sure you're asking the right friend? Wouldn't Lucie be better with this emotional stuff? Now, if you have a question on which oil viscosity suits your car's engine the best, definitely come to me and not Lucie."

Girl talk had always been a mainstay of Natalie's life. She'd grown up with an identical twin, Becks, who was anything but identical in her approach to life. It was more like they were mirror twins than anything else. Then she'd roomed with Shelby at the University of North Carolina, and they'd formed a fast friendship that had endured through Francisco's death and Shelby's pregnancy.

When she had returned to Hollydale without Becks or Shelby, Natalie had latched onto Georgie and Lucie, and the three of them formed a tight new bond. Natalie knew exactly who she was talking to and why, even if Georgie doubted herself. There was always a method to Natalie's actions.

"Although I sometimes question your choices when it comes to men, after you married my brother," Natalie joked and giggled. "You're the exact person for my question. I was there when Mike arrested you, remember?"

Georgie groaned and placed the sandpaper and wood on the picnic table. "That's the last time I help you on my lunch hour, even if it is after two, especially when a '63 Lincoln Continental arrived in the shop this morning." Her green eyes twinkled enough so Natalie knew she was in on her joke. "You had to bring that up, though. Mike's acknowledged he made a mistake, and we've moved on."

Maybe she should be talking to Lucie after all, she thought, grinning. "So, is it better to acknowledge something was a mistake and move on, or is it better to ignore it altogether?"

She threaded more tissue paper through the holes in the chicken wire, alternating the colors so the initials for Hollydale Elementary School would appear on the other side in red and blue with a white backdrop.

Georgie stood and dusted off her baggy shirt and jeans, her standard attire for days when she was working at Max's Auto Garage and even days when she wasn't. "Unlike my teenage self, who should've admitted to Mike how much I liked him, I now prefer to get something out into the open. Better for all concerned. Honesty gets you further than keeping something back."

"Thanks, I think." Natalie rose and stretched, wiggling out her stiff fingers from inserting so many strips of tissue through those tiny holes. "These last two-by-fours will finish up the apron brace so I can start unrolling the chicken wire and puffing out the tissue paper on the other side. Then we can attach this and get ready to build the rest of the structure next weekend."

"That's all you're going to tell me?" Georgie neared and poked Natalie's ribs with her elbow. "If you think I'm letting you off the hook that easily, I'll have to hide the chocolate chip cookies the next time you guys visit Rachel. What's the scoop?"

The student turned the tables on the teacher, and Natalie wasn't sure if she'd created a monster. Threatening to cut Natalie off from her cookie supply was serious business for Georgie. Natalie started unrolling the chicken wire. "For that type of discussion, I'll have to have your help puffing out the paper, so it looks like flowers."

Georgie tilted her head one way, then the other. "Who's SEH?"

"*HES* stands for Hollydale Elementary School." Natalie laughed before she walked around the float. Her laughter died in the breeze. The blood drained away from her face. "Son of a sea biscuit, that spells SEH."

"I know." Georgie patted Natalie's shoulder and glanced at her watch. "The advantage of being the co-owner of my shop is being able to take a longer lunch when there's an emergency. I'll call Heidi and have her tell Travis and Max I'll be back a little late."

The other employees at Max's Auto Repair always had Georgie's back, same as Natalie would always be there for her students. She looked at the ruined display and threw it on the ground, a whole morning's work wasted. At least Danny wasn't here. Instead, Aidan had picked him up and, of all things, the two of them were having tea at the Eight Gables bed-and-breakfast. Natalie swallowed her pride and thought of that boulder. "Don't be silly, Georgie. You have that Lincoln Thing-a-ma-bob to work on. I'll be fine."

"Continental. I'll have it purring before I'm through. You sure?"

The anticipation on Georgie's face was priceless. "Go on with you. I have letters to correct."

"Only you would answer your own question. See, this is a mistake. Now you can figure it out all by yourself whether the other thing was right or a mistake or not." Georgie grinned before her eyes narrowed. "Am I being totally oblivious? Is this about Danny's uncle?"

Natalie shifted her weight, today's cowboy boots being her favorite summer footwear with light blue flowers etched into the brown leather. "Lincoln Continental. Lincoln Continental."

Georgie laughed and reached for her small purse. "Next time you want to talk, make sure Lucie's around. I'll provide the cookies, and she'll provide the advice."

Natalie waved as her friend drove away. She unlocked the utility shed and found a box for the tissue paper she could salvage and reuse. Plucking out each strand of tissue paper from the ten-foot roll of chicken wire kept her mind off the handsome and infuriating soldier. Her fingers cramped, and she stopped for a minute.

Kissing Aidan the other night would have been a mistake. No doubt about it. Getting involved with anyone else in the military was out of the question, let alone the one man who held Danny's future, and her promise to Shelby, in his hands.

Footsteps heralded a new arrival. Glancing up, she found Danny, plus Aidan, standing there.

Danny threw his arms around her. "Aunt Natalie, I don't like cucumber sandwiches," he told her and stepped back. He wrinkled his nose. "But they were a lot better than salmon. Yuck!"

"You tried new food. You can't like something until you've tried it. I'm so proud of you." Natalie wrapped her arm around Danny's waist, keeping him close enough for the smells of tea and sugar to surround her. She might also be using him as a buffer from Aidan, so she let go of him.

"He wanted to try every one of the desserts as well, but I limited him to two." Aidan reached for the chicken wire and glanced around. "Busy morning, I see. Did you store the first roll in the utility shed? I'll go ahead and start attaching that to the apron brace."

Natalie winced and rummaged through her tote bag for her car keys. "Danny, can you get my extra bottle of water out of the cooler in the back seat? Thanks."

Danny ran off, and she turned toward Aidan. "I messed up, okay? I have plenty of time to start over and get it done right."

She reached up for a quick pat of her necklace and gasped as her hand touched bare skin. Her necklace was gone. She clenched her hands.

Aidan stepped toward her. "You don't have to be that upset about the other night."

"That's not why I'm upset." She patted the sides of her dress in case she hadn't clasped it correctly this morning and it had fallen there. Nope. She started scanning the area around her feet. "I lost my necklace."

The grass crunched under her ankle boots as she scoured the ground for any sign of the golden chain with Francisco's medallion. *Where is it?* It had to be here somewhere. She approached the truck and the chassis and circled the area, her steps getting quicker, her heart beating faster.

Danny returned with her bottle of water and handed it to her. "What'cha looking for, Aunt Natalie? I can help."

Her eyes burned, but she wouldn't cry. "My necklace." She choked out the words while grasping the cool, wet bottle, thankful for something to hold.

"Is it the one you always wear? Are you sure you wore it today?" Aidan asked.

"I don't leave home without it. I remember making sure it was fastened securely in the bathroom this morning." Her voice quivered, and she tightened her grip in an effort to stay calm. This necklace couldn't be replaced.

"Then it's here, and we'll find it." He shifted his weight. After a moment's hesitation, he reached out and rubbed her arm. The brief touch calmed her, his composure helping to settle her own nerves.

Danny rattled her keys. "I'll look in the car. I'm good at finding things. My teacher said so."

He trotted off. She and Aidan watched him make his way to her SUV before she turned her attention back to the grass. She wouldn't even think about what creepy crawlies or, worse yet, snakes might make their home in this area.

"Did you go anywhere else before you came here?"

Collecting her thoughts was harder than her emotions. She glanced in his direction, a methodical plan written all over his face. She retraced her steps. "Home, then here."

"If we can't find it at the park, I'm sure it will turn up at your house."

They kept searching, but nothing. Her phone played a familiar ringtone, and she considered letting her mother go to voice mail, but answered it instead. She scooped up her phone. "Hi, Mom. What's going on?"

"What's wrong? You're not your chipper self."

Her loss impacted her more than expected if her mother picked up on it that quickly. She wouldn't lie, but she didn't want her mom thinking she was freaking out over something seemingly simple. "Just a couple of things happening all at once. They should be resolved shortly." She'd fix the tissue paper debacle after she found her necklace. "Danny's looking forward to the picnic tomorrow."

"It's not on the truck platform. I'll keep

looking." Aidan's voice carried over to her and she waved in return.

"Did you invite Aidan? You should invite him." Her mother's insistence came through loud and clear. "We always have two to three weeks of leftovers. Make sure he has our address. See you tomorrow."

Natalie was grateful for her mom's unusual brevity. Aidan kept his nose to the ground until he arrived at her side. "No luck so far. We'll keep looking. It's gold, right?"

"Gold chain with a St. Michael pendant."

"That's the air force good luck symbol. Did you serve in the military?"

She shook her head as Francisco's image, blurrier now, came into focus. "My fiancé was in the air force."

"Fiancé? Was?"

Her chest constricted for a second before peace settled over her. "Francisco died in combat in Afghanistan seven years ago." A lifetime ago, but she'd never forget. "His *abuelita* gave the necklace to him when he enlisted. On his last birthday, he gave it to me. He asked me to marry him before he left for what would be his final mission. We were to be married after my graduation."

"I'm very sorry."

"Thank you." His sincerity meant the world to her.

Danny ran their way. He panted for breath before shaking his head. "Sorry, Aunt Natalie. It wasn't in your car. I found thirty-eight cents." He held out his hand, and she sent him a wobbly smile.

"It's yours. You did a good job."

"What about me? I found a bottle cap but I threw it away." Aidan leaned against a wooden post while he continued to scan the ground.

"You're in luck. I have something better than that as a thank-you for helping me look for my necklace." Natalie tried to inject her voice with its usual buoyancy. "My mother called. She wants you to come to the Harrison Family Barbecue tomorrow. It's extra special this year because it's their fortieth anniversary. What do you say? I can text her and let her know you're coming."

Danny pulled at his uncle's arm. "My new cousin, Rachel, told me it's the most fun ever."

Aidan stopped scouring the ground and looked her way. She ignored the ripples of attraction as much as she ignored the faint trace of stubble on his jaw, which added another level of handsome to his features.

"What about you? Do you want me there?" he asked.

"The more the merrier." The challenge was clear in his eyes and she shifted her weight, too aware her answer was evasive. She nodded. "Yes, I'd like you to come."

"Count me in. What can I bring?"

"Yourself. There's enough food to feed all of Hollydale. My mom goes overboard, and it's really more of a community barbecue. There'll be at least fifty people there."

The prospect of Aidan coming to a family event had her feeling conflicted. On the one hand, she liked having him around and, on that account, his presence boosted her spirits. On the other hand, he affected her like no one had in years.

Normally, she grew on people the more she was around them. One look at Aidan's profile proved she didn't know where she stood in his estimation. That bothered her. Not as much, though, as losing her necklace forever. She headed for the shed, eager to lose herself in work, looking at the grass the whole way.

CHAPTER TEN

HOLLYDALE RESIDENTS OF every age congregated on this Sunday afternoon around Diane and Carl Harrison's house and backyard. They had greeted Aidan like they would a long-lost relative.

This was new to him, and he'd escaped inside while others chose teams for a volleyball game. In the living room, he took a deep breath. Diane reminded him of Cathy, and the inside of the Harrison house had the same floor plan as his father's house in Cincinnati.

Until his father had met Cathy, he and his father were settled in a comfortable routine that centered around the two of them. Cathy had gone out of her way to do everything she could to make seven-year-old Aidan like her. Unbending and inflexible, he'd pushed her away for a good year until his stepmother gave up and concentrated her sunny optimism on his father and their new daughter.

He brought himself back to the present. Pictures of the three Harrison children lined the fireplace mantel and the top two shelves of the built-in bookcases. In every picture, he could tell Natalie apart from her identical twin as their different hairstyles and shape of their eyes gave them away. There was even a recent picture of Natalie and Danny.

It must be nice to know someone somewhere had pictures of you and welcomed your return. With Shelby gone, he didn't have those roots anymore. Shelby had been his last living relative, other than Danny, ever since the plane crash that had taken his father's and Cathy's lives.

He needed fresh air, the beige walls were closing in around him.

Wandering back outside, Aidan admired the crisp, clean lines of the classic Thunderbird parked in the driveway.

"Overwhelmed a little?" Natalie's father, Carl, if he remembered correctly, headed his way, a mason jar of lemonade in hand. "Even I'm surprised at how many people showed up."

From the man's handshake earlier, Carl promised to be a straight shooter.

Aidan kept from reaching out and running his hand over the shiny metal fins of the convertible. "Someone's taken good care of this Thunderbird. She's a beauty."

"Good eye." Carl sipped his lemonade.

"Georgie cares about each car she renovates, but I think she poured her heart into my dad's Thunderbird, which Mike inherited. It saw some hard times. Though TLC and a lot of elbow grease on Georgie's part went a long way to change that."

Those words penetrated deep but not in regards to the car. Years of isolating himself from family activities might have taken a toll on his and Shelby's relationship. Unlike this car, there was no second chance with his sister.

More now than ever, he had to be the uncle Danny deserved. The boy needed a lot of TLC, and Aidan was prepared for the long haul of parenthood. He'd never shirked from hard work and wasn't about to start doing so now.

"And Georgie's married to your son, the sheriff?" Polite conversation was one skill he hadn't had much opportunity to refine as of late. Coming to Hollydale might be the best preparation of all for his return to the private sector next year.

Pride shone on Carl's face. "Best decision of my son's life." Carl walked over and inspected the other side of the Thunderbird, keeping his gaze away from Aidan's. "Tricky business, this parenthood gig. You have to know when to accept what's best for your family, even if it means you can't step in and interfere." He met Aidan's gaze and smiled. "When they're adults, that is."

Aidan nodded, unsure of what to say or do next. "Thanks for the advice. By the way, happy anniversary." Searching for Danny was a safe bet.

Carl laughed as two kids zipped past him and headed for the backyard. "Maybe it's because I have three children, but you're easier to read than you think. Natalie's an adult, and I'm not going to interfere with whatever's going on between the two of you. I'll be here for her regardless of the outcome, but it's a little like this barbecue. I'm just the hamburger flipper. My wife's the organizer and the caretaker. In the meantime, my grill awaits. By the way, last time I saw them, they were almost done with their volleyball game."

Carl walked on, leaving Aidan to ponder the man's words. What did he mean about there being something between him and Natalie? Was the chemistry between them obvious to everyone else? Or had Natalie confided in her parents about Aidan's desire to take Danny to Fort Lewis and assume permanent custody? Judging from the looks of this barbecue, Natalie would have support after he left. She'd be able to get through Danny moving away a sight better than he would.

But what would it be like for Danny to grow up knowing there were so many houses with people who loved him, folks he could always turn to? Homes that would have Danny's picture on the mantel?

No, Aidan wouldn't go there. His nephew needed discipline and consistency, two qualities he could supply. He navigated the path toward the backyard, where shouts of victory arose. That volleyball game must be over. He walked through the fence opening and found a girl with braids whooping for joy, while Danny hung out on the other side of the net, his shoulders drooping with dejection. Aidan increased his pace.

Before he reached Danny's side, Natalie pulled Danny in for a hug. "You were great. I loved how you dove for that last ball. You gave it your best. That's what matters. Keep that up, and you'll always be a winner, I promise."

Promises from other people were feathers as far as Aidan was concerned, light in the air and easy to blow away. He always tried to deliver on his own but held back from assuming everyone else would, too, except for his fellow troops. Aidan could count on them. He clapped his hands. "How about another game?"

Natalie eyed him with some trepidation. "If

you say that with any more enthusiasm, we'll have to restrain you."

Shouts of welcome greeted new arrivals, and Aidan turned to find two bundles of pure energy flying toward Danny. "Hi, Danny. Want to go inside and play video games?"

Natalie moved toward him and grazed his ear. "Remember Ethan and Mattie, Lucie's twins? Well, Caleb's in the process of adopting them."

The softness of her breath tickled his ear, and her strawberry scent reminded him of the best parts of summer.

She stepped away and clapped her hands. "No one's going inside on this glorious afternoon. This is a day made for outdoor games so we can eat all the food. I am the Harrison Family Barbecue Horseshoes Champion. Do I have any takers to try to dethrone me?" She looked at the three kids. "Do any of you know how to play?"

Three heads shook, answering no, and Aidan found himself mimicking their response. Athletic and fit, he'd played a variety of games before, but never horseshoes. If they were pairing up for basketball, however, he'd have chosen Natalie in a heartbeat.

Natalie gathered a group of adults and kids together and headed to the other side of the yard, where a dirt circle contained a large metal stake rising out of it. Natalie led them to a grassy area with horseshoes resting on the ground near a white spray-painted line. Aidan noticed another one ten feet closer to the dirt circles. She explained the rules and asked each child to pair up with an adult. Several kids scattered toward a parent, grandparent or other adult. Danny glanced at him, then at Natalie. Aidan's heart wrenched at the indecision on his nephew's face, although he was making some headway if Danny didn't beeline straight for the beautiful redhead.

"Danny, go ahead and team up with your uncle. He needs some Murphy power to help him combat this fabulous Harrison package." She tossed a horseshoe inches in the air before catching it. She sent a smile in Lucie's direction as the twins argued with their mother about who to pick for her team. "Besides, we girls need to stick together, right, Mattie?"

Natalie reached for Mattie as he did the same for Danny, who tugged at Aidan's T-shirt. "Have you ever played before?"

Aidan wished he could lie and say he was good at this, but he shook his head. "Nope."

"Aunt Natalie's been giving me lessons. I'll cover you, Uncle Aidan."

UNTIL AIDAN CAME to town, Natalie had never been in touch with her competitive side, which was rather surprising, considering Becks's intense drive. Then again, Becks had enough of an edge in that regard for both of them, so Natalie had always been content to let her sunny side shine all the more.

She stood back and disconnected that wire Aidan sparked in her. Life was meant to be savored and enjoyed; it wasn't a game where winners took all.

And life on an afternoon like this? With friends nearby, yummy aromas coming from the grill, a breeze keeping the summer temperatures relatively cool? Priceless. Summer was for the living.

In spite of herself, she felt compelled to look in Aidan's direction, waiting on the sidelines of the horseshoes playing area. If only he could see the positive effect Hollydale had had on him even in such a short time. Already his face was lighter than when he arrived, his shoulders no longer carrying the weight of the world.

Her niece Rachel hooked a sinker, and Natalie cheered. "Way to go." Extending her hand, she gave her niece a high-five. "Great job."

Diane also delivered a high-five to her granddaughter and another to Danny before clutching her clipboard under her arm. "Proud of you, Rachel! Same to you, Danny!" She then cleared her throat. "The two pairs that are moving on to the final round are Danny and Aidan, and Mattie and Natalie. It starts in ten minutes."

Natalie side-hugged Mattie, her kind of girl in those tie-dyed leggings paired with a hot-pink top. "Who knew you had such a good arm? I'll have to talk to Lucie and Caleb about softball lessons." She extended her other arm. "And there's my boy. Way to go, Danny. You've done great with all those horseshoes so close to the stake. Those points really add up."

Danny's eyes lit up like the fireworks that were only eight days away. Aidan stayed on the periphery of the action. Her father yelled out a new round of burgers were hot off the grill, and the crowd dispersed. She stepped toward the food table, hoping enough of the potato salad was left for her.

Aidan blocked her path. "Finals? What did your mom mean about finals?"

"Bragging rights, that's all. Food first. It wouldn't do for your competitor to drop of hunger, would it?" She pressed her arm to her forehead and pretended to swoon before his hand reached around and cupped the small of her back.

Awareness of him flooded her, the same as

his scent, that citrusy smell she now associated with him. Her mother had warned her not to bite off more than she could chew. A relationship with Aidan, worrying about whether he'd be hurt again or worse, would be a gargantuan bite that could consume her whole.

For Danny's sake, and her own, she had to keep her feelings to herself.

Aidan made a noncommittal sound, and his brusqueness was the right reminder of how they saw the world with two different sets of sunglasses, his opaque and hers rosy. Danny joined them in line for the food. Natalie grabbed two plates.

"Two plates? You weren't kidding about how hungry you are." Aidan reached for plastic utensils, glanced at Danny and picked up another handful of napkins. "Must be shooting all those dead ringers."

"Is it wrong to root for you to miss one, Aunt Natalie?" Danny looked at her with his big brown eyes.

Aidan shook his head. "We don't root against the other team. We have to rise up and perform better if we want to win."

"For the record, I worked up an appetite threading all that tissue paper through two rolls of chicken wire earlier this morning, one for each side of the float." Then she laughed and held up the second plate. "This one's not for me, though. It's for Danny."

They piled their plates high with food and found a place to sit on the lawn. Appreciating the creamy taste of the potato salad, she couldn't help but notice the strong family resemblance as Aidan and Danny bent their heads together, discussing strategy for the finals. Someday in the future, if Aidan's high cheekbones were any indication, Danny's chubby cheeks would fade away and become more prominent. He'd be a heartbreaker for sure.

In no time, Danny's plate was empty. "Can I go play with Mattie and Ethan? I won't tell Mattie anything about our strategy, Uncle Aidan."

After they assented at the same time, Danny scampered off.

Aidan leaned back and patted his flat stomach. "If I eat much more today, my commanding officer will have a fit when I come back out of shape. Don't suppose you run."

"For my mom's potato salad, I do." She held up her spoon and licked off the last bit. "And I ran half marathons in college."

"Didn't expect that. Basketball, horseshoes, running. Is there anything you can't do?"

"Painting. My art always looks like stick figures." Rearranging her legs under her, no small feat in this sundress, she turned her attention to her hamburger. "I like surprises, same as I like cowboy boots, long soaks in the tub with a good book and meeting friends at The Busy Bean. What about you? Tell me three things you like."

He raised his eyebrows and glanced at her over his burger. Putting it back on his plate, he shrugged. "Haven't given it much thought."

"What's to think about? By the way, I won't accept calendars, day planners or watches." She eyed the dessert table and decided to wait until after the rest of the horseshoe competition.

"What if those are my three favorite things, though?"

She almost threw the rest of her hamburger at him before the sparkle in his eyes let her know he was joking. Instead, she waggled her burger at him. "My game, my rules."

He bit off a chunk of his burger, a faraway look in that gray gaze.

Before he answered, her mother blew a whistle. "Time for the final round. Everyone gather around."

Aidan leaned over and whispered, "Strawberry scones, strawberry chiffon pie and strawberry shampoo."

She used that type of shampoo, and he'd noticed. If he wanted to throw her off her game, he'd have to rise up and try harder than that. Although, from the way her insides went all quivery, he'd done a good job.

And the day wasn't over yet.

CHAPTER ELEVEN

AIDAN LEANED BACK against the Harrisons' old gray shed, soaking in every detail. Carl and Diane sat in the distance with a photo album, showing off pictures of their wedding day. A few feet away, Natalie laughed with a group of people, her face animated with good humor as her hands moved along with the story she was telling.

A man in a black T-shirt, Natalie's brother and the sheriff, approached him with two bowls. "Do you like banana pudding?"

Aidan hadn't consumed pudding since his wisdom teeth removal. The sheer memory brought a shudder. "Gave it up a while back."

"You haven't tried my grandmother's recipe." Mike shoved one of the disposable bowls with a plastic spoon toward Aidan. "If you don't like it, you won't hurt my feelings, unlike my sister, who wears her heart on her sleeve."

Aidan stiffened his spine and accepted the proffered bowl. "Thanks." He swirled the whipped cream into the rest of the mixture and forced a smile.

"I wasn't always the smart man you see before you today," Mike said.

Self-deprecating humor. Relatable and approachable, Mike was the type of person Aidan could see as a friend if he stayed in one place long enough. Being a loner could get tiring after a while. Still, no real use in making friends here if he intended to leave.

If?

Where had that come from? Leaving was a given, with his itinerary planned for the next couple of years. Aidan blinked and rotated his spoon in the opposite direction. "Hollydale is thankful you've wised up, I'm sure."

Mike ate a spoonful of pudding and pointed at Aidan's bowl. "If you wear a hole in the bottom from all that circling and the pudding falls on the ground, don't blame me. Where was I?" He licked his spoon before tapping it on his chin. "A long time ago, Natalie delivered a note to my now-wife that ended badly. Georgie didn't talk to me for eleven years."

Aidan nodded as if he understood a word Mike said. Six languages with a smattering of a few others, yet the Harrisons confounded him more than any dialect.

Mike finished off the last of his pudding,

while Aidan swirled his spoon around his. "You're diplomatic. I'll give you that. You're willing to play along."

"To a certain extent."

Seriousness replaced Mike's good humor. "Natalie would kill me for saying this, but she's a happy soul and loyal to a fault. When I was stupid and hurt Georgie, Natalie stopped talking to me for a long time."

Mike was a straight shooter, so Aidan leveled with him. "Still not connecting the dots."

"Try a bite, and I'll fill you in." Mike tilted his head toward the bowl. "It's the sheriff and father in me."

Aidan hesitated before curiosity won out. He brought the spoon to his lips. Creamy goodness slid down his throat. Nothing could be that good. He tried a second taste and discovered he was wrong. It was better than good.

He finished the bowl and glanced at the sheriff. "Thanks for the push. Now, what's your point?"

Mike glanced at Natalie. "Natalie has a lot of friends who'll defend her to the ends of the earth. You can have the same people on your side if you let them in. She's a genuinely happy person, and I'd hate to see her hurt."

Mike walked away, and Aidan threw the bowl in the nearest receptacle. Mike was protective of Natalie. Didn't he know Natalie could protect herself?

Aidan searched for Danny, eager to spend some time with the pint-size horseshoe champion. There he was, hanging on Natalie's every word, love reflecting in his nephew's brown eyes.

Mike's point hit home. Aidan could be a part of all of this, and yet, he couldn't. But how could he tear Danny away from Natalie and the home she'd created for him over the past three months, even if he had the best of intentions? If he took Danny with him, ripples of his actions would impact more than his nephew.

Aidan took another look at Natalie, her beauty a true breath of summer. Taking Danny away would hurt her. And it would also hurt the Harrison family, who all seemed to genuinely care for Danny.

Shaking his head, he wandered inside and drank a glass of water. In the kitchen corner, he spotted Danny's bright blue backpack with sharks. *Where did that come from?* Danny hadn't brought anything with him. Aidan grabbed it and headed outside to the front porch. The cool mountain air was fresh and it was relatively quiet. Being alone felt good, and he pulled Danny's backpack onto his lap.

Less than a minute later, Natalie, as lovely

as a sunflower, came around the corner of the Harrison house.

Suddenly, being with Natalie, while not being alone, didn't feel so bad. Nearly perfect, in fact. "I wanted to find you and make sure you're okay. I saw Mike talking to you, and you turned ashen. I'll let you in on a little secret. Mike's really a teddy bear when you get to know him. That's our secret, since it wouldn't do for the town to know that about our sheriff."

Aidan gripped the straps of Danny's backpack. "More of a grizzly bear, really."

"Danny's playing with the twins, and Lucie won't let them out of her sight. All of this must be pretty overwhelming, huh? Wait until the dancing starts in a little while." She joined him on the swing.

"There are worse things." His future stretched out before him, and he liked it. More family barbecues like this. Time with Danny. Maybe even a date with the attractive redhead. Dancing sounded really good.

Plans could change. It might be time to write some of his plans in pencil instead of indelible ink. Take himself for example. He thought he'd serve his full twenty years and retire, yet he was considering the position in DC.

Then he reached for the metal chain attached

to the porch swing and spotted his scar. For years, he'd followed his orders, knew what was expected of him. He also knew his responsibilities and that meant looking after Danny day in and day out. He preferred that more regimented approach while Natalie loved going with the flow. In fact, she deserved someone who was spontaneous like she was and fit in with her family. While opposites, especially his father and Cathy, did attract, wouldn't Natalie be happier with someone who looked at things the same way she did?

"Is this barbecue on your list of worse things ever? Or is it something positive?"

"Danny's having fun."

"I didn't ask about Danny. I asked about you."

He fingered each link, the metal warm to the touch. "I've had some interesting conversations. The day's been rather unusual."

"It's okay to like something. In Hollydale, it's encouraged."

"I'm fond of Danny." *And you.*

She started swinging, and they fell into a comfortable rhythm. She turned toward him, and her leg brushed his. "He's blossoming so much. After Shelby's death, he closed up, and today when he won…"

"Why'd you lose the horseshoes match on

purpose?" The question had been bothering him since she didn't sink two of her throws, one not even coming close to the target. It was the only time since he'd known her that she hadn't given something her all.

She laughed and massaged her arm. "If you'd been on target and hooked sinkers every time before the finals, your arm would be sore and you wouldn't see the need to ask that question."

He scooted away from the strawberry scent of her hair and repeated himself. This time, he sent her another glare his drill sergeant would be proud to replicate.

Same as last time, however, a peek of a smile lifted the corners of her lips. "You have to try harder than that to intimidate me."

"You threw the game."

"Nice pun. I'll have to remember that one." She glanced around as if making sure no one overheard her. "If I did, and I'm not admitting anything, Danny needed it more than me. He'll remember winning with his uncle. That's an important memory for him to have."

Speechless, he leaned back and let the rhythmic motion lull him into relaxing a bit. She picked up Danny's bag and bumped her free hand against her head. "My mom came over to borrow my corkscrew and other things for the party. I'd packed a snack for Danny thinking he'd be over there yesterday afternoon. I'd best throw it away. Excuse me."

She reached in and gasped.

"Food can't go bad that quickly."

He leaned over for a closer look, while she placed the backpack next to the glider and pulled out the lunchbox. Tangled in the zipper was Natalie's necklace. Her fingers shook, and she extended the lunchbox to him. "I'd love some help."

Without another word, he carefully freed the gold chain and pendant from its zippered snare. She turned around and upswept her red locks. "My hands are still shaking. Will you clasp it for me?"

Now he had to work hard to keep his hands from shaking as he hooked the necklace in place.

She faced him, her eyes shining in appreciation. "Thanks."

For what? He hadn't done anything someone else wouldn't have done. He grunted his reply and scooted back to his place. From where he sat, envy spread over him like sticky tar. Her town held her in the palm of its hand. Natalie's brother had gone out of his way to show his protective nature toward her. His nephew loved the woman he called his aunt.

No wonder, with her vivacity and her love of life blooming like a cactus rose.

"You have the funniest expression." She reached over and patted his hand, her imprint searing hot. "You didn't eat Mrs. Norman's fruit salad, did you?"

At last, Natalie had hit upon something wrong with the town.

Then again, the real reason behind his discomfort had nothing to do with Hollydale and everything to do with that necklace around her neck. Her feelings for Francisco still ran deep. What would it be like to know she cared that deeply for him?

"I'm good." He tried to rise but found himself rooted to the glider, wanting to soak up a few more minutes of her rays before he moved on.

"Hold on. You have something on your cheek."

Sitting here, he soaked in the apple pie moment. He wanted to remember everything, from the crickets chirping to the breeze cooling off the night air. She tapped her left cheek near her mouth and scooted closer. "Looks like banana pudding landed in that dimple of yours. My brother beat me to the last of it."

He wiped his cheek and turned so his lower back touched the frame of the glider. "Wouldn't do for a soldier to walk around with banana pudding on his face."

She laughed and pointed again. "Still have a little left."

Her gaze met his, and the laughter faded away from her crystal-blue eyes. Time stood still, and everything happy seemed inches away, his for the asking. In the golden glow of the early evening, she radiated warmth and beauty and kindness. The bronze streaks in her hair were unforgettable, her pink lips too kissable. They moved nearer, and his heart raced until he glimpsed the gold chain and symbol hanging around her neck. As much as Natalie lived in the moment, her heart was stuck in the past.

He shifted away and rubbed his cheek with the back of his hand. "There. I'm sure it's all gone."

He jumped up, and the magic of the evening faded.

She rose, and hurt flashed in her eyes. "I'm happy you were able to enjoy it while it lasted."

She walked away, the slight swish of her hips most beguiling. As much as he longed to run to her and throw caution to the wind and kiss her, he stayed where he was. She stopped at the bottom of the steps and glanced back as if she was about to say something.

Hesitation warred on her face, and Aidan moved to the top of the stairs. "Yes?"

"I forgot to tell you I rescheduled Danny's therapy for Wednesday morning since we're meeting with the attorney Penelope Romano on Tuesday."

Another reason to keep things cool between them. Danny's world was shaky enough without him getting involved with Natalie. Good thing his meeting with Mike and the city manager, Woodley, was scheduled for Wednesday afternoon. "I'll be at both."

Laughter came closer, and Mike and his wife and daughter emerged from around the corner.

Mike waved. "We'll be at the park next Saturday, and we're making brisket in the smoker on Friday."

Rachel bounced up and down. "Daddy said I'm not to let our dog, Beau, near the meat. Beau's marching in the parade! I can't wait."

"If he doesn't stop and sniff and steal every hot dog along the way." Georgie laughed and reached for Mike's hand. The simple display of affection hit Aidan hard.

When was the last time he was involved with anyone to the extent mere hand-holding lit up the other person's face, like Mike reacted to Georgie?

When was the last time he was involved period?

The family walked away, and Natalie returned her attention to Aidan. "If Rachel still has that much energy, I'd better rescue Lucie and take Danny home."

"How about we meet tomorrow at The Busy Bean?" Aidan remained at the top of the stairs. He didn't trust himself if he were near her. "I'd like some strong coffee before I tackle Shelby's. Ginny's brew is great, but Deb's is more potent. Then I could take Danny to that grocery store I saw downtown. Pick out some snacks and food for him to have at Shelby's for his visits."

"I hadn't thought about that." Natalie ran her hand down the white bannister. "Wait a second. That won't work. Caleb is taking Danny and the twins to the Timber River Park Center tomorrow for a morning of camp activities."

"Then Danny and I will go to the store in the afternoon. Do you want to meet me at The Busy Bean in the morning, then?"

"Without Danny?"

"Yes. How does nine sound?"

"Ten would work better since I drop Danny off at nine."

"Ten it is."

Country music started playing over speakers in the backyard.

She tapped her foot. "Want to dance?"

She was a bright ray of summer sunshine, while he'd seen the darker side of life.

He didn't want to cast a shadow over that ray. "I haven't danced in years."

"If you can play basketball that well after not playing for a while, you'll remember how to dance."

She held out one arm, and the porch light activated, shining a spotlight on her necklace. Her reaction to finding that necklace gave him pause. He wasn't sure there was room for someone else in her heart.

"Danny's probably ready for bed. I don't want him to think we deserted him." Those excuses sounded weak even to his ears.

The way she arched her eyebrows showed she wasn't buying them either. "One dance isn't a lifetime commitment, Aidan. Good night."

CHAPTER TWELVE

NATALIE PARKED THE car in the farthest spot from The Busy Bean, preferring to leave the closer spaces for those who needed them. She'd just dropped Danny off at Lucie and Caleb's house, and now she was exactly on time, which was nearly a miracle for her during the summer. Her phone pealed the ringtone for Becks, and she debated answering.

Then again, this might be important.

"What's up, Becks?" She used her best upbeat voice.

"Everything, and nothing." Becks hesitated, not sounding like her usual confident self. "Forget I called. Rough night with Pippa, that's all."

"Make sure Jack gets involved." Natalie frowned, as she had never trusted her brother-in-law more than she could throw him. One of the few people she could say that about. After one conversation when Becks and Jack were engaged and Natalie had said something critical about him, Becks raised a haughty brow in her direction. From then on, Natalie focused on maintaining their relationship rather than signaling any disdain for Becks's choice.

Sniffles came over the line, and Natalie was sure this was about more than staying up with Pippa. "Fireball?" She whispered her special name for her twin, one only she was allowed to use. "What's wrong?"

A long pause came over the line, and Natalie shifted her weight, unsure of whether to break the silence. "Most likely postpartum depression. I miss our talks."

Her intuition kicked up a notch at Becks's winsome voice, which sounded nothing like her. "You're making me nervous enough to drive to Asheville and book the first available flight to California."

"You have enough going on." Crisp authority came back. For a second, Becks almost sounded like Becks. "Tell me about the barbecue yesterday."

The sudden switch in topic sent another wave of suspicion through Natalie. She'd play along, though. Maybe her proud sister would get to the point if Natalie prattled on for a few minutes about Aidan, Danny and the festivities. Usually a little bit of chitchat was all Becks could handle before spilling what was upsetting her.

"Why'd you throw the game?" Becks asked.

"I didn't. Aidan and Danny won outright. My arm was sore." Only Aidan and Becks had guessed. Asking for ice before the final start was a good enough ploy to throw everyone else off track.

"Why does your voice lighten up whenever you say Aidan's name?"

Practical, proud and perceptive. That was her sister. "Does not."

"Does so. It quivers and comes out breathless. Is there something going on between the two of you?"

Natalie reached up to tap her necklace before she remembered she'd placed it in the jewelry box her grandmother had bequeathed her, along with her amethyst ring. Mike had received Grandpa Ted's vintage Thunderbird, Natalie had received the jewelry box and Becks had inherited their grandma's silver tea service, which resided at their mom's house as Becks claimed she had no room for it in California.

Part of her wanted to yell direct questions at Becks, but her twin would only reveal what was bothering her on her own time. "Believe it or not, he's immune to my charms. We sat on a glider on Mom and Dad's porch, and he didn't kiss me." *Or dance with me either.*

That was her cue to concentrate on what was important. Finishing the float, keeping Danny here and making him laugh. Not necessarily in that order. So, Aidan was immune to her? Big deal.

Except it was, for she was starting to care for him. No one else looked that appreciative when he was included in family activities, like the basketball outing or yesterday's barbecue. For the most part, those who grew up in Hollydale and stayed here knew each other so well as to practically take them for granted. People knew Lucie cared for stray animals and would often leave them on her doorstep. Georgie restored machines and helped seniors around town with anything with a motor. Aidan fit right in, helping with the parade details and the float. Of course, Aidan had no intentions of staying, his military career and future position in Washington, DC, precluding any future in North Carolina.

More reasons to keep her distance.

"Be careful, Daffodil." That was Becks's pet name for her. "I don't want Aidan leaving with Danny and your heart."

"What did you say?" Hurt tightened her throat. "You think Aidan should take Danny with him. Aren't you on my side? Shelby named me as guardian."

Another minute of silence, and it was all Natalie could do to compose herself.

"Pippa's taught me there are no sides when it comes to children, but Aidan *is* his uncle. That should count for something. You know better than most about bonds between family members. How many times have you brought up our twin bond?"

Too many, and far more often than Becks.

"That twin bond is telling me something is wrong with you and Jack."

"And it doesn't take a twin bond for me to know you're avoiding any serious discussion about Aidan."

Faint wails came over the line.

"Pippa's awake and due at day care soon."

The line clicked off, and Natalie inhaled. The older twin by twenty minutes, Becks had often tried to shelter Natalie. Had Aidan distanced himself from Shelby in the past few years to keep her from experiencing some of the effects he'd endured on his tours?

She shook off the question and grabbed her purse, already late for a date that wasn't a date.

AIDAN GLANCED OUT the window again, wondering why Natalie was still in her car rather than coming into The Busy Bean. She'd sat there for a good ten minutes. Not that he was spying on her or anything like that.

When she emerged from her SUV, he scanned the perimeter around her. *Uh-oh.* Hyacinth fastened her bicycle to the rack on Timber Road and reached into her basket. She followed inside on Natalie's heels, while he folded the *Hollydale Herald* and placed it next to his breakfast, a vegetable frittata.

Natalie entered, pointed to the front counter and made a beeline for it. Before he could stop Natalie from ordering, Hyacinth headed straight for him.

Aidan inhaled and braced himself. "Good morning."

"Isn't it? You should know, though, as you went for an early run. I can't jog every day like I used to. Athena wanted outside, and it's getting harder for her to go through the doggy door, so I stopped my morning meditation and let her out. She's a darling and, thanks to her, I saw the beautiful sunrise. Do you have any pets, Major M.?"

How did she manage to get all of that out in one breath? "No pets." Although the thought of getting one had crossed his mind.

A dog might help Danny with his therapy. Then again, moving to Fort Lewis and living on base were big enough adjustments.

"That's a shame. Pets are one of life's greatest blessings. Having a pet can help decrease your blood pressure and help you relax. Athena and Artemis soak up the sun and keep me company while I garden." Hyacinth beamed and settled her reusable cotton bag on the table. "Do you mind if I join you? I love riding my bike, but I could do with a minute of rest before I run the rest of my errands."

She plopped herself at the place he'd reserved for Natalie, and her eyes widened. "You're expecting company, aren't you?" She glanced around the coffeehouse and then turned back to him. "You're smarter than you look, Major M. Hi, Natalie!"

Everyone in the coffeehouse stopped and stared.

His cheeks grew hot. Natalie finished ordering and came over to his table, a scone in hand, while Hyacinth brought another chair. Not the cozy seating arrangement for two he'd been hoping for.

Conversation buzzed around them again as Natalie glanced at the strawberry scone and cappuccino he'd purchased. "For me?"

Aidan nodded, and Natalie looked at Hyacinth. "Would you like this cinnamon scone I just ordered?"

"How lovely. What a pleasant way to start the day." Hyacinth beamed.

Natalie settled herself and picked off one corner of the scone. "Thank you, Aidan."

Deb had told him it was her last strawberry scone before she'd sold out this morning. Natalie's sweet expression was all the thanks he needed. Especially after he'd been so rude to her last night.

Hyacinth pulled a long rectangular leaflet out of her bag and handed it to Aidan. "I have a feeling you'll need these soon."

He glanced at Hyacinth's gift, which appeared to be some sort of homemade pamphlet.

"They're babysitting coupons. For Danny." Hyacinth fixed her gaze on him, then Natalie, then back on him. "And the future."

The heat in his cheeks grew to an inferno, and he dropped the pamphlet like a hand grenade. "Thanks for the gesture, but I..."

"Wait, there's more." Hyacinth rummaged through her sack.

"But—"

"Nothing's too good for the brave men and women who serve our country with honor. My pear trees came in so nicely this spring." Hyacinth pulled out a jar of poached fruit and placed it before him before glancing at Natalie. She extracted a second jar and gave it to her. "I appreciate teachers, too."

"The red velvet cake was delicious." Natalie rubbed her stomach and licked her lips.

One thing about all of this puzzled the interrogator in him. "How'd you know I was here?"

Hyacinth cinched the sack tight and rose. "When Artemis, Athena and I took a small walk, nothing like our long weekend jogs, mind you, I ran into Ginny. She told me you had just checked out and were stopping here before you move into Shelby's house. I took a chance you'd still be here. Natalie, too. I was right. I have a couple more deliveries before Artemis and Athena enjoy a beautiful day in the yard while I prune my trees. Toodle-oo."

Her long, wispy floral scarf trailed behind her as she floated out of the coffeehouse.

Unsettled, he turned toward Natalie. "Did I just imagine that?"

She inhaled the coffee he'd bought her. "I haven't had any caffeine yet, so I'll answer your question in a bit. It's the little things in life, you know, that make it so worthwhile."

Natalie stopped talking, picked off another piece of scone with her fingers and popped it in her mouth. Her look of bliss said everything, and he liked seeing that expression too much. That was only one reason he was attracted to her. Going out of her way to help others, which seemed as natural to her as her red hair, was another. Whereas he often kept his distance, she went all in, a worthy opponent in basketball and horseshoes and… That smile and her sunny outlook could impact his every move.

If I let her in. "About last night on the porch."

Taking a bite, she leaned back and regarded him with some wariness. "How about we talk about today instead? Caleb is dropping Danny off to you at Shelby's after the session ends. After that, could you bring him to the park and help me with the float?"

"I thought we agreed Danny would go to the Corner Grocery with me." Besides, he had so much to organize at Shelby's. He also had work to do for Mayor Wes. No time like the present to figure out how to keep an eye on Danny while doing other tasks.

"Oh." She examined her jar of pears and glanced at the door, then at her scone. The scone must have won out because she hadn't bolted yet.

His own jar of pears caught his eye. *Are they a genuine gift or a bribe? Does it matter?* Hollydale residents had opened their doors to him. Already The Busy Bean, with its aromas of coffee and sugary carbs that brought a smile to Natalie's face, was becoming one of his favorite spots. *Where was the last place I went on base with half this enthusiasm?* The Harrisons had warmly included him at their barbecue, treating him as one of the family. And yet he'd rejected Natalie's request a minute ago.

"We'll help for a little bit later this afternoon."

Her smile was his second reward of the morning. He gripped his coffee cup and stopped from groaning. He couldn't let himself get attached to Natalie. The military was his family. He, they, made a difference.

"What time should we…" No sooner did he start to ask a question than Belinda strode into the coffeehouse, her laser beam gaze focusing on him.

Did Ginny announce his location on social media? Or just text everyone in town?

"Good morning, Major Murphy, Natalie."

Belinda hung her large canvas knapsack on the back of Hyacinth's former seat before sitting and reaching for the coupon book. She fanned herself and then saw what she held. Her laugh boomed in the calm atmosphere of the coffeehouse. "Goodness gracious, you want a babysitter, just call me. I'm bursting to overflow with all the love and attention my grandkids have spoiled me with. Least I can do is pass it on."

Perplexed, Aidan kept his mouth shut. *What is at work here? Small-town friendliness or blue-ribbon envy?*

He sipped his coffee the way he liked it, without sugar or cream, and then found his tongue again. "Thanks for the offer."

Why is everyone assuming Danny will remain in Hollydale?

Belinda eyed the jarred pears in front of him and Natalie and then reached for her own canvas bag. She pulled out two jars of preserves and placed one near each of them. "Share it in good health with Danny. Little boys love frog jam."

"Frog jam?" Aidan blurted out while eyeing the glass jar with some trepidation.

"You ought to see your face right now. I've never seen a man turn purple before." Belinda laughed and turned the jar around so the label faced him. "Figs, raspberries, oranges and ginger. It's one of my specialties. Figs come from my sister's backyard. Picked them fresh myself on my last visit."

"Thanks." He and Natalie spoke in unison.

Their gazes met, and humor lurked in the crystal-blue depths of her eyes.

Belinda rose, knapsack in hand. "Wait, one more thing before I go." She extracted a crocheted blanket in varying shades of camouflage green. "I make these and send them to our troops at Christmastime. You can take yours with you."

"This is too much." Aidan fingered the yarn of the blanket, the fine rows consistent and even. It was beautiful.

"Not nearly enough." Belinda smiled and patted his hand. "And it's not on account of anything in the foreseeable future either. I don't know how hard it's going to be for you to say goodbye to that adorable nephew of yours when you return to duty, but we'll all be thinking of you and hoping you come home real soon. My little granddaughter's coming over today. I'm teaching her how to make pie crusts. See you later."

Her words sank in as she left, his jaw clenched. "Would you explain?"

"Explain what?" Natalie's wide blue eyes connected with his gaze, and he inhaled.

Once in the army, always in the army. Once a kindergarten teacher, always a kindergarten teacher, he supposed. He folded his arms. "Explain, *please.*"

She laughed and tossed back her hair. "While you might think I'm being obtuse on purpose, I wasn't. I honestly don't know what you're asking."

"Why does everyone think Danny is staying here?"

Her smile faded from her lips. She propped her elbows on the table and said in a low voice, "Are we back to that again? I thought we agreed you were going to keep an open mind about Hollydale. I don't want Danny relapsing and having night terrors again."

Night terrors. Aidan shuddered. He wouldn't wish those on anyone, let alone a six-year-old. For a while, after his arm injury, his screams would wake him and he'd be covered in sweat. Until he'd been informed of Shelby's death, it had been years since one of those vivid nightmares gripped him. Now it had only been three months.

He toyed with his napkin, shredding the end of it. "You can't go around telling everyone he's staying."

"I've done no such thing." Her indignation was clear. "Well, I told my mom you want to take him to Fort Lewis. While Mom told Dad, I know the two of them. It ended there."

They both held firm, neither willing to concede an inch but both willing to do anything for the boy at the center of it all.

Why did she expect him to blink first? In all honesty, he had expected her to relent by now. On the basketball court, she had committed her all, then moved on. This was a woman whose character he couldn't wrap his head around. What did she expect from him?

What did he expect of himself?

Even a few short days in Hollydale proved he'd better figure that out fast, especially before the next meeting with the attorney on Tuesday, which happened to be tomorrow.

"You really believe Carl and Diane would keep that to themselves? Look at Ginny this morning, giving my itinerary to Hyacinth and Belinda."

"I do believe the best about my parents. What you see is what you get. Kids respond well to that. No matter what happens with Danny, remember that." She reached for her drink and raised her cup. "To Danny."

He also raised his disposable cup, and she clinked hers against his with a smile.

"For Danny's sake, I'll keep an open mind."

"What time is it? I never wear a watch in the summer."

He glanced at the watch his father had given him when he finished officer candidate school. "Ten thirty."

"That late." She scarfed down the last of the scone and grabbed her disposable coffee cup, raising it in his direction. "Thanks for the coffee. Gotta run."

"Wait. After I dropped Shelby's car at her place with my duffel, I walked here to clear the cobwebs. Can you take the bribes, er, I mean, preserves and pears and quilt, with you and drop them off at Shelby's?"

"Do you want a ride back?"

"Thanks, but I need another walk." *And some time alone.*

Once he finished eating, he left the coffeehouse and started out for Marigold Lane. No sooner had he passed City Hall than he noticed Mayor Wes heading his way. Hmm, Ginny probably had him on speed dial.

"Aidan, just the man I needed to see. By the way, Woodley says you're doing a commendable job on the security for the parade." Mayor Wes came up beside him and patted his shoulder. "I'm on my way to the police station, and it was my good luck I ran into you. Where are you headed?"

"To my sister's house." Maybe Natalie was wearing off on him as he offered that without hesitation.

"Want some company for a stretch?" Mayor Wes walked alongside him, as if he didn't expect Aidan to say no.

"The police station is the other way."

"It'll still be there when we're done talking."

Aidan moved along the sidewalk, the steady marching rhythm his standard trade. "What did you need to talk to me about? We're scheduled for a meeting later this week."

The mayor laughed once more, and nervousness welled inside Aidan. "Always straight to the point. Here in Hollydale, we like our visitors to take time to eat at our restaurants and spend time in the great outdoors so they'll come back again. Are you liking our fair town?"

Yes, especially one beautiful whirlwind. "No complaints, although Hyacinth and Belinda are coming on rather strong."

Mayor Wes shrugged and kept a steady pace alongside Aidan. "You're army strong. Judging from your attention to detail, you can handle that situation. By the way, Sheriff Mike and Woodley are impressed with the schematics you emailed them this morning."

They were still a couple of blocks away from Shelby's house. Judging from the mayor's body language, the mayor hadn't revealed the real reason for stopping him yet.

"Good to know." Light conversation wasn't his strong suit, but he could give it a try. "Beautiful summer day."

And it was. The gazebo stood proud in the town square, decorated with bunting and twinkle lights. The mountains provided a shield against the heat and humidity associated with the South, and a cool breeze made his morning run enjoyable earlier. People waved their greetings, and the mayor acknowledged each by name, asking after loved ones and pets before returning his attention to Aidan.

"Guess I'd better get to the point before we're interrupted again. The grand marshal of our parade, a former baseball player turned manager with ties to our community, received an offer to star in an advertisement for Japanese sake. He called me personally to ask for a release from his obligation before he accepted. Nice of him. He threw in a new fire engine, so I could hardly turn the man down, could I?"

Aidan grunted his acknowledgment, unsure of any other response. "Danny won't be upset about that. He's more into fire trucks than baseball at the moment."

"That leaves me in a bind, though. The grand marshal leads the parade, unites the town, so to speak." The mayor paused and dipped his head in greeting to more passersby.

Aidan nodded and pursed his lips in his semblance of a smile, unused to this much attention. "I'm sure you'll think of something."

The mayor seemed bright enough to forge a solution. "That's where you come in." The mayor's soft drawl belied his authority. "You're my top choice."

Stunned, Aidan stopped marching forward and rubbed his ear. Then he started laughing. "Sorry. Heard you wrong. Thought you asked me to be grand marshal."

"I did. The Boulevard of Stars Parade is a celebration of everything good about our country on its birthday." The mayor pointed to Aidan's arm. "You've made sacrifices while serving in more ways than one. You answered my call for a project when you arrived, and your work is top-notch. What's more, I need an honorable man for a day that should bring people together."

Aidan lowered his sleeve. Until now, he'd been unaware he had bunched the fabric around his elbow. "How do you know the scar isn't a personal injury with no connection to my military service?"

"Was it?" The mayor leveled a look at him.

"No. I did sustain it in combat." He shifted his weight, uncomfortable with the subject. "There are other veterans. Why me?"

"You've endured and survived, and I believe you're thriving in these parts."

"That's my point. I'm only visiting these parts. Shouldn't the grand marshal have ties to the community? Be a leader."

"I stand by my choice. In the short time your sister lived here, she made a big impact, thinking and dreaming big about Snickerdoodles. The lunch café would have had a real niche in Hollydale, one not represented by our other fine dining establishments. The other businesses in the area and I were hoping she'd make a go of it. Since her loss, the residents have rallied around Danny. That little boy represents us supporting each other in times of crisis. We want to extend that to you as well." The mayor sounded genuine, and Aidan understood why the man spoke for the town.

A strange feeling came over him as he accepted how much Hollydale was rallying around him. Cathy had once rallied around him, and he rejected that kind of concern and affection, only to realize later that he'd missed out on something special. Still, a town going out of their way to embrace him? When he'd seen the hard truth of life out there? Maybe that was what he was fighting for.

"I can see you're skeptical. I would be, too." Hesitation halted Aiden voicing his concern, and Mayor Wes tapped his chin. "There's a perk I haven't mentioned. Georgie's offering her convertible for the parade. You and Danny would get to ride in a beaut of a fully restored Thunderbird."

"Anything else?" While some operations in the army required split-second decisions when your life and the lives of your fellow soldiers were on the line, others required all the necessary information spread out on the table for an informed decision. Having a backup plan would have prevented the mayor from being entangled in this type of sticky situation, where he was asking a total stranger to be the grand marshal.

"I need an answer about the grand marshal position. Today. Think it over and call me this afternoon." The mayor called out to two well-dressed women, and he crossed the street. "Kitty, Beverly. Good to see you both out and about. How are you on this fine day?"

This was an honor, and Danny loved his aunt's Thunderbird. He'd call the mayor later to accept. Another unexpected turn of events, but he was starting to expect nothing less from Hollydale.

CHAPTER THIRTEEN

"Thanks for your help today, Mike. Glad to know they give you a day off every once in a while." Natalie hammered a stud in place.

Mike wiped his forehead with the back of his arm and swallowed a big swig of water. "The least I can do is help today since I won't be around this weekend."

"You're lending me Georgie. That more than makes up for it." She winked as she struck the last nail in place.

Little by little, the float was coming along. In no time she'd be throwing candy out to the crowd and, with some luck and a lot of patience, she might hear Danny laugh again. Even when he won the horseshoe competition, he'd only smiled and thrown his arms around Aidan.

"If I wasn't so sure of myself, I'd be offended by that remark." Her brother crossed his arms and fell backward into a soft patch of grass.

Natalie laughed, hopped off the platform and extended an arm to assist him up. "Nice to see your sense of humor's returned since Georgie came back to town."

"I'd be offended by that if you weren't right. Getting a second chance with Georgie was the best thing that's happened to me." He wiped the grass off his shorts. "That and Rachel."

"The float's coming along, don't you think?" She tilted her head one way, then the other. "It'll come together in the end, right?"

Mike shrugged and picked up the hammer off the grass. "Most things do. I didn't feel like it would when I arrested Georgie, but it did. I think you're finally returning and coming back together, too."

She slipped back to the pavilion area and started cleaning up around them in case Danny and Aidan arrived earlier than expected. Mike followed and waited on the edge.

"I don't know what you're talking about." Natalie tidied the piles of scrap wood.

"Part of you has been AWOL since Francisco died. You've been so busy throwing yourself into everything and urging others to have fun. Anyone not close to you wouldn't guess anything was wrong, but I've seen the faraway looks and the longing glances at Rachel."

She hadn't hidden her feelings as well as she thought, and he knew she'd thrown herself into a haze of productivity to balance out the grief. Staying busy and living in the moment only worked up to a point. There was a time everyone went home and she had to be satisfied with silence.

It was taking some getting used to, but she was making progress. With a quick glance at the sky, gray clouds on the horizon, Mike shook his head. "Looks like it's going to rain. Maybe we should move it back into the shed."

She checked the weather app on her phone. "The system's heading our way, but there should be enough time to get more accomplished."

"Seems like you're throwing your whole self into this." He headed to the toolbox and traded the hammer for a wrench. "Whirling dervishes are a force of nature, little sis."

Leave it to her big brother, the class clown turned sheriff, to know her so well. "Forces of nature make things happen. Nothing wrong with that." There was an edge in her voice that wasn't normally present. Now he was talking to her one-on-one and she realized Mike was the last member of the family she'd have expected to confront her. "Danny needs a force of nature in his life, one that will provide him with sunshine rather than a constant deluge."

"When Rachel burned herself in that accident, I wanted to take away her pain, endure it for her, scream, but I couldn't. She faced it with me at her side. I was so proud of her. I've learned the best I can do is make sure she has an umbrella and knows how to use it."

She sat on the nearest bench. He came over and settled next to her. She clenched her jaw and fists, anything so the tears burning her eyes wouldn't fall. "Do you believe Aidan would be a better choice to teach Danny how to use his umbrella?"

"Did Mom say something to you?"

"So Mom and Becks are both against me keeping my promise to Shelby?"

If she sat here any longer, she'd start crying. She walked over to the chicken wire and unrolled the spool. One by one, she twisted and fluffed the tissue paper loops poking out of each hole until they formed beautiful flowers.

Mike followed her and watched for a minute before imitating her actions on his end of the wire. "I haven't talked to Becks about it but, judging from the way you said that, I assume she said something to you. On the record, neither Mom nor Becks has said anything to me. The way you said 'too' made me think Mom had talked to you since you two are so close. You take after her the most."

His words soaked in, and she took a moment

to absorb everything around her. On a normal day, the birds singing and the kids playing boosted her morale, pushed her a little more to finish what was in front of her. Today, they were reminders of what she stood to lose. She glanced at the ceiling of the pavilion with a myriad of initials written in Sharpie, a couple of spiderwebs and more than enough gum to keep her kindergarten class in ecstasy for several hours. "What do you think?"

One look at his face, more serious than she'd seen in some time, and her stomach dropped. "You'll make a great mom…"

She finished his sentence for him. "For someone else, right?"

"That's the most pessimistic thing I've ever heard you say." Creases lined Mike's forehead, getting deeper with every word. "It doesn't take blood to make a family. It takes love."

And those might be the wisest words she'd ever heard her brother say. If anyone could say that, though, he could, considering her parents adopted him before they found out they were expecting twins. She slugged his shoulder. "And fun."

"And jokes."

Shelby's compact pulled into the parking lot. A few seconds later, Danny emerged and ran to Natalie. He wrapped his arms around her, and she breathed in baby shampoo and pine trees. "Smells like you did something outdoors. Did you have a good time with your uncle?"

"We went for a hike near Sully Creek after our trip to the Corner Grocery." Aidan shrugged and gave a clipped nod to Mike.

Danny broke away, and she flicked off a pine needle from his mop of brown hair.

"I saw a deer and a baby fawn at the nature preserve this morning. It was so neat. They ran away before I could pet them. Then me and Uncle Aidan saw some neat flowers at the creek. Next time, you have to come with us, Aunt Natalie." Danny's smile tugged at her heart, and she glanced at Aidan.

"You and your uncle need time together," Natalie said.

More than ever, she understood the fear of missing out. She wanted Danny to live his life, and she wanted to be there right alongside him.

Aidan walked toward the truck chassis, and they followed. "I'm impressed with the progress."

"We worked on the support frame. Mike helped since he has to miss out on the work party this weekend. Something about commitments as the sheriff and all that." She elbowed her brother in the ribs and winked. "This afternoon, we're going to get the background built so it can be in place for this weekend."

Mike's phone buzzed, and he glanced down. "Hold up a second, little sis." Without another word, her brother headed to the pavilion.

Danny tugged at her sundress. "Uncle Aidan's gonna take me to Timber River Outfitters this afternoon."

Mike came back, shaking his head, his face lined with disappointment. "Sorry, but I have to bail out. Duty calls." He hurried to his squad car.

After he left, Aidan turned to her. "What can we do to help?"

"I'm still your bestest helper." Danny hugged her waist. "And your most favorite, too, right?"

She winked at him. "And the cutest."

She looked Aidan's way. Danny might be the cutest, but Aidan took her breath away. Over the past week, he'd lost some of that straitlaced exterior. Not that a person could change who they were on the inside. He'd always plan everything to the nth degree. Still, some time with Danny loosened him up enough to make this casual side of him that much more appealing.

"What's in store for this afternoon?" Aidan stepped to the toolbox.

"Mike and I were going to lift the superstructure, which is basically that wooden thing that looks like a cross between a stage and a platform, onto the chassis and connect it to the rectangular wooden area we cut out of the red fuzzy fabric that's the base covering most of the float."

He looked impressed but then folded his arms. "Would we get in the way?"

"Most likely."

Without saying a word, Aidan seemed to understand her dilemma. Before she knew it, they dropped Danny off at her mother's, where her niece Rachel offered to teach him how to draw cats and cows. Back in front of the park shed, she wondered if this was a good idea. The gray clouds passed overhead with swiftness, and she wasn't sure if the weather would hold off long enough to get anything done.

Aidan looked at her and pointed. "Something's better than nothing."

No sooner had they fastened the superstructure onto the platform than the distant rumbling of thunder crackled in the air. The wind picked up, the tips of the pines swaying. Nearby, the splash fountains faded away to nothingness as car doors slammed with parents and other caregivers urging their charges to hurry before the storm arrived.

"Where's your tarp?" Aidan yelled as he hopped off the platform to the grassy flat.

"I think there's one in the shed. Wouldn't it be easier to back the truck in?" Natalie disembarked, taking care when she landed. Her ankle boots left an imprint in the soft grass.

"We don't have time. Besides, the truck might not fit. We should have measured the height of the tiered rainbow frame you designed. The rain'll be here soon." He ran to the shed and brought out a bright blue tarp.

He unfolded the plastic, and they worked together, making sure every inch of the truck was covered, securing the corners with rocks. The wind now swirled all around them, leaves hitting her face. No sooner did they pile on the last stone than fat raindrops began to fall. Her car and the pavilion were farther than the shed, so Natalie grabbed her bag from the side of the float and rushed inside the makeshift building. She and Aidan made it inside the second the skies burst open with a deluge.

Rain poured forth, coming down sideways, lightning flashing across the dark sky. She shivered.

"Are you cold?"

His words drew her attention to him standing a good ten feet away on the other side of the utility shed. He shook some water droplets off his cropped dark brown hair.

"Not really." She removed the elastic holding her messy bun in place. She then shook out the rain from her hair. "I feel like a dog after a bath."

She only hoped she didn't look like one.

The rain pelted the roof, the constant pitter-patter almost a melody. She exhaled and looked around for a place to get comfortable. The smells of fertilizer and paint weren't her favorites but, with the doors wide open, fresh air and rain dispersed the strong aroma. "Mountain storms tend to last longer than a pop-up shower." She found a bucket and upended it before pointing to its twin. "Do you prefer to sit or stand?"

"I'm fine." He glared outside as if that would stop the storm in its tracks.

"I'll text my mom to let her and Danny know we're okay."

"Good idea."

She rifled through her purse until she found her phone. After a quick text to her mother letting her and Danny know they were safe, she searched through the rest of her bag. With a triumphant cry, she produced a deck of cards. "What's your poison? Poker? Gin rummy? Crazy eights?"

"Solitaire."

Thunder boomed in the distance, and she kept herself from tumbling off her makeshift chair. "Meet me halfway."

Rain started coming inside the shed, and he backed away, closing one of the doors while keeping the other open. Then he approached her. "What's with you and games anyway? Basketball? Horseshoes? Cards?"

"Would you prefer to talk? I've been known to do that on occasion."

"Hand me the cards. I shuffle well."

She smiled as he upended the other bucket. "Whoa. Someone's found his confidence. Pride goeth before a fall, and notice I'm the one who travels with a deck of playing cards."

A clap of thunder directly overhead elicited a gasp, and she jumped off the bucket, knocking it sideways. He dropped the cards and stood.

In two steps, he closed the distance. "Are you afraid of thunder?"

Nervous laughter passed through her lips. "Of course not. Who'd be afraid of a natural phenomenon?"

"I'd classify you as a natural phenomenon in a second."

He was close enough for his breath to tickle her cheek, the warmth of it warding off the cooler air rustling in from the storm. The rain pelted the roof, but the coziness of the dry, isolated spot embraced her. He moved even closer, and his hand tilted her cheek upward.

"Most natural phenomena, though, are scary. I'm harmless." The deep gray flecks of his eyes stood out like charcoal.

"You're anything but harmless."

That was something, considering all he'd seen and done. However, at this point, he was harmful to the careful equilibrium she'd rebuilt for herself. "Why didn't you dance with me at the barbecue?"

"Maybe because I didn't expect to find anything like you in Hollydale. On the flight, I figured everything out about my life with Danny. Serve one more year, accept the job in DC, then meet someone who's like me. Being attracted to you wasn't on that list."

So he was attracted to her, but he had come up with a convenient checklist for a relationship? "Relationships aren't necessarily something you can plan, although it's nice to know you feel something for me. Can I claim that dance now?"

"There's no music."

"There is if you listen." She wiggled her finger, and he moved closer. "The rain and the wind are providing a melody of sorts."

"May I have this dance?"

Her stomach fluttered, and something in his face let her know the chemistry between them was mutual. She stepped toward him and reached for his free hand, pulling him toward her for a slow dance. They swayed for a minute before his gaze met hers, and she nodded. His lips claimed hers, and the tingle traveled to her toes. This kiss was everything a kiss should be. Fun enough to keep it light but with enough emotion to make it count, make it real. Make him matter.

A faint whimper caught her ear, and she laughed. "I didn't expect that sound from you."

He broke away and shook his head. "I thought it was you."

They both laughed before the sound returned, a little louder this time, more of a mewing than a whine, coming from the direction of the far corner.

Aidan beat her to the corner, and he held out his arm. "Stand back until we know what made that noise."

A small bundle of fur caught her eye, and she reached for the kitten hovering there, wet and scared, covered in mud. "Ah, the poor little thing."

"It might hurt you." He blocked her hand

before she could pick up the animal. "Or the mother might be around searching for it."

"*It* is a kitten and if the mother cat were in here, *it* wouldn't be dirty and mewling. Poor thing probably got lost or separated."

Brushing Aidan aside, she made soft, cooing sounds and bundled the cold kitten in her arms. The kitten put up a valiant effort and unsheathed its claws for a second before Natalie held it to her chest and it purred. "Danny will love the newest addition to our family."

The "our" slipped out, but she could hardly take it back now. The kitten protested its hunger.

"I'm not sure introducing Danny to the kitten is a good idea." He backed up until his rear smacked the back of the shed.

"Why not? Little boys like cats, too." She had no idea if Danny was a cat or a dog person, but there was no reason why anyone couldn't make room in their hearts for both.

"He can't take a kitten cross-country."

AIDAN HAD BLOWN the moment with a simple sentence. The look on Natalie's face changing from wonder to cold, hard reality reinforced what he already knew. They could never work, not with his pragmatic, nose-to-the-grindstone approach against her breezy light self. Storm clouds blocked sunlight every time.

Besides, Danny would be the one most devastated if Aidan tried to turn that kiss into something more and he failed. He'd failed to stop his arm from getting sliced open, despite all his training. He'd failed at being a big brother to Shelby and making sure she went to the doctor for annual checkups. Not many others could warp a kiss like that into a monumental disaster, but he'd succeeded.

He couldn't fail as Danny's co-guardian. The stakes were too high.

In the privacy of Shelby's house, he shook off that train of thought as he twirled his pasta with his fork. Dinner for one wasn't as much fun now. Should he go next door and check on Natalie and Danny? Or would that look too pathetic? The doorbell rang, and he jumped to answer it. There on his doorstep stood Danny, bouncing with excitement.

"Can you come with us? Aunt Natalie said it was okay to invite you."

Aidan glanced out the door and found Natalie in her driveway, her cream floral sundress cool and breezy, her ankle boots slightly edgy and all charm, same as her. She waved, and he hurried over, glaring at her all the while.

"I thought we agreed you wouldn't say anything about the cat until the veterinarian was sure she was going to be alright." He kept his voice low enough for her ears only.

Her chest rose and fell before she rolled her eyes. "We're not going to the vet's office. We're going out for ice cream, and Danny wanted his uncle to join us."

So, the invitation came from Danny and, from the tone of her voice, Danny alone. He shuffled his feet and kept his gaze at the ground. "If I jumped to conclusions, I'm sorry."

Her head jerked back as though his apology was the last thing she expected. "Apology accepted." Her face brightened as Danny neared. "We're walking downtown if you'd like to come with us."

"Then this really has nothing to do with the kitten?"

She laughed and shook her head, folding her arms across her chest. "You don't get it, do you? And by the way, the vet called. Stormy's a little fighter. She'll be coming home tomorrow. This isn't about that or anything, really. My parents took the three of us siblings to Miss Louise's once a week during the summer. It's just a way to be grateful for today."

"Maybe we should go back and get the frame finished first. That was your goal for today, wasn't it?" At this rate, the float would be ready for the Christmas parade.

She linked her arm through his and then disconnected from him like she'd come in contact with a hot iron. "I'll have time to work on it tomorrow. Going out for ice cream tonight is totally unplanned, totally unexpected, totally wonderful."

Their gazes met, and her cheeks reddened into a most becoming shade of pink. Two surprises on this day, three if you counted the kitten. "I haven't finished my dinner yet."

"Come on, Murphy. Live a little." She stood back and tilted her head. "Hmm. Cup or cone? If I had to guess, I'd say cup since it's neat and organized and not prone to drip."

She nailed his usual choice, but he refused to answer.

Danny tugged at his hand. "Uncle Aidan, it won't be the same without you."

Looking at Natalie, Aidan begged to differ. He and Danny wouldn't be the same without her. With every passing minute, he connected more and more with the vivacious redhead who made every minute lighter, happier.

"Isn't it a little late for ice cream?"

"It's never too late to celebrate a beautiful day."

"Just so this doesn't become a nightly occurrence. Wait here a minute." He hurried back to his house, grabbed his wallet and locked up.

They strolled along Oak Street, and he absorbed everything around him. He'd spent time on almost every continent, but this place seemed different. A band tuned their instruments in the gazebo, and Natalie tapped her forehead.

"I forgot about the Summer Country Music Series. It happens once a week until Labor Day. The line at the ice cream parlor will be a little longer, but we'll enjoy some good country music while we wait. The Smoky Sirens are playing tonight. They do covers of Keith Urban and Tim McGraw. Do you mind?"

Danny looked at him as if expecting Aidan to throw water over his bonfire.

He couldn't disappoint either of them again today. "Not at all."

Old habits died hard, though, and he scanned the perimeter. A father threw a blanket over the last patch of unclaimed grass. Nearby, a young couple clinked tall glasses of what looked like champagne. A group of kids danced as the band tuned their instruments. To his surprise, people greeted him by name. He nodded in return.

"You've made quite the impression." Natalie kept up with his brisk pace, not winded at all.

"So have you." The words slipped out, but he wouldn't take them back. "I met most of those people while working on the parade security project."

"Which, according to Sheriff Mike, is now ahead of schedule. Why doesn't that surprise me?" The twinkle in her eye matched her tone as they arrived at Miss Louise's Ice Cream Parlor.

He ushered them inside and didn't have far to go as the line wound around several ropes and back to the entrance, with half of Hollydale already ahead of them.

She held Danny's hand and smiled. "It's worth the wait. I promise."

The person in front of them turned around and greeted Natalie, and the two started talking. Danny released Natalie's hand and joined him. "This could go on awhile."

He spoke from experience, it seemed.

Aidan stifled a laugh and nodded. "Natalie likes to talk. Nothing wrong with that."

"What was my mommy's favorite flavor?"

The breath escaped from Aidan's lungs. Shelby had only been gone for three months, and Danny had either forgotten or never had time to find out.

"When she was your age, it was chocolate.

When she was ten, she tried butter pecan and never looked back."

Danny squeezed his hand and looked at him with those big eyes. Shelby's eyes. Danny must have been satisfied with the answer because he started talking about his time at Diane's that afternoon.

Finally, the people ahead of them placed their order, and Natalie returned her attention to them. "What did I miss?"

"Uncle Aidan told me Mommy's favorite ice-cream flavor was butter pecan."

Natalie smiled and nodded. "When your uncle was on a date, she tagged along as sort of a reverse chaperone, perfect, really, since she was younger and constantly asking questions. She thought Aidan would like her more if she ordered the same flavor. Turned out, she loved it."

He'd never known Shelby's side of the story before as he'd been rather upset at Shelby's presence as a third wheel. They stepped to the counter and ordered from a harried-looking teenager, while another scooped out cones and handed them over. With no empty tables remaining inside the parlor, Natalie suggested they walk and lick at the same time, and he agreed. She grabbed bunches of napkins and stuffed them into her purse.

Outside, soft music filled the air, and Aidan swayed to the tempo, although he preferred jazz to country. They strolled along, and he kept a close and constant eye on Danny, with crowds of people milling about.

The sight of his nephew walking and trying to lick at the same time brought out a tenderness he'd never felt before. Drips of ice cream melted down Danny's cone, and Aidan noticed someone leaving a nearby bench. Before anyone else could take the spot, the three of them squeezed in tight. From the looks of it, it was the only open spot around.

"Danny, watch me." He demonstrated how to lick the side of the cone.

The expression of pure concentration on Danny's face touched something even deeper, and Aidan knew there was no way he'd ever give up his nephew. A musician started plucking a banjo, and someone introduced a new tune. Dusk surrounded them, the warm pink rosy glow from the mountain sunset bringing out the burnished auburn of Natalie's hair. Twinkle lights switched on.

She wasn't part of his plan. He'd had everything tied up with a nice neat red bow on that flight, and she made him question every dotted *i* and crossed *t*.

"Penny for your thoughts." Her voice held

bemusement, even though her eyes reflected something deeper, almost contemplative in nature. "Or, in your case, a nickel and a day planner."

Was he that obvious about everything?

He pointed toward her cone. "Vanilla ice cream? That's the last flavor I would have expected you to order."

"So, I'm a woman of mystery?" She licked her cone, bliss coming over her heart-shaped face. "Vanilla gets a bad rap as plain and boring. There's nothing boring about rich texture and delicate flavors."

He could say the same about her.

Danny held up his cone. "Butter pecan is my new favorite, Uncle Aidan."

His nephew wore most of his ice-cream cone on his face and hands, and Aidan restrained his laughter. Natalie shoved a wad of napkins their way. He wiped Danny's face while fiddles and guitars melded together for a smooth sound in the background.

During a lull between songs, Danny bounced on the bench. "Gigi's waving at me. Can I talk to her before we go home?"

Danny looked at Natalie, then Aidan, before biting his bottom lip as if he didn't know whose permission to ask.

"Of course. Have fun," she said.

"Stay on the green where we can see you. A moment of safety is an hour of security."

Their voices overlapped, and Danny came close to tears, obviously unsure of what they said.

Natalie waved at Gigi's mom, who nodded and pointed to Danny, then Gigi. Natalie leaned over and kissed Danny's forehead. "Stay with Miss Kris until we get there. We'll join you as soon as we're done with our cones."

Aidan watched Danny join Kris and Gigi. Then he focused his attention on his cone as the next song started. Anything to keep his mind off Natalie as she scooted closer to him to make room for someone else on the other side of her. His awareness of her heightened in the damp coolness of the evening.

She crunched into her cone as a couple passed and waved their hellos to him. Aidan remembered the woman from the security assignment and responded accordingly.

"One week and you're already beginning to fit in. Isn't Hollydale wonderful?" Natalie spoke loud enough for him to hear but not in a way to disturb those around them. She lifted her cone and polished off the rest.

Aidan savored the next lick, the buttery richness of the treat melting in his mouth. "Natalie..."

"Hold that thought. I like this song." She held up her finger, a napkin attached to it, and her slight laugh broke the growing tension. She swayed in time to the music, and he enjoyed watching her.

He crunched the last bite of the cone, while she handed him a napkin. The song ended. She turned to him, his gaze still on Danny sitting still next to Gigi. "By the way, a bunch of tomorrow's volunteers had to cancel."

"What about finishing the float? How will you get it done in time?"

"It's coming along, and there'll be more volunteers this weekend. We still have a week left to finish it. It's going to be beautiful."

"But you mentioned that Stormy's coming home tomorrow. Where will the kitten stay while you're at the float?" His palms itched at Natalie's easy acceptance of two things that needed serious focus and engagement. "The framework isn't completed, and an abandoned kitten needs care."

The band announced intermission, and people started standing and stretching. Natalie rose from the bench and Aidan followed suit. She faced him. "I'll love the kitten and give her a good home. Isn't that what's important? Speaking of home, it's time to get that little boy and head that way ourselves."

They collected Danny, thanking Kris and Gigi before Danny yawned, a sign they'd best be going.

Aidan gripped Danny's hand as the three strolled along Maple Drive. They turned left onto Hollyhock Street, which would lead them to Marigold Lane. Danny reached out to Aidan, and he picked him up. The faint chords of the next song filled the air, and Danny nestled in, his head fitting snugly on Aidan's shoulder.

This was what he didn't know he'd been missing.

Before he knew it, he was in Danny's room, helping Danny into his dinosaur pajamas. He was about to tuck in his nephew when Danny looked at Aidan through half-slit eyes. "I want Aunt Natalie to do it."

Natalie brushed past him, and Aidan backed away. That was probably his cue to head next door to Shelby's, but he didn't want to leave just yet.

A minute later, she settled on her couch, and he lowered himself onto her comfortable love seat.

"Aidan, I'll figure out a way to take care of Stormy and finish the float."

He lifted one eyebrow, and she clutched a bright purple throw pillow to her chest.

"Before I go to sleep tonight."

"A kitten is a big responsibility."

"I'm more than capable of taking care of a kitten." She huffed out a breath and threw the pillow aside. "And Danny. Everything doesn't fit into a nice neat package, Murphy. Take tonight. Danny now has a new memory of his uncle, and you had a good time, whether you want to admit it or not."

Fun only went so far, though. It didn't keep people safe. It didn't help him sleep at night. It didn't last.

One look at Natalie's face made him wonder if what they had, what they could have, might have a chance at being long-term. Nothing came with guarantees, but was that any reason to give up something that held so much potential?

As it was, he was choosing to take the job in DC since it was a solid idea with a low degree of risk. There was no use in changing that plan and having something else possibly go wrong. Even if he did change his plan, where was the certainty that would work out in the end either? "My service to my country makes a difference. My next job will also make a difference."

"What does that have to do with admitting you had a good time tonight?"

Everything, and nothing.

"I guess it doesn't."

She tilted her head as if waiting for more of an admission from him.

"Okay, I did enjoy myself, but I have to keep an eye on what the future holds. For me, that's in Fort Lewis and then DC."

Inspiration struck him.

He should ask Natalie to move closer to them next year after he received his honorable discharge and accepted the job in Washington, DC. That plan made sense. In a year, she could reconnect with Danny and also be part of his own life as well. The thought both terrified and captivated him.

Was it too soon for that kind of commitment? Unsettled with all the recent events, he'd almost abandoned his steady self. No one rearranged their lives for someone else this quickly.

Surely Natalie would come to the same conclusion?

"It's okay to keep one eye on the here and now every so often." Her voice softened. "And you're not doing a disservice to your fellow troops. You deserve this time to grieve for your sister and make some new memories."

"How did you know what I was thinking?"

She shrugged and picked up the pillow once more. "I did have a heads-up on your personality from Shelby, you know. Did you know I lived in Raleigh for five years? I was even Teacher of the Year there. As soon as the Dalesford County School District posted the kindergarten teacher position, though, I submitted my application, and they snapped me up. I missed my friends and family too much to stay away."

One more reason she couldn't move to wherever he and Danny lived. She needed her support system. People she could depend on. People who loved her.

Unlike him, she couldn't flourish where those were nonexistent.

"You can choose where to teach and serve others." Come to think of it, though, they had that in common. They both wanted to help make the world a better place, him through service and her through education. "The security firm has government contracts and is centered in Washington. It doesn't have branches in Hollydale."

"Serving people is what counts. Serving people you care about while helping them enjoy their lives is a bonus."

They were at yet another impasse. Any chance of her relocating to Washington washed away before it had any chance to take root. He should have known the evening's cozy glow wouldn't last. Cease-fires often preceded renewed combat.

"That's my cue to leave." He rose, and she escorted him to the door.

"I haven't told Danny about Stormy. I'm not seeking your permission either, because I think having new life around will help his therapy. He still hasn't laughed, you know, and kittens bring smiles and giggles to most. Who knows? A kitten might break through his defenses."

He opened the door, and she reached out and touched his arm. "Do you want to take him to his therapy session tomorrow while I pick up Stormy?"

He recognized her peace offer. Nodding, he looked back one more time before entering the cool comfort of Shelby's house.

"AUNT NATALIE, MY tummy hurts."

Natalie rolled over in her bed. Just five more minutes. She reached for the pillow to put it over her head when Danny's words registered in her brain. The minute they did, she jerked to a sitting position in her bed and turned on her lamp. Hunched over, Danny stood in the doorway, pain etched on his face.

Aidan had told her it was too late for ice cream. Why hadn't she listened to him?

She bolted out of bed, the cherry hardwood

cool against her warm feet. Running over, she reached Danny and led him to the bathroom.

"Wait here a minute."

Taking her phone off the charger in her bedroom, Natalie dialed and waited. Her mother had raised three children and would know best even if it was one o'clock.

"Natalie. What's wrong?"

"It's Danny." Retching noises came from the bathroom, and she winced. "I let him eat ice cream too late, and now he's sick. What should I do?"

Sure, she had taught enough kindergarten classes where she'd witnessed a similar scene before, but this was Danny.

"I'll be right over."

Natalie replaced the phone on the charger before running to the bathroom.

The second Danny saw her, he cried. "I want my mommy."

Her heart broke as she held him, sitting on the edge of the bathtub, his tears gushing out along with choking sobs of anguish. She tightened her grip and rocked him, singing to him in a murmur as soft as a mountain breeze.

"Natalie? Danny? I'm here!" Her mother must have let herself in with her spare key. Her mom's head popped into the bathroom doorway.

Tears burned Natalie's eyes, and she did everything in her power to stem them. "It's my fault, Mom. Aidan warned me it was too late for ice cream, but I forged ahead."

Danny was paying the price for her impulsive ways. He shivered, and she clutched him to her chest.

Diane came over and placed the back of her hand on Danny's forehead and then on the nape of his neck. "He's hot. I think this is a stomach bug, not something he ate."

"Oh." Natalie repeated her mother's actions and blinked. The teacher in her took over, and she helped Danny to his feet. She and Diane cleaned him and helped him change into fresh pajamas. "Back to bed with you."

A quiet rap on the front door startled her, and she glanced at Diane. "Did Dad follow you over?"

"He would have let himself in. I'll check the peephole." Diane hurried away.

Natalie ushered Danny to bed and looked up to find Aidan in the doorway. "I heard a car pull in and looked out the window. I saw the lights go on and recognized your mother's car."

So he was a light sleeper? Was that tonight or every night? Nightmares or his natural habits? Their gazes locked, and a tingle of awareness made her admit he was far more complicated than he appeared.

"What if I had invited a male friend over who had the same make and model as my mom?" She pushed a lock of Danny's wet hair off his forehead.

Aidan shoved his hands in the pockets of his black sweatpants. "You wouldn't have kissed me if there was someone else in the equation."

Her mother appeared behind Aidan carrying a tray with crackers and water, her face giving every impression she'd heard about the kiss.

Aidan reached for the tray, and Diane smiled. "Now that Danny's in such capable hands, I'll be going."

Natalie flinched, her jaw tightening. Diane found Aidan capable, but not her? *Ouch* didn't begin to cover the gaping hurt inside her.

"Aunt Natalie?"

She shifted on the bed and reached for the glass of water on the tray. After he took a small sip, she sang a soft lullaby.

He squeezed her hand. "Thank you, Aunt Natalie. I love you."

Within minutes, his steady breathing filled the room, and she extricated herself from his grip. At the doorway, she soaked in the sight of him, calm and content in his bed. She clicked off his lamp and found Aidan in the living room, pacing.

"Your mother said she was sorry. She realized she sounded like she was being critical of you and promised she'd call later today." He stopped pacing the floor long enough to look at her. "How's Danny?"

"Asleep. Did she really say that or are you being nice?" She folded her arms and stood back, her eyelids growing heavier by the minute.

"Yes, she said that." His eyes gave no appearance of being sleepy. Military background and all that, she supposed.

"Why did you leave Danny's room? Why didn't you come in and comfort him?"

He halted and sat on her couch, his shoulders slumped. "My mother sang that same song to me."

His voice was so low, it was almost imperceptible.

She sat next to him. "Thank you for telling me that." She yawned, unable to hold back any longer.

"You need sleep. Call me in the morning with an update on Danny."

The morning! She was supposed to pick up Stormy from the vet's office. "Could I ask a favor of you? Can you fetch Stormy and take her home with you for a few days? Just until Danny's better."

The long pause grew into silence. "As long as you don't repay me with cake, preserves or blankets, we're good."

And his sense of humor might be the part of him that was stealing her heart.

"Thank you."

"Lock up behind me."

He gave a longing glance in her direction but left without another word. She hesitated at the front door, the chain in her hand. While caution was part of his inner self, his words about security were his way of showing he cared.

At least her heart started to hope he did.

CHAPTER FOURTEEN

WHAT HAD AIDAN gotten himself into? He'd survived in the military, fifteen years in a world of order and teamwork. Now, in the comfort of Shelby's living room, everything he'd accepted about himself was up in the air.

Except for Stormy, who mewed on his lap after he'd fed her a bottle with formula mixed with chicken from a blender. He'd have never guessed the kitten had orange-and-white fur when it was all dirty and wet.

One, two, three swipes on the kitten's back with his pinky, and then the kitten circled once before making herself comfortable, snuggling into him, the mews turning into soft purrs. Within minutes, she was asleep. He transferred her to a box filled with one of his old T-shirts. Wasn't like he was going to use it anymore.

"Rest well." His whisper was rusty from disuse, but he managed anyway. "Glad you're safe from the storm."

The kitten stirred, and Aidan hovered over

the area for a second until she nestled in and resumed its nap.

Aidan went to Shelby's bedroom, the box on the bed already half full of clothes to take to the local women's shelter. After knowing Natalie a little over a week, he saw the box as half full. Heading to the closet, he reached for another armful of clothes and deposited them in the container. That was the last of Shelby's closet. A long rectangular teak box on the floor caught his eye, and he reached for it at the same time the front doorbell rang.

He still held the box in his hands when he opened the door and found Natalie on his front porch.

"Thought I'd check on my kitten. How's she doing?"

"Where's Danny?" He searched the yard, alarm rising.

"My mom came over to check on him and is with him now. Don't worry. His fever broke. I did tell you Penelope Romano can't fit us in until after the Fourth, right?"

"Yes. I made a note of the new appointment with the attorney on my phone." He shifted the wooden box from under one arm to the other. "Were you able to reschedule his therapy appointment since you canceled it?"

"No. They'll see him next week as usual unless there's anything before then that causes too much concern and…" Natalie pointed at the box in his hands. "What's that?"

Whatever it was wasn't heavy. Bulky but not heavy. "I don't know. I found it in Shelby's closet."

He led her inside, and they sat on Shelby's leather couch. He placed the box on the coffee table and stared at it for several minutes.

She tapped his knee. "Do you want to open it? Or shall I?"

Aidan breathed in and exhaled, rolling his neck around, popping sounds filling the air. Nothing came out of his mouth. There was so much he hadn't known about his sister. The superficial things like butter pecan ice cream? No problem. As far as her hopes and dreams, he had no idea, no answers for Danny when he was older.

Although he might, in fact, find out something in a minute. Would this box hold answers about what was important to her?

Natalie picked up the box and extended it to him. For all he knew, it might be empty, waiting for a lifetime of treasures from Danny. He accepted it and opened the lid. There, stacked with a ribbon tied around them, were all the letters he'd written and sent to Shelby during basic training. Gingerly he untied the ribbon and fingered the first one.

"I wrote her every week. I had no idea she kept them." The lump of emotion in his throat made it impossible to talk.

Shelby had written him every other day, sending him doodles and long chatty stories. He'd only replied out of guilt, and his letters, more like postcards really, were brief, to put it politely. Butter pecan ice cream, these letters, the Christmas care packages. His sister cared more than he'd known, and he'd failed her.

Natalie's arms wound around him. "She saw how your father was emotionally distant at times, and she once told me she'd never give up on you."

Soldiers weren't supposed to cry. He hadn't cried when he'd seen unimaginable atrocities. He hadn't cried when the young enemy sliced his arm.

And he hadn't cried when he received the news of Shelby's death.

Now, one tear, then two, then an avalanche fell. For what he'd seen, for what he'd lost, for Danny. Natalie held him close as waves of grief crashed over him.

PUSHING AROUND HIS macaroni and cheese, Danny sent Natalie a look of pure defiance. Bored at the curtailment of activity from the past two days, his message was clear. He needed to get out of the house, and soon.

Truth be told, she could use a change of scenery herself. The float showed some progress today, but the only places she'd been over the past couple of days were the park, Aidan's home and her own.

Funny how she already considered Shelby's place Aidan's.

She rose from the small table in the breakfast nook and clapped her hands. "Time for a walk."

For the first time since his stomach bug, light flashed in Danny's eyes. "With Uncle Aidan?"

She hesitated. She'd like nothing more than to spend time with the handsome soldier who was close to claiming her heart. He was sensitive and direct, and the heady combination intoxicated her more than two glasses of her favorite zinfandel. He'd be leaving soon, and the question still remained whether he'd take both halves of her heart, the half that belonged to Danny and the half he was close to occupying.

Still, there was no reason not to include him. After a little more than a week, his seriousness and dependability were becoming bedrocks in her life. Problem was, another military bedrock had been ripped away from her once before.

"Aunt Natalie?"

Danny's voice pulled her back to the breakfast nook, and she nodded. While Danny fastened the Velcro on his sneakers, she slipped into her favorite ankle boots. They headed next door, where Aidan didn't answer when she knocked. Danny's face fell, and a twinge of something missing tickled her spine.

She chucked his chin. "We'll tell him in advance the next time so we can include him."

They set out for downtown, his little hand tucked in hers. She refused to think this might not be the case in the near future. Aidan and she would work together in a way that would benefit Danny in the long run. For Danny's sake, they had to agree rather than take sides against each other.

Stretched across the top of the two-story brick storefronts were lines of twinkling white lights. Hollydale bathed in the happy glow of the last day of June. Holiday excitement took hold, smiles on more faces.

Even now, though, the mountain air and altitude provided a welcome respite to the heat that often gripped the South. She was glad for the light sweater she had donned before they left.

Near the gazebo, college-aged students joked

and one or two strummed guitars while families dotted the lawn with their picnic blankets and coolers. Strolling along, she stopped and chatted with a former student about her summer.

She and Danny approached Timber River Outfitters, run by a former classmate of her brother's. The backbone of the town, small businesses were some of her favorite places to shop. While she'd normally prefer to check out her favorite dress shop, Odalie's Dresser, or Miss Louise's Ice Cream Parlor, or even the nearby art gallery, Danny's face lit up at the new window display at Timber River. "Let's go inside."

Danny's smile was enough reward for her. Her eyes adjusted to the lower level of fluorescent lighting, and she smelled Aidan's citrusy scent before her gaze fell on him. Aidan wasn't home because he was here.

"Natalie! Danny! What are you doing here?" His gaze met hers, tentative with a touch of disapproval.

After everything between them from kisses to tears, he still didn't trust her. Then again, he might not know Danny's tummy trouble was normal for someone his age.

"I should have realized right away what was up. I'm a kindergarten teacher. I see this type of stomach bug all the time. Sick for a couple of hours and climbing the wall the next. He's feeling much better." Reassurance lined her voice, and she leaned against the display of lanterns.

"I've been better since yesterday morning." Danny backed up her claim and mimicked her gesture, his arms tight against his chest. "If I didn't walk, I'd be a real crab. Aunt Natalie said so."

Out of the mouth of babes. Natalie's cheeks warmed even in the coolness of the air-conditioning.

Aidan closed the gap and ruffled Danny's thick brown hair in need of Mitzi's services at A New You salon. "I stand corrected. Anyone who can put two adults in their places like that is on the road to recovery."

"What were you looking at?" Natalie asked.

"Canoes."

They strolled over to the section, and Aidan ran his hand over the smooth contours of one at the end of the aisle, his longing and desire clear.

"Timber River has some great spots for canoeing and kayaking. I have a friend who runs a tubing and canoe station."

"Do you know everyone in Hollydale?"

She shrugged and stopped from whistling at

the price of the canoe Aidan was eyeing. "That was one reason I moved back. Homesickness can gnaw at you."

"You need a home for homesickness."

The electric current between them rushed along like class five rapids. She accepted there was something between them, but until Aidan admitted love didn't run on a schedule, she wouldn't make the next move. "Home starts with people who care about you. It's within your reach if you want it."

Her heart raced as it sounded like she was proposing he settle here and create just that, a home. Then again, when it came to push and shove, why else would she have been singing Hollydale's praises all along? She wanted Aidan to love it here and put down some roots.

Danny bounced up and down before reaching for a paddle. "I've never been canoeing. Is it fun?"

"Depends." Aidan gave Danny a slight nudge to place the paddle back on the shelf.

Danny did just that, and Natalie stepped away, admiring Aidan. That was the type of person Aidan was, encouraging others to do the right thing without coming straight out and saying it. Instead, he gave careful prompts to the person so they'd consider their actions for themselves. Same as her teaching style in kindergarten, although there were times she had to break down and flat-out state the moral in simple terms as clearly as possible.

Natalie stopped looking at the canoes and patted Danny's arm. "Hey, Danny. We've been out long enough. Time to go home. Staying well for the Fourth is our main priority right now."

"I'll walk with you," Aidan said.

"That would be nice." She winced at how bland she sounded.

As they edged toward the exit, he slipped his hand in hers, and giddiness spread through her as she entwined her fingers with his. This felt like home.

THERE WAS NOTHING like breaking down and showing your innermost weaknesses to someone to pull two people closer together. With his hand joined in hers, he and Natalie walked along Maple Drive. Dusk was fast approaching. He almost let her go but didn't want to.

Could love and acceptance be in his grasp?

They turned north on First Avenue.

"Natalie! Aidan! Over here."

Natalie's friend Lucie stood on a blanket spread over the grassy area near the gazebo and waved her arms. With some reluctance, he let go of Natalie's hand first and they strolled over to Lucie.

After greetings were exchanged, Lucie held out a pink cardboard box with Night Owl Bakery scripted in black, adorned with a whimsical owl. "Caleb's taking an overnight expedition of possible donors for the nature conservancy out camping. He won't be home until tomorrow. I'm sending him in my place on Saturday to work on the float, since I have to be at the Wellness Center. As a consolation prize, can I offer you a cookie?"

Danny looked at her pleadingly. "Please, Aunt Natalie. I haven't had a cookie for two whole days."

Her conflict played out on her face, Danny's wants against what was best for him. Her shoulders slumped before she perked up. "We'll split one. That shouldn't be too rough on your stomach."

Danny's lower lip jutted out, and he pouted. "I want a whole one."

"Half or nothing." Her usually sunny tone contained a warning.

Danny kicked at the grass. "Guess I'll have half."

Lucie broke one in half and extended a piece to each of them.

"What do you say to Miss Lucie?" Natalie nudged his ribs.

"Thanks."

They reclined on the picnic blanket with the twins and two dogs. Lucie offered Aidan a cookie as a bulldog came over and sniffed him while the border collie circled the group as if shepherding them before settling back in place.

"Have you met Ladybug before?"

Ladybug was the bulldog's name? He'd have remembered the name, let alone that face. Ladybug sat on her haunches until he petted her.

"I promise she's harmless." Lucie laughed. "She's really hoping you're a pushover who'll give her a cookie. She knows better than to beg from me since these are my favorites. Oatmeal chocolate cherry."

If the smudge of chocolate at the corner of her mouth was any indication, Natalie's friend told the truth. Lucie waited beside Aidan as if seeking his approval, and he decided to take the plunge. The texture of the oatmeal complemented the cherry chunks, and he held up his thumb for approval. "Thanks. These are really good."

"Be sure to visit the bakery before you leave." Lucie reclined on the blanket between Mattie and Ethan, and Ladybug followed while wagging her tail.

Aidan munched another bite, unused to evenings like these. He savored the rest of the cookie before resting his gaze on Danny.

Natalie rose and wiped her hands. "Busy day tomorrow. Come on."

He and Danny stood, and Aidan stretched his back.

"But I want the last cookie." Danny stomped his foot into the ground. "Mommy would have let me have it."

A pure look of hurt shadowed Natalie's face before her ankle boots dug into the grassy knoll. "Shelby would have said 'no way' simply on that reaction alone. We're going home."

"I don't like you anymore." Danny ran ahead, and Natalie glanced upward before turning on her heels and following him.

Aidan passed her and looked over his shoulder. "I'll talk to him."

She pushed aside her hair, the curly strands swaying in the breeze. Without a word, she nodded. Aidan hurried and reached Danny, both of them shoving their hands in their pockets.

This guardian act was new and frightening, in some ways requiring a different sort of bravery than what he was used to. "You should always be respectful."

"She's not my mommy." The catch in Danny's voice was too real.

Aidan wished he knew how to comfort his nephew. He reached into his memories of his father after his mother's death. Nothing. His father had relied on filling every minute of the day with organized activities covering the gamut from archery to zoology. Cathy had tried reaching out to him, and he'd rejected her. He wouldn't let Danny make the same mistake.

"Your mommy wouldn't want you to be disrespectful to the person she chose for you." Seemed like the catch in Danny's voice was contagious. For Danny's sake, and Natalie's, Aidan pulled himself together and showed Danny his arm. "You know, some days I think about this scar over and over, and I have to stop myself from feeling sorry for myself."

"What does this have to do with my mommy?"

Straight to the point. He liked that. "There are other days when I see it and remind myself I have work to do, important work, just like there'll be days when you miss your mom a lot and other days you'll remember how much she loved you and that will wrap you in enough love to keep you going."

They arrived at Natalie's gate, and Aidan stopped.

Danny jutted his lip out. "It's not like you're staying here. If you don't stay, I don't hafta stay."

Aidan's breath caught in his lungs and burned. "You need to apologize to your Aunt Natalie."

"Are you staying, Uncle Aidan?" Danny's big brown eyes filled with tears.

He slowly shook his head. "I have to return to Fort Lewis in three weeks."

The use of the singular pronoun didn't escape his translator mindset.

"Are you taking me with you?"

The sweet smell of strawberries filled the air, and Aidan didn't have to look back to know Natalie was behind him and probably hanging on his every word. "Your aunt and I will figure out what's best for you before I go back. She loves you and deserves your respect. You have something to say to her."

Danny stomped his foot once more before tears streamed down his red cheeks. He tried the door, but it stayed closed. Natalie must have locked it. She unlocked the door and stood back. Danny ran inside the house, and Aidan heard the boy's bedroom door slam. She moved past him.

"Natalie."

She paused and turned, her eyes full of a

weariness he'd never seen in them before. "Don't you need to check on Stormy?"

"You did the right thing by not giving in." The admission tore out of him.

If she was a good guardian for Danny, where did that leave him?

She shrugged and gave him a half smile. "I see kids with meltdowns on a regular basis during the school year. His grief is going to keep coming in waves. Some will fade quietly onto the shore, while others—" she pointed upstairs "—will come like tsunamis."

"Would you have given him the cookie a week ago?"

"Probably." She hesitated and held on to the door. "Good night, Aidan."

He walked over to his house and checked on Stormy, mewing for her next feeding. Without a word, he prepared a bottle and cuddled the kitten on his lap.

NATALIE STARED OUT her living room bay window and wrapped her hand around her cup of herbal tea. Bright stars illuminated the dark sky. During the school year, she rarely saw this many stars as she and Danny shared the same early bedtime. Now, sleep eluded her. Aidan's reminder that he had to leave soon burst her bubble already deflated from Danny's resentment of her.

She didn't want to take Shelby's place, but she did want to forge her own path as his guardian.

Moving to her couch, she placed her tea on the end table and cuddled with a pillow. She stared at her fireplace, the gas logs pretty even without the flames and heat of winter. A week ago, she'd have given in and allowed Danny another cookie in a second. After holding him in her arms and singing the lullaby, however, she had realized parenthood was more than just fun and games. She had to put her foot down when health and safety mattered.

Whether that would cost her her contact with Danny in the long run, she wasn't sure, but she was sure she wouldn't have kept her promise to Shelby if she allowed Danny whatever he wanted, whenever he wanted it.

Then again, Dr. Laurel, his therapist, had warned her this type of outburst might happen. Whether this fresh moment of grief was a result of missing Toby this week or a result of the hard weeks leading up to now, resuming visits next week after the holiday was a must.

"Aunt Natalie." Small sniffles came from behind her, and she whipped around to find

Danny there in his dinosaur pajamas, wiping his nose on his sleeve. "Yes, darlin'."

"I'm sorry." He launched himself at her from his corner of the living room, and she pulled him close on the couch, breathing in essence of little boy. "I love you, Aunt Natalie."

Hiccups replaced the sniffles, and she waited for a glimmer of a laugh from him. Before Shelby died, he had always laughed whenever he suffered a case of the "hiccumps," as he called them. No laugh, but his arms wound around her, holding her tight.

"No one can take your mommy's place, but I'll do my best to be the best auntie I can be."

That was, if Danny remained here when Aidan returned to Fort Lewis. His even breathing, a sign he had fallen asleep, calmed her, and she continued to stroke his thick hair. Ever since Francisco died, she relegated planning to the curb, preparing everything, except her lesson plans, on the spur of the moment. There were times that worked, but this wasn't one of them.

She was in this for the long haul. Danny deserved her best, and he deserved her fighting for what was right. This was right.

CHAPTER FIFTEEN

AIDAN RUSHED INTO the Timber River Counseling Center, concern marking each stride as he made his way to the front desk. Of all the mornings to forget to turn his phone off "do not disturb" after his run. Only after he'd finished playing with Stormy had he realized his mistake and found his phone had several text messages from Natalie telling him of today's unexpected visit during the Friday lunch hour.

"Aidan Murphy." He introduced himself to the receptionist, Jean, and almost saluted.

"I remember, Major. I never forget a face or a case. That's why they keep me around here." Jean nodded. "Go on back. Danny and Natalie are in room C with Dr. Hargraves and Toby."

Hurrying through the hall, he stopped abruptly in the doorway with the three faces, four if you counted Toby's, staring at him. "Sorry I'm late."

Upset at his failure to turn his phone back on, he sat in the empty chair just as Toby laid his head on Danny's knee.

Next to him, Natalie sat on the low aqua couch with plump yellow and white stripped pillows. Her red hair was pulled back in a messy bun emphasizing her wholesome beauty, which didn't stop at the surface. He expected reproach or something similar in her eyes. Instead, she radiated a message of laid-back forgiveness. She was easier on him than he was being on himself.

He could understand why he was attracted to that. Also, why he and Natalie mixed like oil and water with two such different approaches to life.

The doctor, tall with straight black hair, rose from a bright green chair and extended her hand. "I'm Laurel Hargraves." In contrast to Natalie's bubbliness, the young therapist conveyed an air of calm capability, the image of what he thought he'd be drawn to once he retired.

Still, for some unknown reason, Natalie was the one who had caught his attention and held it.

He accepted Dr. Hargraves's handshake and noted a dollhouse nestled against a blue wall beside built-in shelves filled with toys. "I rushed over once I realized Natalie texted, Dr. Hargraves."

"No need to stand on such formality. Call

me Laurel." She pointed toward the hall. "A word, please." Natalie started to rise, but Laurel shook her head. "Just Aidan."

"I'm his co-guardian. If it's about Danny, I deserve to know."

Laurel walked to the door. "I'd like to catch him up on today's session and get to know him a little better."

Without missing a beat, Toby nudged Natalie's hand, and she petted him before Toby returned his full focus to Danny. It was as if Toby knew Natalie's and Danny's sense of well-being depended on each other.

In which case, where did that leave him? He'd messed up his relationship with Shelby. He couldn't let her down by forsaking her son.

Perhaps a solid plan and the promise of continuing therapy at Fort Lewis would convince Laurel he had this under control. Aidan followed the doctor out of the room.

Laurel swiped on her tablet and, from the looks of it, brought up Danny's file. "I heard you and Natalie found a kitten. Studies have proven the positive effects of owning a pet. Decreased loneliness, increased responsibility for children, and cats are particularly effective in lowering stress levels, all of which should bolster Danny's self-confidence in the upcoming months before he starts first grade."

Aidan didn't think she pulled him out into the hall to explain the benefits of pet ownership. "What's the real reason you brought me out here?"

"I was on vacation, and my partner saw Danny last time. I wanted a minute to find out more about you. It was either move the three of them or the one of you. I chose you." Her steady brown eyes gave nothing away.

"I don't have a good excuse for not being here." He shoved his hands in his pockets. "Playing with Stormy is hardly justification for missing this."

Laurel kept her gaze on the tablet, although he guessed she registered his every move. "Interesting. Go on."

At that moment, Natalie cleared her throat and approached them. The door remained open, his view of Danny and Toby clear. "Sorry, but I couldn't sit still any longer."

Laurel glanced at Natalie, then Aidan. "Danny's torn at the uncertainty between the two of you."

Finally, someone in Hollydale was blunt. He wouldn't have minded, though, if she'd beaten around the bush a little longer.

"I have a couple more weeks before my leave is over. I promised Natalie I'd take that time and assess every detail in order to make an informed decision about the future." Promises should matter to a trained therapist.

"While that's commendable—" Laurel lowered her voice "—Danny needs stability at this time."

"Exactly what I've been saying." Natalie inserted herself into the conversation. "By the way, thank you for thinking of Danny when you had a cancellation so he wouldn't miss this week's session. I imagine it's quite busy the Friday before the holiday weekend."

"He also needs wise counsel and solid guardianship." Laurel tucked her tablet under her arm. "He's making progress, but it's slow going. Anything disruptive might slow it even more."

Aidan's gaze was drawn to Toby, whose head still lay on Danny's leg. His nephew stroked Toby's fur, nervousness in those familiar brown eyes.

Aidan returned his attention to the adults. "Is Toby helping?"

"It's early yet, but I see small and positive changes. He's a little boy who lost his mother not that long ago. You need to present a united front when you're with him." Laurel looked at him, then Natalie, and back at him again. "In the long run, Danny has the potential to thrive, but he needs a support network. He needs to know there are people who are there for him and who will let him be himself in a manner that's not rude or harmful."

Aidan faced Natalie, and his gaze went to her neck.

She wasn't wearing Francisco's medal.

"Is Hollydale providing that support network? Should he stay in his established home?" Natalie's words were a bombshell to his heart.

It would be hard for a court to go against Shelby's decision and the advice of a therapist.

Laurel adjusted the tablet to make another note in Danny's file. "Based on today's session, that's something the two of you need to discuss and decide."

The more Aidan tried to find reasons to justify taking Danny with him, the more there were for Danny to stay.

NATALIE TRACED HER finger around the mason jar of sweetened iced tea, her favorite drink at the Holly Days Diner. Rather than meeting Aidan at The Busy Bean, she opted for comfort food and lots of it. Located across from her sister-in-law's garage, the diner was a local Hollydale institution with its old-time jukebox and milkshakes so large she'd always split one with Mike and Becks growing up. The posters of movie stars from the fifties might be fading, but the delicious aromas of the best biscuits this side of the Mississippi never did.

Most of the lunchtime crowd had dispersed, and they'd been lucky enough to score her favorite booth next to the huge pane of glass overlooking Maple Drive. She loved watching people stroll by, and more people were arriving to enjoy the weekend's festivities and local natural amenities.

"Thank your mom and dad for watching Danny and Stormy at the last minute. Again."

"My parents love Danny as much as they love all their grandkids."

His jaw clenched, and he picked up a menu from behind the metal napkin holder. "What's good here?"

"Everything." She didn't even pick up a menu as she knew it by heart. "What's something you've never tried before?"

"One advantage of being a translator is getting to try a variety of foods in different regions." He opened the menu and perused the selections.

She used her deep supply of patience as he kept the menu aloft. It was all she could do not to snatch it so he'd have to look at her. "What's been your favorite?"

He exhaled and lowered his menu. "You're

going to keep harping on food rather than discuss Danny?"

She put her elbow on the table and rested her chin on her upturned palm. "I like finding out new things about you." One look at her reflection in the glass confirmed her suspicions: her cheeks matched the color of her pink sundress. "And we need this out in the open. There's something going on between us."

He replaced his menu with some deliberation behind the napkin dispenser and leaned forward, intensity emanating from him. The waitress must have sensed the mood between them because she took one look at them and hustled back to the kitchen. Natalie met Aidan's gaze, and they burst out laughing.

He stopped chuckling first. "I didn't plan for this to happen."

One more giggle escaped her. "You can't plan attraction. It either happens or it doesn't. When it's right…" Her words faded away as she wondered if she should count on his being here tomorrow.

She had to face it. He wasn't in a safe profession. If this relationship progressed, she'd have to find a way to deal with that.

Memories might have to suffice once again, and she didn't know if she wanted to take that chance, even for something as beautiful and rare as love.

Love?

Who said anything about love? He planned everything down to the minute. He probably even wore his watch to bed. She flew through tasks by the seat of her pants, and yet, the truth of the matter was, none of that mattered. What mattered was the connection between the two of them, a connection that was more than Danny. They laughed no matter the outcome of a hotly contested game. They liked slow, long dances with the rain falling. Somehow, they fit together, his gray eyes never missing a beat, taking in everything while she was already halfway to the next thing.

And there was something about a man petting a kitten and nursing her to health that might be the sweetest thing she'd ever seen.

Aidan had swooped into town and restarted her heart. Sitting there, he made her world better just by being himself. Sometime during the past couple of weeks, she'd fallen in love with Aidan Murphy. Love didn't have a time frame, and it sure didn't pick the person with the same outlook on life. Maybe that was the best part of all—love had sneaked up on her and scored a slam dunk.

"When it's right… What else were you going

to say?" Aidan prodded with a gentle way about him, another unexpected layer to the man she hadn't known a long time although, through Shelby, it was as though she'd known him forever.

"Um, uh, well." For someone who taught kindergarten and had been on the receiving end of questions about nearly everything, she rarely became flustered. There would have to be a first time for everything. "So, what's on the menu that you've never eaten before?"

"Diversion. An effective strategy at times. Hmm, let me see…" Aidan moved his elbows off the table and reached for the menu again.

The waitress appeared, fanning herself with her order pad. "Natalie, the heat coming from this table is hotter than our barbecue sauce, which is hot enough to scorch the toupee on Ed Hicks's head. Of course, every true North Carolinian knows vinegar-based barbecue sauce is the real deal." She glanced at Aidan. "Well, hello there, Major Murphy. I'm Jolene. Pleasure to make your acquaintance at last. Just to let you know, the betting pool around here is an even fifty-fifty."

"What betting pool?" Aidan leaned back, and Natalie recognized the instant worry on his face. Endearing.

Jolene plucked out a pencil from the front

section of her apron. "For who'll win the pie contest. Now what'll you have? You look like a daily special man to me. Our cook has a real nice grilled catfish sandwich on Fridays."

Natalie glanced at Aidan, who was almost salivating at the words "daily special."

"I've been dared to try something new and adventurous, so I'll take the fried green tomato sandwich with pimento cheese."

"One antacid special for you." She turned to Natalie. "What can I get you, hon?"

"I'll have the Friday special with a side salad instead of fries. Thanks, Jolene."

The waitress strode toward the kitchen, and Natalie leaned forward, her chin resting on her hands again. "It seems like we both did something unexpected. You ordered something unusual while I went for the daily special."

"You mean, we did something the same?" He straightened the white paper placemat on the red-checked tablecloth, good humor radiating from the slight crinkles around his gray eyes. "For the most part, I eat whatever's available from the commissary. There's nothing I like better than a hamburger, hot off the grill, but I like experiencing whatever's around me. Bibimbap in South Korea. Cheese soufflé in France. Personally, I'm a big fan of the Italian tradition of an alcoholic cordial with break-fast."

Layers of the more complicated soldier emerged with every passing day. Problem was, the days passed by with increasing speed. The waitress delivered their meals, and their conversation remained light.

Aidan polished off his sandwich, and she leaned forward. "What did you think? Worth the trip?"

"I wouldn't have missed this for anything. That meal was certainly..." He reached for a napkin and wiped his cheek, that left dimple downright appealing. "Interesting."

"I can't tell if that's a good or bad thing with you. You always make every situation seem more complicated than it really is."

"With you, nothing is simple."

Jolene came over with her notepad. "Can I tempt either of you with the last slice of lemon meringue pie? It's famous in these parts."

Aidan screwed up his face. "Anything but pie."

"I've got just the dessert for you two to split." Laughing, Jolene marked something on her pad. "It's one of Natalie's favorites, chocolate cake with Cheerwine cola frosting. We only make it on Fridays. Be right back with a slice and more tea to top off your drinks."

Natalie crooked her finger toward Aidan, waiting for him to get closer. "Shh, don't tell Jolene, but all the desserts here are my favorite."

"What's Cheerwine cola?"

"It's a local drink."

Aidan reclined against the bright red vinyl pleather of the booth. "You love this area, don't you?"

She sipped the last of her tea and considered everything. "I can't imagine living anywhere else."

AIDAN REACHED FOR Natalie's hand. Natalie walking alongside him should make everything worse, but it didn't. He liked this far too much, considering they were heading in different directions. Even now, they were leaving downtown for their respective homes. Though they were next door to each other, they were miles apart.

They passed the Corner Grocery and headed for Hollyhock Lane. She nestled her hand in his, a small gesture but a welcome one. His turmoil about Danny and the future dwindled to a trickle, their long strides matching, hers in ankle boots and his in sneakers. After this, his first extended leave in some time, he'd have to adjust to military gear again.

They arrived at her porch, and she sighed. "We still haven't discussed Laurel and her suggestions." Natalie's eyes lost a little of their usual sparkle. "Why don't we talk it out here where we can watch the town go by?"

They settled on the swing, her presence already a steady marker in his life. This close, her strawberry scent filled the air with sweetness. "Is it a requirement that all porches in Hollydale have swings or rocking chairs?"

She pumped her legs, the silk fabric of her sundress rustling in the summer breeze. "My dad's hobby. You know he likes you when you get one of these for a birthday or Christmas present."

The litmus test for Natalie's parents. Good to know.

"Maybe you, Danny and I should do something on Tuesday the fifth. Just the three of us. Provide stability together. Work for him, not against each other." His stomach clenched. He'd just suggested they do something, and it sounded like he wanted them to be a family. Sitting on this swing with her might not have been a good idea after all. Whenever they were alone, they either fought or kissed.

And Natalie was a good kisser.

He saw the uncertainty written on her face. "Maybe we shouldn't plan on something happening. Maybe we should go wherever the wind takes us." Natalie's musical voice was lower than usual.

"What about that stability Dr. Hargraves said Danny needs?"

"I don't think that comes from planning every minute of every day. Danny needs to know that, no matter what we decide, he can always depend on us. Both of us. We need to commit to both of us being a part of his life."

He let the hot metal of the chain links slide through his fingers. One way or another, he finally accepted Natalie was destined to be a part of Danny's life. Something else gnawed at him. "What do you have against plans?"

The air between them crackled, yet there were only blue skies on the horizon, no lightning in sight. "Why do you like plans so much?"

"They represent order and purpose. After my mother died, my father planned every minute of the day. When he met Cathy, that stopped. I missed our closeness." His sleeves hiked up, and he let go of the links to push them down but decided against it. She knew about his scar and accepted him anyway. "Now, what's so bad about plans?"

"Before Francisco died, we made plans for our future together." It was her turn to twist the metal chain links together before letting them go. "After he died, it seemed more important to make each minute count to the fullest."

"Burn me once, shame on you. Burn me twice?"

"Interesting take, but something like that."

Natalie's mother, Diane, stuck her head out the doorway and took one look at them. "Don't mind me. Danny's fine. Take your time."

Diane disappeared back inside.

"Guess I should follow her." Natalie paused and smoothed her skirt. "Otherwise, I'll hear about how I'm spreading my eggs too thin or something like that."

Aidan touched her arm and liked the feel of her skin under his. "She loves you. That's her way of showing it. About next Tuesday. You, me and Danny. Plans, real plans." He released her and still took comfort from her having sat so close. "You haven't worn Francisco's chain in a while."

"I won't forget him, but it was time." She traced the outline of the links with her fingers. "Time to make new memories and be happy without feeling like it's a compulsion."

Enjoying being happy. It was what he'd found in this short time with Natalie.

"Interesting. You're being yourself because you're you, and not to please anyone else."

"Thanks for understanding. I'm glad you're not one of those people who insists everyone else should wear a watch because it suits you so well," Natalie admitted with a wistful look. "I think that sums up the attraction between us. You'd think those kisses would have gotten you out of my system."

He'd be lying to himself and her if he denied that. "One more kiss ought to get each other out of our systems."

"I agree. We should test your theory."

They moved closer. Rather than anything awkward or clumsy, their lips joined as if by some invisible spark guiding them together. The feeling ignited embers in him he never knew existed. Chocolate cake had never tasted so good as now.

After a minute, they backed away from each other, retreating to their own sides of the swing.

"Totally out of my system." Her words were more of a croak than her usual melodious voice.

"Liar."

She shrugged and laughed. "Maybe, Murphy, maybe not. While I'd be a bad role model for my kindergarten students and Danny if I went around lying all the time, sometimes it's not a lie if it's for everyone's best interests."

She licked her lips and wiped her palms on her sundress. "Next Tuesday. What's your pleasure?"

"Or my poison?"

"Tsk, tsk. Fun isn't overrated." She rose and popped her hands on her hips. "If I can finagle a canoe rental from my friend, how about it? You, me, Danny and a day on Timber River. I'll plan everything, and you do nothing but show up prepared for a day you won't soon forget."

He blinked. He'd been so sure she wouldn't go through with actual plans. Letting go and counting on others?

If he trusted Natalie, would she give up when the going got tough? Would she let him down?

Or was trust like swimming? No matter how meticulous he was about practicing, he hadn't gotten the hang of it until he plunged off the deep end.

Natalie extended her hand, and it was his turn to hesitate. "Do I have to dare you?"

The swing squeaked like Stormy did when he fed her. A reminder the kitten was due for her afternoon meal. "I'd better say hello and goodbye to Danny and take Stormy back to my house for her next feeding."

"That kitten has downright entranced you. What about Tuesday, then?"

The kitten isn't the only one. Aidan gripped her hand in his, her lightness filling him with something close to hope.

"It's a date."

CHAPTER SIXTEEN

AIDAN CHECKED HIS detailed set of float blue-prints while shifting his weight in Shelby's compact. Using her car had allowed him to return his rental, but he'd had a good seven inches on his sister.

Mike hadn't batted an eye when Aidan enlisted his help the other day to drop off the rental at the nearest location in Asheville, a good thirty-mile drive via US-25. On the way back, Aidan tried to talk to the sheriff about the city's emergency plan and offer some new insights and suggestions. Mike waved him off, preferring to shoot the breeze, even inviting him out for a night at the River Bar and Grill with him and his wife.

If he didn't know better, he'd almost think he'd made a friend.

The Harrison family was becoming part of his life quite fast. Diane was taking the morning to prepare food for those who showed up this Saturday morning, the big day to work on the float at Hollydale Park, while keeping an eye on Danny and Stormy.

Climbing out of Shelby's tiny compact, he debated whether to shed the windbreaker he'd worn over his short-sleeve T-shirt. Other volunteers might want to make light talk about his scar. He hated to draw attention to the fine line, a sliver of white against his tanned skin. However, the early morning breeze made his decision easy. He'd wear his jacket for now and finagle his way next to someone who wouldn't make a big deal of his scar when the day grew warmer.

The open green field separating the pavilion area from the playground was empty, and he shook his head. So much for the legion of volunteers promising to help with the float. No volunteers, no food, no Natalie.

Natalie's SUV approached and he snapped to attention. She parked and ran over to him, a wide smile beaming her welcome, her red hair pulled back in a messy bun. A cold glass of lemonade in summer didn't look half as good as her in a yellow top with matching daisy capris. Pink sneakers replaced her usual boots.

"Why am I not surprised you're here an hour before everyone else?" While she used her kindergarten teacher voice, her twinkling eyes told the real story.

"I'm on time. Ten hundred, just like you said."

"Aren't you on my group text?"

He shook his head, and she pulled out her phone and checked something. "We pushed back the start time to eleven a couple of days ago. Thought you knew. Please help me with the food."

Natalie opened the back doors of her vehicle, and he beheld stacks of plastic containers on one side and a bushel of apples and other snacks on the other.

"You were busy," Aidan said.

"Not all my doing. Some of my students' parents, who are out of town this weekend and can't help, dropped off fruit, cookies or other items. It takes a town."

Yet another reference to the town's involvement in her life and, by connection, Danny's. If he heard one more reference today, he'd…

Do what? Scream? Kayak in the upstream rapids? Concede and agree to this co-guardianship idea and revisit it after he received his honorable discharge?

He kept his composure and loaded his arms. It took them a couple of trips to transfer it all. Once the final container was on the picnic table, he wiped off imaginary dirt from his hands. "How about we take the tarp off the float and figure out what absolutely has to be done so it'll look decent on Monday? Then we'll divide the work and conquer."

She laughed and organized containers. "You have no idea, do you?"

"About how many signed up? Are we talking one person? Two?"

"Try fifteen in the first shift alone."

She strode over to one side of the tarp and waited until he stood in place on the other.

"It's been my experience people will often tell you something to get you off their backs. This is a three-day weekend, family time."

"Party time, community time. They'll come." She smiled.

Together, they removed the tarp, and he clenched his fists by his sides. Little, if any, progress had been made since the last time he'd been here. "Natalie." He waited until she met his gaze. "The parade is Monday. This float…"

Words, his stock in trade, his lifeblood, escaped him as he stared at the float. If his calculations were right, only a third of the work had been completed. "Did you amend the tiered structure for the frame? The way you planned it, we'll have to keep it covered as it won't fit in the shed. Did you decide to go for something a little less?"

"A little less what? A little less wonderful?" She ran her hand over the wood. "Nope. We're on schedule. Trust me."

"There's no way the design we created will come together."

How was she so good at leveling looks like that? He had to contact his former basic training instructor and ask for tips.

She approached from his side of the truck and patted his arm. "It will. The primary colors on the boxes with the school's mascot will pop, and the rainbow of stars will let the kids know to always aim high. Sometimes it's hard to believe anything beautiful will emerge out of something this messy. I see it all the time, though. I had a student with dyslexia. Everyone said it would be years before he'd read anything. Each afternoon, we sat down with his favorite comic book and by the end of the school year, he was reading." She wiped away moisture from her eyes. "You get the general idea. Sometimes you have to dream big and then back it up with action."

"But surely, you've also seen the worst. The kids who come in without lunches. The kids who lose someone and are grieving."

They both knew he referred to Danny.

"Even then, I try to make a positive difference. If I see something amiss, I have a duty to report that. The safety of each child comes first. Our school also has a wonderful counselor, who helps, but sometimes a hug or finding a way to make a day a little brighter? That's how I make sure each child knows someone cares. That's why I want them to reach for the stars, hence the theme."

A beeping horn drew his attention to the parking lot. A newer model bright green smart car with pink flower magnets dotting the passenger door swerved into a parking spot. Hyacinth emerged and waved. Then she reached into the car and pulled out a small structure like none he'd ever seen before.

She rushed over to them. "What a glorious day! You couldn't ask for better weather for a group project. Isn't this a gorgeous birdhouse?"

Aidan stared at the birdhouse, wondering how many North Carolina license plates had been sacrificed for this. "I don't remember that as part of the design."

"It's not for the float. It's for you when you return to your base. A little reminder of home." Hyacinth handed it to him.

His mouth gaped open. Of all the surprises in Hollydale, this one might take the cake, or pie, as the case might be. Hyacinth's expression changed to hurt, and he clamped his mouth and tried a smile. "This is too generous. I won't be able to look at it without thinking of you."

Beaming, she fiddled with the end of her scarf. "I knew you'd love it." She turned to Natalie. "I brought my CD player and a nice collection of soothing, relaxing music. I'll be right back."

"Hyacinth, thanks." Now it was Natalie's time on the hot seat. "I'd hate for anything to happen to your CD player. You know how it is at a party. People accidentally spill their drinks, and then I'd be responsible for buying you a new one. I have a cheap Bluetooth speaker that connects to my phone. It's easily replaced."

"Major M.?" Hyacinth jostled his arm.

"What?"

She waggled her finger at him. "You haven't taken me up on my offer on babysitting Danny." She reached into her purse and pulled out another sheaf of long rectangular paper strips stapled at one end. "I'll need your address for the cookie-of-the-month club."

"What?" He sounded like a schoolboy rather than a major, repeating himself like a parrot.

"It's something special I do for my grandnieces and grandnephews who are in the military. I think you rate that kind of privilege, if I do say so myself. My email address is on the front of that. Email me your address as well as any allergies or special requests." She patted his arm again. "There's nothing like a package in the mail to make you feel special."

Before he fashioned a response, a flood of cars arrived in the parking lot. More people waved and greeted each other while pulling out coolers and casserole dishes.

His mouth gaped open.

Again. Hyacinth went to the pavilion while Natalie went to welcome people before bringing him a bottle of water. "Here. I figured you'd need this before you assign tasks in a minute." She grinned and reached into her satchel, handing him a clipboard. "I bet your improvisational skills are also impressive."

"This is your show, though. Won't it mean more if the instructions come from you?"

"Since you've been here from the beginning, it's our show. I'll start, and then you elaborate."

In no time at all, everyone knew their jobs. The sounds of hammering and sawing filled the air, while others added to the tissue paper and chicken wire for the sides. From atop the platform, where he was assembling the riser where the students would stand, he searched for Natalie. Over the past hour, he'd seen her glancing his way, and now he returned the favor.

Knowing someone with her ability to bring

people together like this made his world feel a little happier, a little more secure.

"Major Murphy!" Belinda's no-nonsense voice made him blink until she came into focus on the other side of the truck.

Her gray sweatpants and sweatshirt were the complete opposite to Hyacinth's multicolored polka-dot dress. Belinda thrust a knitted scarf in the air.

He was afraid to ask for he already knew the present was for him. Politeness still demanded a response, and he laid down his tools and jumped off the float. "Belinda, what a surprise."

Not really, considering neither could bear to let the other one get the upper hand. The birdhouse caught his eye, and he considered how to play this. He wouldn't choose favorites, same as Danny didn't play favorites with him and Natalie.

"It matches your blanket. Wear it in good health." She stormed back toward the pavilion before he could end this escalation of gifts.

He had to put a stop to this, one way or another.

But how?

HIP-HOP MUSIC FILLED the air, drowning out the laughter from the splash fountains. Nearby, Lucie and her husband, Caleb, took turns at the grill, along with his cousin, Jonathan Maxwell. The smell of those hamburgers was too tempting to resist any longer. Grabbing a paper plate, Natalie headed toward the food line, where her sister-in-law, Georgie, tapped her fingers against the wooden table.

"Serious decision?" Natalie breezed over and fanned herself with her empty plate.

"If you call deciding between a cheeseburger and a hot dog serious, this has the makings of a doozy." Georgie shrugged and chose the burger option. "Tell Aidan I'm giving the Thunderbird the total works tomorrow. Detailing with my favorite chenille washing mitt, using the best professional car wash soap and washing the wheels last to ensure no grime or brake fluid of any kind. Nothing but the best."

"For Aidan or your Thunderbird?" Natalie couldn't help but interject a teasing tone.

Her sister-in-law was a bit on the serious side, a good balance to her laid-back brother.

"Your Aidan as well as my classic convertible."

Natalie stopped her hand halfway to her mother's contribution of potato salad. "Huh? My Aidan?"

"Don't sound so surprised." Georgie moved down the line, plucking a handful of chips and a scoop of pasta salad. "Rachel's upset she won't get to play matchmaker again as the two of you are doing fine on your own."

Even her niece Rachel had noticed sparks between her and Aidan? Natalie gulped and was about to refute Georgie's claim when loud voices came from the other side of the picnic pavilion.

"A scarf is useful and utilitarian! Why on earth would a bachelor soldier need a bird-house? It's not like he can carry it through the airport without everyone and their cousins looking at him." Belinda's raised voice sent shivers down Natalie's spine.

Of all the places for Belinda and Hyacinth to finally have it out, why here? Why now?

Natalie placed her still-empty plate on the table and rushed over, meeting Aidan, who came from the direction of the float.

"My birdhouse is beautiful." Defensiveness laced Hyacinth's words. She pointed at her gift for added emphasis. "It'll remind him of his home. There's little more beautiful in this world than home. A colorful home full of spirit and liveliness can brighten anyone's life."

Hyacinth raised her chin, and Natalie stepped in the middle.

She handled kindergartners, and these two were acting even younger than her students. "Ladies. Let your pies do the talking."

Belinda pursed her lips into a straight line. "Tell *her* that. Coupon books, birdhouses, cake. Humph."

Hyacinth shrugged. "If some of us manage to combine simple ingredients into an edible work of art, so be it. Pies are art in their special unique way and can put a smile on anyone's face." She arched her eyebrow and sent a scathing look Belinda's way. "Besides, I know I'm not the only one who bestowed a cake upon our grand marshal."

This time, Aidan folded his arms. "I can't return the cakes as those have already been consumed, but tomorrow I'll be returning the other bribes."

"Bribes!" Both women spoke at once, horror reflected in each of their voices and faces.

Natalie turned to Aidan as Hyacinth stumbled toward them. Her plate flew through the air and landed on Belinda. Potato salad, baked beans and mustard dotted Belinda's sweatpants.

Fire shot out of Belinda's eyes. "You did that on purpose, Hyacinth Hennessy."

Without another word, Belinda tipped her plate onto Hyacinth.

"Food fight," yelled someone in the crowd.

Natalie scrambled onto the wooden bench seat and placed her index finger and thumb in her mouth, emitting a loud, shrill whistle. All eyes turned her way, and she stopped the music. "There will be no food fight."

Aidan scrambled up next to her and glared at the two women covered in food. "If you two continue this, I'll disqualify you both from the pie contest."

Belinda stiffened her spine, her regal manner showing through as much as it could with baked beans dripping off her sweatpants. "You don't have that kind of authority."

"As judge of this contest and grand marshal, I do."

The gasp of the crowd heralded silence. Mayor Wes pushed his way to the front of the pavilion. "I agree with Aidan. Enough is enough. You two will apologize to each other and Natalie, or you'll be disqualified."

"Well, I never," Belinda started but then looked around and hung her head. "I'm sorry, Hyacinth and Natalie."

Hyacinth's cheeks reddened. "Oh, sweet Natalie, I'm most grievously sorry for our behavior. It was disgraceful and not befitting to the tradition of the Fourth of July pie contest." She reached up and helped Natalie down before turning to Belinda and extending her hand. "Please accept my most humble apology."

"Why does everything have to be so flowery?" Belinda grumbled before shaking Hyacinth's hand.

"Because life is all the sweeter when we strive for that extra flavor. You, as a fellow baker extraordinaire, should understand that." Hyacinth continued to shake until Aidan stepped in.

"Maybe you two ought to call it a day."

Hyacinth and Belinda broke away and sized each other up before going to their respective cars. Everyone seemed stunned, the mood much more somber than minutes before.

Aidan's mouth brushed her ear. "How do you want to proceed? I can make an announcement if you'd prefer any bad news to come from me."

Thankful for his offer, she shook her head. "My party, my disaster."

No sooner had she finished her speech than most of her friends collected themselves and went back to work. Within an hour, though, the pavilion had cleared out, except for a faithful few.

Caleb came toward her. "Normally it takes Fred and Ethel at a wedding to make everything this quiet. I didn't start on the big 'Happy Fourth from Hollydale Elementary' sign for the front yet, but I have plenty of time. One of Lucie's coworkers is watching Mattie and

Ethan at the splash area, so I'll stay and knock that out."

"Thanks."

Aidan approached with a plate of food, and Natalie couldn't look at him. Not after her big plans were derailed in a split second. That was the problem with plans. Sometimes they went horribly wrong and she had to clean up the aftermath.

Georgie completed the circle of four and stared at the truck. "Monday morning before the parade I'll come and give everything a once-over. I'll make sure those tires are properly inflated for the adjustment in the hauling weight for Carl, since he's driving you in the truck and I'm taking the grand marshal here. I'm not trusting anyone else to drive the Thunderbird in the parade."

Aidan pushed the plate in Natalie's direction. "You haven't eaten. You seem fond of potato salad."

She glanced at four different types on one side of the plate with a chicken leg, a hot dog with relish and mustard and a taquito on the other. Aidan covered all her possible taste preferences with this selection. It was more food than she could ever eat in a day. The fact that he'd noticed she hadn't found time for a meal yet struck her to her core, as much as the thought behind his food choices.

Natalie smiled, a real smile this time. She had the best friends, ones who had her interests at heart.

They'd taken Danny in, too.

Her heart swelling, she glanced at the float. A couple of weeks ago, her mother was right. She had taken on more than she could chew, but now she'd corral every resource, rely on every volunteer and make this happen.

AIDAN APPROACHED MAYOR WES, who stood on the edge of the play area, talking to a young couple. The man pushed a stroller back and forth while the woman sat perched on the edge of the rock-climbing wall, keeping an alert gaze on the young girl of not more than four on the swings.

Mayor Wes waved him over. "Aidan, come meet my son and daughter-in-law, Leo and Zoey." With fondness, he pointed to the stroller, keeping his voice low and steady. "And my little namesake and first grandson is asleep in there. That's my granddaughter Halley on the swings."

After the introductions, Aidan shifted his weight, a polite way of trying to get the mayor alone for a few minutes to discuss Hollydale.

Natalie must be rubbing off on him if he considered tactfulness in his approach.

The mayor patted Aidan on the back. "This great guy's keeping me on my toes. We've accomplished more with him at City Hall in the past week than in the past three months, but let's keep that our little secret so we don't all look bad! Nancy and I'll be over tonight, kids. I have a feeling Aidan wants a minute of my time." He turned toward the swings. "Bye, Halley. See you later."

Within minutes, they strolled along the outer perimeter of the park, the trail almost deserted with the heat of the day bearing down on them. Aidan shed his windbreaker, tying it around his waist.

The amiable silence lasted a couple of minutes before Aidan got to the point. "Something's got to be done about Hyacinth and Belinda."

Mayor Wes pointed to the flowering bushes blooming nearby. "This part of North Carolina's famous for our rhododendrons. My wife, Nancy, is especially fond of the purple ones, so a couple of years ago she and the other ladies in her garden club planted them along the path."

"Nice." Did anyone in Hollydale respond to a direct statement?

"Take that spiky white flower growing over

there. Do you know its name?" Mayor Wes waited until Aidan shook his head.

Even with all his training in local flora and fauna, he was unfamiliar with this one.

"I'm not making this up, but it's turkeybeard. I'm especially fond of them. Not normally a flower one would plant near rhododendrons. They look a little like weeds, but Nancy knows they're one of my favorites. She accommodated me and blended the two in an artistic way. Fast forward a couple of years, and this trail is more calming than I envisioned after signing off on the artistic renderings."

The mayor guided them toward a cast-iron bench and fanned himself with his hand. Without a hammer in hand, Aidan itched to get back to something, anything. Sitting around watching flowers grow wasn't his passion.

"Sir, with all due respect, do I have your permission to disqualify them? That would send them a strong message about their conduct."

"Permission denied, Major." His firmness, so unlike his usual geniality, caught Aidan off guard. "Permission, however, to sit back and enjoy the flowers, granted."

He sounded like Natalie. Was there something in the water here in Hollydale? Didn't they know how precious life was? How it could be snuffed out in a second? First his mother and then the rest of his family, including Shelby, all gone too soon. There was a limited amount of time in a day with so much on the agenda.

Aidan blinked. He'd been coming at everything from the opposite point of view. Had he been filling every minute of every day with plans and schedules to avoid coming to terms with life?

Natalie had told him she tried to live each moment to its fullest, but had gone overboard to make everything fun for everyone else. Was he also avoiding real emotion in an attempt to shelter himself? Was he distancing himself from caring?

As his gaze fell upon a deep purple rhododendron bush, its small blooms so deep a purple as to almost appear black, he knew he'd done just that.

But that didn't excuse people from acting badly. Belinda and Hyacinth had created a real mess, and he refused to have this carry over to the Fourth's festivities.

"How do I avoid any further trouble?"

"You want to know something else about my wife, Aidan?"

Not particularly. He wanted a solution about Hyacinth and Belinda, but the mayor seemed to like talking in circles. He'd just have to wait until the mayor made his point. Same as almost everyone else around here, as opposed to the straightforward style he loved about the military. Settling in, he leaned back against the hard rail. "Sure."

The mayor laughed. "Thanks for humoring me." He leaned forward, his gaze trained on a white bush on the other side of the trail. "She's a master of compromise. She took all the suggestions and blended them together, designing the trail so the scent would linger while not being too strong, so there'd be enough visual stimulation without being overwhelming." He tapped his fingers together and turned toward Aidan. "I don't want you saying no right off, but will you consider something for me? As a personal favor."

"Depends on the favor."

"Apply for the city manager position."

No. Nyet. Nada. Nein. Not about to do that in a million years. He gave himself points for admirable restraint for not blurting out his answer. How soon did the mayor consider "right off" anyway?

"Thanks." The "but" was in his voice as Aidan wasn't that good of a liar.

The mayor rose and gestured for Aidan to follow. They walked along companionably.

"You're at the top of my list of candidates to replace Bob."

"How many others are on the list?"

"You get straight to the point. I like that. That's why this town needs you. We're growing, and we need strong leadership and wise planning."

"I'm honored." To his surprise, he was, but that wasn't enough to make a difference. "However, I have another position lined up when my discharge goes through next year." One that would make a difference in so many ways.

"I'm not from these parts. Grew up in Nashville. It took some of the old-timers quite some time to get used to me. It helped I married Nancy, who's a cousin of Frederick Whitney. Timber built this town, and the Whitney family made their money in that industry and then converted to furniture. Frederick and Agnes are now turning toward more philanthropic pursuits, especially given that their daughter, Charlotte, has no interest in settling in this area."

Not once had Aidan thought the mayor's accent was different from the one in these parts, and he'd had quite a bit of training in that respect. "Couldn't tell you hailed somewhere other than North Carolina." Aidan took a second glance at the turkeybeard on the trail. Darned if it wasn't growing on him.

"Nancy wasn't interested in me at first. She calls me an acquired taste. However, there was something about Hollydale that appealed to me. Besides her, that is. Long story short. I had connections and could have been on the fast track to the mayor's seat in Nashville that would have been a springboard to other political aspirations. Never regretted being a small-town mayor, though. Pay's not the best. Hours are a sight better here, though. People give Nancy and me some of their best casseroles, too." Mayor Wes stopped walking, and Aidan did likewise. His face grew somber. "I remember one tornado warning when I flagged down a woman who had made a U-turn at the high school, which was set up as a shelter. She'd brought her dog with her, and she was going to go home when she realized they wouldn't let him in. I convinced her to stay and settled her and the dog away from anyone who might have allergies. When she left the school, I held her hand when she found her home a pile of rubble. I know every resident by name, and I listen to their stories. Someday, I want to hear about that scar when you're ready to tell me. As far as Belinda and Hyacinth are concerned, you'll figure it out."

Humbled, Aidan walked back to the picnic pavilion without saying another word, the mayor joining him.

NATALIE YAWNED AND STRETCHED, her muscles rebelling. She lifted the star fashioned out of bent wire hangers and outlined with red garland. Stripes of blue pipe cleaners divided the middle. She placed it carefully on the pole.

She gasped and hopped off the platform. Dare she even think it? With a little over thirty-six hours to spare, the float was finished.

"Aunt Natalie!" Danny skipped along the path, dripping wet from his time at the splash area with Aidan, who trailed behind the boy.

She ran forward and hugged Danny. "It's done! Come and see."

"Now you're all wet." Aidan handed her Danny's dry towel. "You need this, seeing how he didn't wait to use it."

"Thanks." She accepted his offering and smiled.

Together, the three of them stood in front of the float, and Danny clapped. "It's happy, just like you, Aunt Natalie."

That might be one of the best compliments she'd ever received. "What about you, Aidan? What do you think?"

She tried to see it through his eyes. Sure, it

was a little gaudy and over-the-top, but a country didn't celebrate its birthday every day. The silence stretched out until it was almost overwhelming.

"You brought everyone together, and it works." Admiration laced his voice, and that approbation also meant the world to her.

She approved, too. She was proud of this, and hoped the volunteers were, too. It might only be around for one day, but what a day.

To celebrate the moment, Natalie motioned for Danny and Aidan to stand together in front of the float. "I'll take a picture of the two of you." The photo could act as a bookend for the one she already had on her mantel of Shelby and Danny.

She snapped the handsome pair and viewed the result on her phone. The handsome visage of Aidan's strong features, his stoicism on full display, almost leaped off the screen. Even now Danny showed signs of being a heartbreaker, so like his uncle. Their family resemblance revealed much more on her screen than in the flesh.

A sobering thought, indeed.

CHAPTER SEVENTEEN

AFTER YESTERDAY'S COOL, refreshing rain, Aidan didn't quite know what to expect on this Fourth of July. His morning jog had promised the beginnings of a sunny day, and now walking along the group of floats and past the high school band congregating in the parking lot of Hollydale High, the starting point of the parade, he checked the skies. That promise had come to full fruition. Blue and clear. The same as Natalie's eyes.

He reached Natalie's float, and he couldn't help his broad smile. There, atop the float, stood Natalie in a red dress with white polka dots. Somehow, those blue ankle boots should clash but, on her, they didn't. Instead, everything eccentric and quirky about her fit together, and he liked what he saw more and more every day. Returning to Fort Lewis a few weeks from now would be a sight harder. Either he'd break Natalie's heart by taking Danny with him or he'd break his own if he left Danny with Natalie.

Before he was able to herald Danny to join him in the lead grand marshal convertible, Aidan realized his cell phone was ringing. Speaking of the military, it was Lieutenant Colonel Thrasher, his superior officer. Aidan ducked behind a utility pole and answered the call. Minutes later, he pocketed his phone, his new orders clear. He and Danny were expected to return on Wednesday, two weeks early. A top-level security meeting requiring his translation skills was scheduled for Friday at the base. Lieutenant Colonel Thrasher had ordered him back. Aidan had no choice. That was all there was to it.

There'd be no day trip tomorrow as he and Natalie would have to make a decision.

Around him, people waved flags, popped in and out of shops, carried coolers and camp chairs, staking out their spots on the parade route. They blurred. How was he going to break the news to Natalie?

He caught sight of her emptying bags of candy into a pillowcase and knew he couldn't ruin her day. She'd put so much work into this, and Danny deserved a holiday to remember. He'd tell her tomorrow morning.

They'd work out what was best for Danny, maybe a transition where she accompanied him to Fort Lewis before school started, so Natalie could see Danny was in good hands.

Guilt ripped through him. He should just tell her now. That way, they'd both have time today to think about Danny's best interests.

Emerging from his spot, he swallowed that lump in his throat. Natalie waved at him, her smile lighting up his day more than any firework finale.

"Aidan!" She jumped off the float. "You look like you've lost your best friend."

In a way, he had. He'd be losing this town sooner than anticipated, and that loss was almost as devastating as not spending the next two weeks with her. He'd lost his chance at a future with Natalie. However, he was a soldier. He'd made sacrifices before. He'd make sacrifices again.

He tightened his facial features into a faux smile. "That wasn't the right look for the grand marshal?"

Natalie's eyes sparkled even brighter. "Only if you want to scare everyone. This is the Fourth of July, not Halloween."

"Aunt Natalie, help me down." Danny's voice tugged at Aidan's heart as Natalie lowered him to the gray asphalt.

"We have an important job, Danny. We have to give your uncle real smiling lessons so he makes a positive impression on Hollydale as the grand marshal. Come on, show him a Murphy smile."

Danny rolled his eyes in the age-old expression of humoring an adult. "Okay. Funny faces are always good." Then he lifted one side of his face and stuck out his tongue. "Natalie's dad likes it when I make good funny faces."

"That would leave an impression alright." Aidan nodded and folded his arms, his blue Oxford shirt stiff and starched. He'd decided against his full-dress uniform. "Not quite the one I'm going for, though."

"I'm the queen of funny faces." Natalie wiggled her fingers above her ears, twisted her tongue and scrunched her face.

He snapped a picture, and she reached for his phone. "No fair! Delete that!"

"It's totally fair, Harrison. Come on, Danny. We have a parade to lead."

Natalie's protests followed him. He merely grasped Danny's hand and led him to the front of the procession, where Georgie stood beside the beauty of a restored Ford Thunderbird he'd seen once before at the Harrison family barbecue.

Danny squeezed his hand. "I wish my mommy could see this, but I'm glad you're here, Uncle

Aidan." He gazed at him with big eyes. "Is it wrong to be happy without her?"

Aidan's heart clenched at the concern and depth pouring forth from such a young boy, a mirror image of him as a child, only wiser and more accepting. This time he accepted the lump and merely shook his head, adding a mental snapshot of Danny to the actual one he'd taken on his phone of him and Natalie.

"Ladies and gentlemen, thank you for coming to the twenty-seventh annual Hollydale pie contest." The mayor's announcement brought cheers from the crowd.

Aidan met Natalie's gaze, her happy smile buoying him for what was coming. It wasn't going to be popular, but it was the best solution he had come up with and the mayor had agreed on. He braced himself for the crowd's reaction.

The mayor introduced Aidan, and a hushed silence fell over the crowd as he stepped onto the dais and the podium.

"First, thanks for the privilege of being your grand marshal this morning. It was an honor I'll never forget." He came close to letting his secret about his new departure date slip from his mouth. He couldn't tell Natalie this way, though.

"Get on with the pie judging. Who's it gonna be, Hyacinth or Belinda?" someone yelled from the crowd.

Seven pies sat on the long table, only identifiable through a number, with slivers of slices already precut. The rest of the slices would be sold later with the proceeds going toward park improvements. Aidan had loaded up on protein this morning to combat the sugar rush the mayor warned him about. Between the slices sat a small tumbler of coffee and a few saltines so he could judge each pie on its own merits. One by one, he sampled pie, the stares of the crowd on him the entire time. Somehow, he kept it together when he bit into an egg shell in one piece and then discovered something that tasted like vinegar in another.

The bite of pie with colorful cereal circles was more sugar than he normally ate all month, and he deserved all the credit for widening his fake smile and keeping it intact.

Natalie mouthed something and pointed to her left cheek. He squinted until her message of *no dimple* came through loud and clear.

No one had ever known him this well.

He shook it off as he arrived at the last three slices. Plump cherries winked out of lattice work that looked like it came from a 3D printer. The smooth velvety texture slid down his throat. Without thinking, he reached for another bite, flavor filling his mouth with delight. This was heaven on a plate. After the third bite, he stopped with two slices awaiting him.

While he sipped the coffee, his gaze fell on Belinda, her plain blue shirtwaist dress offset with a red-and-white scarf tied around her neck, preening like the cat who came upon an unattended koi pond. A few yards away, Hyacinth stood, her gauzy red scarf a headband in her hair with her light blue tank top flowing into a white vintage flared skirt with yellow lemons, concern overriding her usual laid-back features.

The penultimate slice was lemon meringue and, from all accounts, this must be Hyacinth's contribution. He slid his fork and expected another bite of hometown goodness; instead, he tried to keep his composure. Someone forgot to add sugar. This was lip puckering failure at best, plain awful at worst.

The pressure must have gotten to Hyacinth. That was the only explanation he came up with that made any sense.

It also made his decision easier.

At last, he came to the final slice, his childhood favorite, strawberry chiffon pie. He hadn't had a slice of this in years. To be exact, since a few days before his mother passed away unex-

pectedly. He glanced at Natalie, wondering...
As expected, she seemed able to read his mind,
and she shook her head. *I didn't enter the contest.* She formed the words so clearly he had no
trouble at all reading her lips this time.

Hints of fresh strawberries peeked out of
the sides with one plump strawberry half atop
the sliver. His first taste brought back the last
pie his mother had ever baked for him, and he
hurried for another bite before letting out a soft
sigh. Then he took one final bite. Perfection in
a flaky graham cracker crust.

Aidan walked along the row of pies and
handed the results to Mayor Wes behind the
curtain. Then he approached the podium with
the mayor, who adjusted the mic.

"The moment you've all been waiting for."

Before the mayor announced anything, it
was as if the crowd separated in half, with half
standing behind Belinda and the other half behind Hyacinth. Natalie and Danny stood in the
middle, not taking either side. She smiled at
Aidan, a slow, steady current of calm in a sea
of turbulence.

The mayor joked for a couple more minutes,
prolonging the suspense before holding up two
envelopes. "The blue ribbon for best fruit pie
goes to number five, cherry lattice pie." Grumbles and a few boos could be heard as people

patted Belinda's back. The mayor opened up the envelope with a big five printed on it. "Belinda Chastain, come get your blue ribbon."

She jogged up the steps and clutched the blue ribbon to her heart. "Number fourteen is as sweet as number one. Thank you. Enjoy the fireworks, and I'll see you next year." Victory tinged her words, and the crowd started dispersing with several patting Hyacinth on the back and murmuring words of consolation while shooting Aidan daggers.

The mayor leaned over. "Wait a minute. I'm not finished. That was the award for best fruit pie. There's another award."

Gasps filled the crowd with everyone filing back into the area. Belinda shook her head. "For twenty-seven years there has only been one blue ribbon. There can't be another one."

The mayor arched his eyebrow. "Are you arguing with me and the grand marshal of our fair parade?"

Belinda gripped her blue ribbon, her lips turning almost as blue as the ribbon. "I won this fair and square." She lifted her chin. "Besides, I saw him taste that lemon meringue pie. Hyacinth won't win this year."

The last part was for his and the mayor's ears only. She left the stage to cheers and whistles from her friends, and she raised the blue ribbon in victory.

"This year there will also be a blue ribbon for best soft pie." The mayor looked at the index card and then at Aidan. "There's been some mistake."

He approached Aidan and whispered in his ear. "Hyacinth always makes lemon meringue pie. This says the strawberry chiffon is the winner."

Aidan shrugged. "No mistake."

The mayor pled with his eyes. "This will cause a huge rupture in the town. I agreed to this compromise to keep the peace."

"No mistake."

Mayor Wes glanced at the sky before resuming his place behind the podium. "The winner for best soft pie is number seven, the strawberry chiffon pie."

"What?"

"No way!"

"He needs his taste buds examined."

"Hyacinth was robbed!"

Aidan shifted his weight on the podium, but resolve flowed through him. He'd made the right choice, despite the protests. The mayor ripped open the envelope, and his jaw dropped. "Hyacinth Hennessy."

Hyacinth breezed up to the stage and shook

Aidan's hand. "I might have taken advantage of the fact that a certain redhead smells like strawberries."

"That fact had nothing to do with my decision."

His gaze met Natalie's as murmurs of reluctant approval rippled through the crowd. More than one person's face relaxed, and it was as if peace settled the feud for this year. Accepting change fashioned a compromise that crowned two winners. Somehow, he and Natalie had to hammer out such a solution to benefit Danny.

If she was still talking to him after he announced his new departure date and how long he'd known about the new orders, that was. Sunlight reflected off the golden glints of her red hair, same as her happiness radiated out of her and spread to others, including himself.

He was betraying the one person who had accepted him, external scars and all.

If she took his news as expected, he'd be returning to Fort Lewis nursing an internal scar much deeper and painful than the one on his arm.

DUSK FELL OVER the town square, excitement building for the main event. In front of the gazebo, families and couples rested on blankets while children played Frisbee and tag, or lit sparklers. Glow stick necklaces illuminated the night.

"Loved your float!"

Several people held up their thumbs while others waved. Some of her students from last year came over and hugged her, their parents waiting for them to rejoin them. This town was the best.

The pink and orange ribbons streaking the horizon faded, leaving only the dark firmament of night. The time for fireworks was fast approaching. Where was Aidan? Natalie searched the crowd while Danny played with Lucie's twins. She wanted to spend time with the soldier and give him a sneak peek at some of her plans for tomorrow. He'd discover an invigorating but relaxing family day in front of them.

Family. For a long time, she hadn't dared dream of her own family, content with popping in and out of everyone else's. Why be a legal guardian when ol' Aunt Natalie was so much more fun? Why care on a deeper level when something might be ripped away from you on a minute's notice?

Aidan was part of the answer, but the truth came from something inside her she'd buried long ago. She could care and still let herself be attached to something real and worthy. Look at Aidan. He'd lost his mother and sister when they were so young. In spite of that, he went out of his way for others and attached himself to matters of weight and significance. He could have come to Hollydale and kept to himself, yet he got involved in float preparation, the parade's security plans and the pie contest. The balance between him and her worked well, so well she wanted to see if they could work on something permanent instead of a temporary stopgap for Danny.

With a nip cooling the mountain air, she reached into her tote for a light sweater and shrugged it on. Aidan came toward her, carrying two necklaces with red, white and blue light-up stars similar to Christmas bulbs. She patted a space beside her on the blanket, while Danny ran over. Aidan handed him one necklace and her the other.

"For me?" She reached for it, downright giddy at receiving an unexpected gift. "What does this button do?"

"Don't know. It looked like you."

Natalie pressed a button, and a patriotic song played. Giggles filled the air. Goose bumps dotted her arms under her sweater. She wasn't laughing. She glanced at Aidan, the sound not coming from him either. Her gaze fell on Danny, who slipped onto his bottom as waves of laughter came out of him as though every pent-up giggle from the past few months wiggled out of him.

Danny was laughing.

A loud boom filled the air before she could hug him. She started to move down when Danny snuggled into his uncle's side, the necklace looped around his neck. Immediately Aidan relaxed and gripped Danny's hand in the twilight.

The sky flashed as ribbons of white light spiraled down with plumes of red on the outer edge. Several bursts came together, and Danny leaned into his uncle again. Green and red flares burst into spectacular displays of color until multiple pops in succession heralded the finale, light coursing across the sky in a magnificent array. Wonder and awe filled Danny's face, and there were no two other people she wanted to share this moment with as much as the two Murphy males.

Once the last ribbon faded into a plume of smoke, people folded lawn chairs and gathered their supplies for a quick mass exodus. Danny rolled over and reached out his arms to her. "I'm tired. Let's go home now, Aunt Natalie."

Her heart lifted as the little boy managed to bridge her and Aidan.

Smart little boy.

"You set up. I'll clean up." Aidan took charge, but she didn't mind as it was her turn to snuggle with Danny.

In no time, they headed toward their houses at a slow clip, staying to the side as others passed them. The twinkling white lights strung overhead flicked on. They must have been on a timer for after the fireworks display. Surprisingly, even Aidan managed a turtle's pace in keeping with Danny's sleepy progress. Natalie stopped when her phone pinged with a text. She responded with a smile emoji and caught up with Aidan.

"Dad wanted to let you know that Stormy is fine and he'll be at your place later to drop her off. He also said to thank you for letting him cat-sit."

"Why did your father agree to stay with Stormy during the fireworks?"

"He wanted an excuse, and he loves animals. Big crowds aren't his thing. The barbecue is his lone exception, and he goes along with it for Mom, since that's how she wanted to celebrate their anniversary."

Her mother tended toward splashier displays. For years, her parents had proven the adage *opposites attract*, meshing their styles for a successful partnership and a loving marriage. *Could we do the same?*

The three of them turned onto Marigold Lane. The promise of tomorrow's canoe excursion was uppermost in her thoughts.

"Natalie." Aidan's voice made her pause three houses down from hers.

"Yes?"

"There's something I need to tell you…"

Her heart leaped at the expectant tone in his voice, and she touched the stars around her neck. He halted as a plain blue sedan pulled into her driveway, and Natalie turned toward him. "Are you expecting someone?"

"No. Besides, it's your driveway, not Shelby's."

She held Danny back, expecting the driver to reverse and head in their direction, lost after the fireworks.

Instead, the taillights extinguished, and Aidan forged forward. "I'll check it out."

The glow of the lamplights caught the glint of familiar red hair. Natalie blinked, unsure of why her twin would be here in North Carolina, rather than in California.

Natalie reached for his arm. "It's okay. That's my twin sister, Becks."

As they approached, though, it was clear the situation was anything but okay. The streetlights provided enough illumination to make the red blotches on her sister's ashen face stand out. Natalie was instantly on alert. Becks showing up unannounced was unprecedented. While Becks reached into the back seat, no doubt for Natalie's niece Pippa, Natalie turned to Aidan, her hands still on Danny's shoulders. "Can Danny sleep with you tonight?"

"About that and tomorrow." Aidan fidgeted, but his face softened. He exhaled a small sigh. "It's for the best we cancel the outing now, what with your sister here and all. Any chance we could meet for breakfast, though?"

Natalie shook her head. "I promised you and Danny I would plan something and spend the day with you. I'm sure Becks will want to see Mom and Dad, and I don't back down on a promise." *Not to Principal Garcia, not to Danny, not to Shelby.* "I'll text you in the morning, though, to let you know if we'll be starting later than expected."

Danny faced her, his big brown eyes transfixed on her. "Who's going to read me a bedtime story? Who's going to tuck me in?"

Natalie ruffled his hair, then brushed her hand over his matching light-up star necklace. "This is a special day." And it was, considering she'd heard his laughter for the first time in ages. "You'll be back home tomorrow night. For tonight, though, I bet your uncle is a great tucker-inner."

"He probably won't make funny voices for

every character like you do." Danny's pout played with her heart, but she stayed firm.

"Then you'll have to teach him how, okay?" Natalie kissed his cheek. "I'm not going anywhere. I promise you'll be back in your own bed in no time."

Aidan opened his mouth as if to speak, but Natalie rose and put her index finger over his lips. "This must be important. You and Danny will be fine. Becks needs me."

CHAPTER EIGHTEEN

AIDAN FLIPPED PANCAKES on the griddle. He hadn't cooked his mother's special recipe in forever. Stormy had awakened him hours before dawn, and he'd held her an extra-long time before taking every precaution to be as quiet as possible while packing his suitcase. Once he'd finished, he found Stormy again, until it had been time to make breakfast. He wouldn't leave Danny, so he'd canceled his morning run and turned to comfort food instead.

All his plans were out the window, and it was time to be honest with Natalie.

Could he take Danny away from this town without notice? No, he couldn't. Hence the comfort food.

A soft knock at the kitchen door almost leveled him. It could only be one person. Natalie.

He flipped the pancakes off the griddle and added them to the stack on the plate before answering the door. In place of her usual sundress and ankle boots, she wore a light blue

University of North Carolina T-shirt with short floral athletic leggings.

She leaned against the doorjamb. "I have good news and bad news."

"What's the good news?" He could use some before he shot the cannonball through her plans.

She sniffed the air and smiled. "Are those pancakes I smell? My absolute favorite breakfast ever. I'll trade you news for a Stormy sighting and some pancakes."

Breakfast was the least he could do, considering everything they'd have to get settled today, from relocating Stormy to mapping out Danny's future. He stalled, though, unable to move, wanting this moment to last longer. If he willed it, maybe she wouldn't reject him the way others had in the past. Though Danny would be part of their lives always, he acknowledged, he wanted more than a shared custodial arrangement with her. Maybe she'd still stay after he told her everything, so they could work out something together.

She nudged him and pointed inside. "Late night impacting you, too? I guess Danny's still sleeping, huh? Pretty soundly if the smell of pancakes isn't waking him. Glad I reorganized everything for early afternoon."

"You haven't mentioned your sister yet. Is she okay? Why'd she arrive last night?"

"Stormy, food, news about Becks. In that order, I think."

He led her into the living room, where Stormy lay sleeping in a curled ball. Natalie reached for his hand and squeezed. "Seeing a kitten like this makes me believe everything's going to work out for the best."

"Natalie."

"*Uh-oh*. I don't think I can take whatever's coming on an empty stomach." She headed toward the kitchen. "Mind if I help myself to pancakes and syrup?"

It was next to impossible to say no to a whirling sandstorm. "Want some coffee?"

"I'd love some."

He filled two cups and sat at the table, his appetite diminished. She settled in and poured syrup on her pancakes. "Thank goodness we're canoeing later today. Becks, that's my twin sister, said she'll watch Stormy." She cut her stack into big pieces. "Before you say anything about canceling, hear me out. She and Pippa flew in from California yesterday. Becks found out Jack cheated on her. She's utterly devastated and wants a day to herself with Pippa. My mom and dad will descend on her anyway, and that's a conversation best between her and them, without me getting in the way."

"Canoeing today isn't a good idea." The scar on his arm throbbed, and he rubbed away the pain.

"It's a perfect plan. Because you need to know you deserve this. We can make this work somehow. We can't throw something like this aside. Danny's only part of it. This type of attraction doesn't come along every day. And those kisses?" She lifted a bite to her lips and smiled while he struggled to pull himself together.

Those kisses were part of the reason this was so hard. Everything about her had brought what he'd lost back into his world. Most of all, he cared for Natalie, the pure essence of her. She played basketball with her whole heart. She dropped everything to raise her best friend's child as her own. She even changed breakfast from something ordinary to something special just by being her. Here he'd thought he could make everything fit into a comfortable timetable. A relationship with someone safe, a more traditional career with a security firm with military contracts and raising Danny in a convenient setup. He was wrong.

If only he had more time to find out if whatever was starting between him and Natalie could last.

As she chewed, she looked at him, waiting for some response.

"Relationships take time." Something he didn't have, thanks to his new orders.

"Anyone who can make pancakes this good is worth keeping around. You haven't listed Shelby's house yet." She sipped her coffee, bliss coming over her face. "These next two weeks are a perfect opportunity for us to start building on what we have. You're a planner, and I like more spontaneity. A nice compromise, don't you think?"

"I have to leave tomorrow." He'd blurted out the words.

She blinked, pushed that stray curl behind her ear and slumped backward. "I didn't hear that right. It sounded like you said you're leaving tomorrow."

Her voice was small, almost as though she'd uttered the words in a tunnel.

"I did."

She set her fork and knife on either side of her plate with deliberate precision. "What time did your commanding officer call you? Isn't he in Seattle? I thought it's still before dawn there."

His hands turned to ice, and he tugged his

long-sleeve T-shirt over the scar before giving up the effort. It was part of him forever. "He called yesterday morning."

Standing, she disturbed the table, and her plate clattered to the floor. They both looked toward the direction of the hallway as if expecting Danny to materialize. No sounds came from his room, and she turned back. Their eyes locked, anger coming from hers.

"You knew all day yesterday?"

"I didn't want to upset the festivities." That sounded lame even to his ears.

Natalie huffed out a deep breath. "When you care about someone, you include them in decisions. You include them period. Love isn't about control or about dictating who knows what, when. Love is about taking risks, something I haven't done in years. Love is about two people buoying each other up, rather than sinking, a support in the storm."

Love? Falling in love would require letting go of any control he had over a situation. When he let go, bad things happened to those he cared about. Like his mother. Like Shelby. Even his father and Cathy.

"Love takes time."

"Anything can happen in an instant. Love, death, laughter. Any of it. We can't control everything, just like you can't plan for every scenario. But I love that you're a planner because together our strengths added up to a beautiful float that made people happy, that gave Danny the freedom to be himself and laugh again." She broke the gaze and strode to the back door.

"Natalie."

She stopped at the mention of her name and turned toward him.

"In spite of that, Danny is my only living relative, and vice versa. I know he should stay here, but he belongs with me." He couldn't let him go. Not if something bad might happen and he wasn't around. "I want Danny to go with me tomorrow. Maybe you can fly to Seattle before school starts and make sure you're happy with the arrangement."

He came forward, but she held out her arm, keeping him a good length away.

"How magnanimous of you to let me fly out after you've taken him from his home. Danny finally had the courage to laugh again."

"Well, that's a good thing, isn't it? So he'll be fine at the base. I'll make sure of that."

Tears welled in her eyes. "Whether you like it or not, Shelby named me as co-guardian. Someone has to think about Danny's best interests." The tears flowed down her pink cheeks, and he hated himself for placing her in this position. She reached for the knob and opened the door. "He needs to stay here. For his continued therapy and well-being. I'll call Penelope and text you the time she can meet with us today."

If she walked out, another person in his life would once again be leaving him. "Come to Seattle with me tomorrow. You're on summer break. We'll see then if this is real. Right now, it almost seems surreal. You're mentioning love, and everything's been so fast. We need time to make sure this can be manageable and not messy, make sure no one gets hurt."

"I don't need time to know I love you. There. I love you. I said it." She wiped away her tears with the back of her hand. "As far as getting hurt, I think it's too late for that, but I'd rather put myself in a place where I hurt and feel the emotion. It's the only way I can be myself. Becks needs me."

Natalie slipped out the doorway, and took part of him with her, too. He should go after her. Danny, though, slept nearby, and he couldn't leave him alone. Waking up to no one in the house would scare him too much.

He walked over to the table and collapsed in a chair. He'd always bounced back before, emerging from his losses strong and in control. *No, that is a lie*. He'd thought he'd been in control since he quit relying on emotion, using the convenient excuse that being in the military demanded that kind of discipline. In fact, he'd relied on that as a crutch, burying feelings that became messy, that hurt too much.

While he assumed he'd find someone staid, someone who wouldn't challenge him to feel again, someone who'd accept security in exchange for companionship, he hadn't counted on Natalie.

He hadn't counted on Natalie in so many ways, but she'd proved herself time and time again. Once more, Aidan had taken the safe way out. This time he'd hurt both him and the whirling sandstorm.

CHAPTER NINETEEN

NATALIE PICKED UP the picture of her, Shelby and Danny, all smiling in happier times. She'd met Danny the day he was born, and her heart had belonged to him ever since. She'd cemented her promise to Shelby that day.

What was the exact promise?

If anything happens to me, make sure Danny is taken care of. Promise me, Nat. The words flooded back, and Natalie's legs collapsed under her. In the picture, Danny was almost a miniature version of Aidan. Someday, he'd resemble his handsome uncle with high cheekbones, eyes that read a person like no other, with a tall stature and a whole lot of honor.

Aidan hadn't stayed away from their lives out of anything other than duty, she reminded herself. Over the past couple of weeks, he'd proven he'd always do what was best for Danny. The bond between uncle and nephew tightened yesterday, with Danny's small, fragile hand in Aidan's strong larger one, Danny's laughter ringing out during the fireworks display.

Aidan would not only take Danny with him when he flew to Fort Lewis. He'd be taking her heart, too.

The cry escaped her throat as the notion of what was right washed over her. Aidan needed his nephew. She knew him well enough to believe he would form a support group at Fort Lewis for Danny. Aidan was a man of his word.

Yesterday showed how much Danny needed Aidan. Unlike the pie contest compromise, this situation resembled the basketball game where only one of them could come out the victor, except there wasn't a winner or loser here. This was all about Danny.

She wanted to be upset with Aidan for marching in here and stealing her heart and Danny, but she couldn't. The ache was too raw. She loved his commitment and the way they grounded each other while pushing each other to new limits. Too bad he hadn't trusted her with his heart or even told her the truth about when he'd received his orders.

Every inch of her screamed with a deep-down hurt, but she knew what she had to do. As much as she dreaded relinquishing custody of Danny, it made sense. For both Aidan and Danny. They understood each other on a basic level that would serve Danny best for the long run.

Finding her phone, she dialed Penelope's office. To her surprise, Penelope had a spare moment, and they talked. Natalie outlined her plan and hung up after assuring Penelope she'd be there at one to sign the necessary papers.

Her couch never looked so inviting, and she clutched her big, fluffy purple pillow to her chest. Her mother stepped forward from the back hallway, Pippa in her arms.

Natalie gasped. "Mom! Where did you come from?"

"Didn't you see my car in the driveway?" Diane sat next to her on the sofa, taking care with Pippa.

"I used the back door."

"Becks called. Thank goodness Mike wasn't operating the speed gun in one of his usual spots today." Her mom jostled Pippa on her lap, her niece's thin, downy red hair lying flat on her small head. "Who's a good baby?"

Last night was her first introduction to her niece, and she'd instantly flashed back to Danny's full head of brown hair and his small features. Somehow, Pippa therapy might be the right answer to losing the two Murphy males. Natalie wasn't quite sure yet. She'd have plenty of time to find out the answer.

Why had Aidan assumed she wouldn't want

to know right away about his orders to report back two weeks ahead of schedule?

Maybe because he hadn't wanted to ruin her favorite holiday. Maybe because the second he told her, she gave up and took the easy way out. She'd left his house faster than a college track star.

Considering how Cathy stopped trying to draw him out after Shelby was born, she could see how fear played into his response. Hadn't he helped her work through her fear of committing to anything on more than a superficial level?

Didn't he deserve the same consideration? Someone to show him he was worthy of the kind of dedication he put into everything?

"Becks filled me in while you were gone." Diane cooed at Pippa, her gentle tone soothing. "I know you need to talk, too."

What is there to say? Natalie clutched the pillow tighter against her chest, the ache growing instead of subsiding. Aidan would leave, and she'd rally her troops around her. Wasn't that what she did best? Retreat to home base when her world fell apart?

"Hard to talk about myself when Becks is hurting."

Like Jack breaking his vows to Becks, Natalie would also be going back on a promise, sort of. No, she wouldn't. She'd be fulfilling hers to Shelby. Promising to do what was best for Danny always. In the process, though, she'd risked her heart again, but she wouldn't have had it any other way. Because in the end, every life had to have an anchor, purpose and meaning in the midst of the storm.

"I listened to Becks. Now it's time to listen to you." Diane continued the same low, rhythmic sound, careful not to disturb Pippa, who mirrored Diane's facial expressions. "I heard you on the phone a couple of minutes ago."

"I'm signing over full custody to Aidan. Danny belongs with him. You were right." *Doesn't every parent want their child to admit that?* "I bit off more than I can chew."

That's me to the core. Dive in and hope for the best. Her hometown would help her heal. She counted on the residents to shelter her and provide her enough room for her big ideas and bigger dreams.

Diane moved Pippa to her car seat and carried it over before opening her arms to Natalie. A hug never felt so good.

"Darling, that's your personality. Becks is cautious and independent. Mike's funny and driven by duty." Diane leaned back from Natalie and chucked her under the chin. "And you're the one who created a beautiful float that was my favorite yesterday. You're my dreamer who brings energy to everything and everyone around her."

Natalie hiccupped and squeezed the bright purple pillow, her new best friend. "Danny laughed at Aidan, not me. Danny needs Aidan more, and Aidan needs his plans more than he needs…"

More than he needs me. She lowered her gaze, not wanting to look into her mother's wise eyes right now.

Her mother tapped her arm. "Those aren't exclusive things, you know. You can like plans and be in love with someone who's a dreamer at the same time. Once I almost gave up on your father."

Natalie froze. Her parents were an institution to her, one of her anchors. They'd just celebrated their fortieth wedding anniversary. "But you didn't."

"Actually, I did. He wanted to go on a trip around the world, get away from Hollydale. I took that as a rejection of our life, a rejection of my desire for children after my miscarriages."

Natalie glanced at Pippa, her eyes closing as she rested in her car seat. Then she inched toward her mother. "I can't stay away from Hollydale. I tried. I really did, but everything I love is here."

"I think that was true a year ago, but I also think you're stronger than you realize."

"What are you saying?" Natalie failed to grasp her mother's meaning.

"If you love Aidan, and I believe you do, you have to decide where your heart lies."

Becks staggered into the living room, her eyes bloodshot and tired. "Did I hear the word *love*? You want my opinion?"

"Later. Much later." Diane rose and guided Becks into the kitchen. "After a nice cup of coffee."

"Coffee is full of caffeine and chemicals, and I'm breastfeeding Pippa." Becks narrowed her eyes. "Herbal tea is much better for a person. Someday, not today or tomorrow or next month even, I'll look back and realize I stayed true to myself. That's the only way I'm going to get through this."

Her gaze connected with Becks, her usually unperturbable sister adrift but still her twin. Becks scooped up her daughter and left the room. Someday she'd have her ducks lined up and when that happened, the world had better watch out.

Staying true to myself. Home was family, and family was home, no matter the location. She loved Hollydale, but dreams and people mattered more. A year ago, she'd been homesick something awful for the town, for the people, for her family and friends.

However, family wasn't just the people related by blood, and dreams weren't tied to a geographical core. She kissed her mother on the cheek, and something shivered inside of her. "Mom, I might be jumping off the high dive."

Her mother patted Natalie's cheek and smiled. "That's the Natalie I know and love. And whether Becks realizes it or not, she'll have to jump off the high dive someday. It's the only way to live." A small crash came from the kitchen. Diane stopped halfway there and looked back, rolling her eyes. "Becks, let's get you that herbal tea."

Her mom strode into the kitchen. Natalie understood her mother. When Becks finally absorbed the shock of the water when she dove off that board, it might be the biggest belly flop of all, but she'd survive. Meanwhile, Natalie had performed her own disastrous dive this morning. She gritted her teeth. She might not be in Hollydale to help Becks out of the pool.

Then again, that was what video calls were for.

"Wish me luck. I'll be online," Natalie called out.

Her mother ducked her head into the living

room and winked. "Any school in Seattle will be lucky to have you."

AIDAN WALKED DOWNTOWN hand in hand with Danny. The familiar storefronts welcomed them, Timber River Outfitters, Miss Louise's Ice Cream Parlor and A New You hair salon. Though he'd memorized the layout and security details of each retail establishment within a day of his arrival, they'd become more than bricks and mortar in the past couple of weeks.

This sense of community, prevalent in the military, had never centered in one place for him before, since his service was spent in Texas, California, Germany and Iraq, among many other spots. In a short amount of time, however, Hollydale had imprinted itself on his heart.

So had a certain redhead, whose bangle bracelets, cowboy boots and sundresses matched her personality.

Shelby once warned him that nothing could prepare him for meeting Natalie.

Shelby had been right.

Danny squeezed his hand. "You make good pancakes. Not as good as Aunt Natalie, though, cause hers are in the shape of dinosaurs and flowers. She knows I like the dinosaurs better.

She makes both, but she always laughs when I bite the head off the T. rex first."

He giggled at the memory before his face scrunched up, almost like he was in pain.

Aidan squeezed his hand in return, understanding what Danny was feeling. "Your mom wouldn't want you to second-guess yourself every time you laugh. She loved you, and she'd want you to be happy. To live life to the fullest without holding back." He could say the same about his mother, too.

They arrived at the storefront that would have been Snickerdoodles had Shelby lived. Would he have made time to visit when his half sister opened the restaurant?

Deep down, he knew the answer was no.

The Realtor insisted he had to come right away as he'd never believe who'd made an offer this morning for the property. Robin herself didn't believe it, and Aidan had shaken his head at that. Realtors should be prepared for every contingency.

He and Danny walked into the establishment, and his jaw dropped. He didn't believe it either. Next to Robin stood Hyacinth and Belinda in the same room. Hyacinth noticed him and clapped her hands together. Her free-flowing dress, a kaleidoscope of color, contrasted with Belinda in her navy capris and matching T-shirt.

"Major Murphy! How delightful to see you again so soon. Isn't it wonderful!"

Robin stepped forward, her black leather portfolio in hand. "I thought he needed to see both of you ladies in the same room when I filled him in on the details."

Belinda folded her arms and pursed her lips. "How was he supposed to make a decision without the pertinent information?"

"Because it's going to be beautiful, and the fall crowds are going to be utterly delighted with our new tea room." Hyacinth went over and hugged Belinda. "You were so right, suggesting we turn professional."

"Tea room?" Aidan echoed, still getting over the shock of Hyacinth embracing Belinda as if they were old friends instead of sworn enemies.

"Sweet Shelby's Tea Room," Belinda blurted out before her gaze softened. "With your permission, of course."

Hyacinth hooked her arm through his. "It's our way of honoring your sister."

Danny shifted his weight, and Aidan removed the backpack from the boy's shoulders. "Why don't you go over to that corner where I can keep an eye on you?"

Danny didn't need a second invitation. He accepted the bag and darted to the corner.

Robin opened her portfolio and glanced at the papers. "I'll email you everything, but the two of them arrived at my office with a reasonable offer. You can take your time to look it over, and we can discuss it at your leisure."

Aidan hesitated. Leisure was the one thing he didn't have since he'd be leaving for Seattle tomorrow. His afternoon meeting with the lawyer loomed large. And he still hadn't told Danny of his impending departure.

Natalie was right. Danny was flourishing here. He couldn't take his nephew with him. Danny's best interests had to come before his own.

How could he go into Penelope's office, though, with Natalie's rejection stinging worse than the knife wound had? How could he ever face her again?

"Major M.?" Only Hyacinth called him that, and he looked her way. "Do we have your permission to use your sister's name? When you visit Danny in Hollydale on your leave, you'll have to come by and make sure we served her memory with honor."

"And for some of the best pie you've ever eaten." Belinda nodded firmly. "It's always about the pie."

"And the ambience. A hot pot of soothing tea, cute little finger sandwiches and…" Hyacinth giggled and shrugged. "Maybe we'll create a special corner for little boys and girls to dream and create."

He'd miss seeing these strong women butt heads. "I don't know when I'm coming back."

Hyacinth moved with him toward the large front window, smudged, but clear enough to see out onto the street. "Of course you're coming back soon. You'll be flying home the first chance you get. Many come in the fall to see the gorgeous display of color with the oaks and maples showcasing their glorious red, yellow and orange foliage. For them, Hollydale is just one day, a temporary respite from their everyday lives. You, however, have put down roots here. You've found your heart, and I daresay you've claimed someone else's heart. You'll be back."

For so long, he'd depended on the rigor of schedules and planning as those were a constant in a world of change, a world of emotion. Now he wasn't sure of anything. Even something as scheduled and planned as the military came with no guarantees, a built-in danger in its very existence. He'd seen too many casualties to not realize the truth in that statement. His own arm proved that.

"Natalie walked out on me." He stared out the window at the bustling sidewalk of Maple Drive, a hive of activity on this gray day. "She doesn't want to come for Danny at the end of the summer. She won't meet me in the middle."

Hyacinth tapped his shoulder, and he faced her. "For so long, Belinda and I made everything about competition, trying to one-up the other. Last night, she came over to my house with this plan for a tea house that sounded preposterous, but it was genuine. It captured my heart. When something's right, competition flies out the window. This is about us coming together and bringing something fresh to Hollydale. If you search your heart, you'll find the truth. You and Natalie will be a family, not just for Danny, but for you and her as well."

The mayor and Hyacinth both believed he had something valuable to contribute to the town, but what about his country? For fifteen years, he'd served his country, and he wanted to continue doing so in a vital way.

He glanced at Danny in the corner, playing with Aidan's tablet, laughing at the screen. It might seem like that change had happened in him overnight, but Aidan knew so much of that groundwork was laid while he was overseas, with Laurel, Toby and especially Natalie pouring a solid foundation.

Natalie. Everything always came back to her. Two weeks ago, life was simple, comforting in its predictable pattern. She'd turned his life upside down with her spirit, kisses and heart.

Did he have the capacity to be so much more if he didn't hold back? His parents had given up on him because he'd mistakenly given up on them. This time, he wasn't going to give up on love, because he loved her.

He loved Natalie.

What?

He couldn't love someone he'd just met. He didn't have "fall in love" circled on his calendar for this month or any other month, and he wouldn't have chosen someone who had big dreams and a hug for every situation, someone who brought a room to life, someone who made the world better with her rays of sunshine.

Until now.

The thought of going to Fort Lewis without telling her they should turn this fledgling relationship into something substantial tore at him. This time, he wouldn't make it sound harsh and cold but make it what it really was about: home and stability and a purpose. This time, it would be about love.

Danny might be the reason they first connected, but what he felt for Natalie went beyond that. It was about finding his family, his home, a love that spread light in those dark times.

He always thought he had to have an exact strategy to make a family, yet what he wanted was so much more than any idea. He wanted a future and love and a warm, gregarious redhead who would remind him about spontaneity in a world where control could only go so far.

Natalie provided all that, and so much more. He had to talk to her about her and Danny waiting here at home for him, a permanent base at the end of his service.

If it wasn't too late.

CHAPTER TWENTY

NATALIE CLIMBED THE steps up to the gazebo for the few minutes until she had to be at Penelope Romano's law office. She sat on the bench and from this vantage point, she had the best view in Hollydale to gaze out at all the storefronts of the town she loved. Mrs. Glisson swept the sidewalk in front of the floral shop where Natalie had worked summers in high school. Miss Louise cleaned her windows, wiping the glass in big circles. Deb made changes to the placard in front of The Busy Bean.

Her heart swelled, but it wasn't the town itself she loved so much as the people, her friends. They'd be here when she left, and most would be here when she visited often. She'd carry Hollydale in her heart, same as Shelby, same as Francisco. All this time, though, she'd thought she could only function in Hollydale, yet the past year had given her a wake-up call. It wasn't that she couldn't function elsewhere, it was that her heart hadn't belonged to Raleigh.

Even a month ago, saying farewell to Hollydale would never have crossed her mind. Now? The two Murphy males made the decision easy—emotional, but easy.

She'd used the rest of the morning to think through her decision to be with Aidan and Danny, since she'd be leaving her principal in the lurch. Marisa could find someone to take her place. Until that happened, though, Natalie would remain here, packing and getting everything in order.

That was, if Aidan agreed they had something worthwhile, something rare and precious. She had to hear his feelings for herself to make any of this work.

Something told her she wouldn't have to wait long. His familiar form strode toward the gazebo. She glanced around, looking for Danny, but not seeing him.

"Is everything okay?" She jumped to her feet, the silk of her sundress rustling, her pink cowboy boots clattering against the gazebo floor. "Where's Danny?"

Aidan started to roll down his sleeves and stopped in midaction, and she hid her smile at having some effect on him. Then she met his gaze, his gray eyes as tumultuous as the clouds hovering over Hollydale. Her smile faded. More than anything, she wanted him to face every moment with the strength he gave so freely to others.

"Danny's fine. He's at Hyacinth's." Aidan settled in the middle of the bench, and she scooted to the far end, not trusting her reaction to him, for good reason. His citrusy scent filled the air, and she longed to inch closer until there was little separating them. However, there was too much on the line for her to waver.

"Danny's helping her with birdhouses destined for the children's area of the new nature conservancy. In her words, 'Only a child can do justice to those dwellings, which will provide nourishment and edification to so many of nature's creatures.'" Aidan sighed.

In spite of everything, Natalie laughed. "That definitely came from Hyacinth's mouth, but why? Why is Danny there instead of with you?"

"Because he might get the wrong idea when I kiss you." Aidan closed the gap and placed his warm hands on her cheeks. "May I? One kiss and then we'll talk."

She hesitated. Whenever they kissed, she lost track of everything around her. "That doesn't sound like the stoic soldier who arrived in Hollydale."

"I'm not the same person. A certain redhead told me today there's strength in confronting your emotions. I thought she'd run out on me, but it turns out, I didn't follow her."

"Aidan. I'm going to find a job in Seattle, near Fort Lewis."

"Or my heart, but there's no time like the present to institute plan B."

Their words overlapped, and they met each other's gazes.

"What?" Once again, they talked in unison, and she pointed to herself.

"I know you think I run on emotion." She breathed in deeply as if she'd made a dramatic statement, but that was the simple truth. She did, and there was nothing wrong with that. "And it might seem like a spur-of-the-moment decision to follow you, but there's no better time, really. My sister can rent my house from me while she adjusts to her divorce, and I'll come out West as soon as Marisa has a replacement for me and I have a new job lined up. First, though, I need to talk to my boss and post my résumé online."

"I can't let you do that." His husky voice made her heart sing. "You love Hollydale."

"I love you more." He needed to know this was all about him, someone loving him enough to not let go, someone loving him enough to not hold back or run away. "And this isn't to do with Danny. I love the solidness of you, the way you concentrate on every task, the way you devote yourself to what you hold dear." She kept her gaze on him. She needed to know if he loved her.

Small lines crinkled around his eyes, genuine surprise flowing out of him. "That's a lot, considering we've only known each other a couple of weeks."

"I know it seems strange, but there are times you know when something's right." She reached for his hands, grasping them.

"This isn't right."

Her heart thudded. She'd been so sure he cared for her, even that he loved her.

"Oh." The word slipped from her mouth.

He gripped her hands and squeezed. "You're right for me, but what you're prepared to do for me, for us? That's not right." He slipped one of his hands out of hers and ran his fingers down her cheek, wiping away her tears. "You came into my life like a breath of fresh mountain air, sweet and revitalizing."

"There's an us." That sounded like a question and a statement rolled into one.

"I want there to be an us. We're both right. We need time to grow, to test the waters, so to speak, to make sure we don't screw this up for Danny." His shoulders began relaxing as if he'd realized he didn't have to carry the weight of the world on them.

"That's what I'm saying. I'm going to move to Seattle."

He shook his head. "Shelby had the right idea. Danny should stay here until I'm done with the military. By then, we'll know everything about each other."

She laughed again, the colors of the world becoming crisp and clear again. "I can't imagine a military man without a few good secrets."

Aidan's face sobered. "It's true I'll have to keep some information classified, but I'll share everything I can about my present, and I'll talk to you about my past. In return, you'll tell me about Danny and Stormy." He paused, and she saw the first hint of a smile. "And Hyacinth and Belinda."

"What about them?" Natalie winced.

Aidan explained about Sweet Shelby's Tea Room, and her mouth dropped open. He leaned over and kissed her, and she pulled him close, the kindness and bravery of him irresistible. For seconds, maybe minutes, the kiss swirled everything inside her into a kaleidoscope of color and wonder that this man wanted her in his life.

She pulled back and gasped, reveling in the taste of coffee and Aidan remaining on her lips. "Penelope!" She glanced at her phone and moaned. "We need to be there in five minutes."

"That should be enough time for us to make a plan together."

As they walked hand in hand, he talked about the tea room and a series of his own phone calls, including one to Mayor Wes and one to the firm in Washington, DC, which agreed to having him act as a consultant on a contractual basis after his discharge. He'd live here but fly out when needed.

They arrived at the lawyer's office with no time to spare. In a mere five-minute walk, they'd settled Danny's future, at least as far as the next year was concerned. She'd stay in Hollydale with him, while Aidan would visit when he could do so. Once his discharge came through, he'd move here permanently. Until then, Becks could rent Shelby's house. Her sister being close by would help out not only her sister, but all of them. And Bob Woodley, the current city manager, would stay on long enough to get his full pension and benefits before Aidan arrived to take over the job.

"You thought of everything, Murphy," she joked as they climbed the stairs to the front door.

"Well, I didn't know if you'd give me another chance, Harrison."

She went up on tiptoe and he lowered his head as their lips met for a brief kiss.

"I think the grand marshal, who helped a small kitten survive and negotiated a truce in the town, deserves one more chance. Heroes don't come along every day, you know."

"Neither do vivacious redheads who turn my life upside down." He smiled.

EPILOGUE

AIDAN CHECKED HIS duffel bag in the parking lot. New cat toy for Stormy, check. Lego set for Danny, check. His honorable discharge papers, check. Until last week, he hadn't expected the military to release him from his duties three months early. However, the JAG attorney who'd met with him had explained he received credit for his medical injury, which had pushed up his discharge date to March instead of June.

Spring break never looked so good as it did at Hollydale Park, with green shoots coming out of the hickory tree branches and the red maples in full leaf. Working with Diane and Carl Harrison, he'd arranged a surprise for Natalie and Danny.

A knock at his window grabbed his attention. There was Danny with a load of balloons. Aidan jumped out of the car and hugged his nephew.

"Surprise, Uncle Aidan!" Danny held him tight while the sunlight streamed across his face.

Somehow, he should have known he couldn't catch Natalie and Danny off guard.

Barking filled the air. A puppy on a leash was headed his way, tugging Natalie along the path. His breath caught. For a minute, he wanted to check to make sure this was all real. Despite everything thrown at her, she hadn't given up on him. Her bangle bracelets provided a soft melody, and she stopped and smiled as he soaked in her yellow sundress with matching yellow-and-brown cowboy boots. He'd dreamed of this moment, but nothing beat the reality of coming home and being with her.

He was thrilled to see them both. He dropped his duffel bag on the sidewalk. "Is this the puppy we talked about adopting?"

A tan puppy sniffed him and decided he liked Aidan as he licked his leg and flopped onto the sidewalk for a belly rub. Aidan complied.

"I know it seems like I talked you into it," she began. "But someone dropped a litter of puppies off at Lucie's house, and she's eight months pregnant, so we all pitched in. Georgie and Mike took one, Becks took two—she's such an overachiever—and who could say no to this face? Even Stormy approved."

He stopped any other words with a kiss, a long one he didn't want to end.

Danny hopped up and down beside them. "I got to name him, Uncle Aidan. He's Edison cause we were studying him at school, but Aunt Natalie shortened it to Eddie."

He grinned and met her gaze. Sparks zinged the air.

"Welcome home, Aidan."

Diane came out of nowhere and grabbed the leash. "Come on, Danny. Come on, Eddie. Let's get this party started."

Natalie moved into his arms, and he held her tight, the strawberry scent soaking into him. He knew he'd never forget this moment as long as he lived.

"I've missed you," she said.

"I love you." The words spilled out of him as he repeated himself in five other languages for good measure.

She cupped his face and kissed him. Seconds passed, and he gave in to the sweetness and the love. Breaking away, she took his hand and pulled him toward the pavilion, where half the town seemed ready to welcome him back officially.

"You knew, didn't you? Who told you? Your mom? Your dad?" After all, when he'd called her parents to tell them his intention of asking Natalie to marry him and sought their approval—rather old-fashioned but something

Aidan felt compelled to do—he had revealed his homecoming date.

"When you Skyped me last week, the discharge papers were on your desk. So was the airline ticket." Her eyes twinkled. "It's hard to fool a kindergarten teacher. You might want to remember that."

Tonight he'd surprise her when he proposed. He knew she'd say yes. The look in her eyes communicated enough love for a lifetime and then some. In Hollydale, he'd found a home. He'd found Natalie.

She tapped his shoulder, and he leaned over. "By the way, I'm going to knock your socks off when you see me in my green cocktail dress at Hollydale's new fancy restaurant tonight." She beamed. "Just in case any important questions get asked."

His laugh was full and rich. One day he'd surprise her, although he didn't know when and he didn't know how. After all, unexpected twists had made his life that much fuller, starting with his nephew, and the redhead who was leading him into the pavilion to share her friends and family with him.

Natalie was the bright star that would always guide him home.

* * * * *

*For more great romances from author
Tanya Agler and Harlequin Heartwarming,
visit www.Harlequin.com today!*

HARLEQUIN SELECTS COLLECTION

19 FREE BOOKS IN ALL!

From Robyn Carr to RaeAnne Thayne to Linda Lael Miller and Sherryl Woods we promise (actually, GUARANTEE!) each author in the Harlequin Selects collection has seen their name on the *New York Times* or *USA TODAY* bestseller lists!

Visit
ReaderService.com
Today!

As a valued member of the Harlequin Reader Service, you'll find these benefits and more at ReaderService.com:

- Try 2 free books from any series
- Access risk-free special offers
- View your account history & manage payments
- Browse the latest Bonus Bucks catalog

Don't miss out!

If you want to stay up-to-date on the latest at the Harlequin Reader Service and enjoy more content, make sure you've signed up for our monthly News & Notes email newsletter. Sign up online at ReaderService.com or by calling Customer Service at 1-800-873-8635.